</p>
I0580022

DESTINY'S CHILD

DESTINY'S CHILD

BARRETT MAGILL

SAPPHIRE BOOKS

SALINAS, CALIFORNIA

Destiny's Child
Copyright © 2019 by Barrett Magill. All rights reserved.

ISBN - 978-1-948232-65-4

This is a work of fiction - names, characters, places, and incidents are the product of the author's imagination or are used fictitiously. Any resemblance to actual persons living or dead, business, events or locales is entirely coincidental.

All rights reserved. No part of this publication may be reproduced, distributed, or transmitted in any form or by any means, including photocopying, recording, or other electronic or mechanical methods, without written permission of the publisher.

Editor - Heather Flournoy
Book Design - LJ Reynolds
Cover Design - TreeHouse Studio

Sapphire Books Publishing, LLC
P.O. Box 8142
Salinas, CA 93912
www.sapphirebooks.com

Printed in the United States of America
First Edition – July 2019

This and other Sapphire Books titles can be found at
www.sapphirebooks.com

Dedication

This series is dedicated to the men and women of the FBI and all of the other agencies who put their lives at risk every day. We are grateful for your service.

And a special dedication to those who have discovered and pioneered the remarkable healing available with our equine partners.

Acknowledgments

First and foremost, I am immensely grateful to the team at Sapphire Books Publishing, especially Chris, Schileen, Lori, and the readers who worked to get the re-issued Damaged series—including this new novel, Destiny's Child—ready for you.

Special credit goes to Treehouse Studio and the very talented Ann McMan for providing the perfect covers for almost all of my books since 2012. Team: May your faith be greatly rewarded.

Once again I need to acknowledge the important work and generous suggestions from Nancy De Santis (Horses for Heroes), and Melisa Pearce (Touched by a Horse), whose work with Equine Gestalt Coaching has saved lives and brought a new understanding of the healing gifts available through our equine partners.

My inspiration to write fourteen novels is thanks to the amazing people at the Office of Light and Magic who annually manage the NaNoWriMo (National Novel Writers Month). Bravo! Another important inspiration came long ago with the very first publication of Damaged in Service; that was my very first review from The Rainbow Reader and Salem West. Her excellent observations and comments were exactly what a new writer needs for inspiration.

Many thanks to my diligent and eagle-eyed beta reader, Mary Ann Bosworth. Your careful and thoughtful evaluation was invaluable. Thank you.

I am so very fortunate and grateful for my brilliant editor, Heather Flournoy—you are an inspiring teacher, editor, and the wind at my back.

As always, my work doesn't happen in a vacuum, and for the many folks who take the time to buy the books, provide their feedback, and continue to believe in these beloved characters...I am in your debt.

(Psst—Stay tuned. Who knows what's next?)

Thank you,
Barrett

Chapter One

Anne Reynolds fidgeted with a loose thread on her jacket. Another jet roared over her head as she waited in the cell phone lot of the Albuquerque Sunport. Much of the ten-year history she shared with Zeke Cabot had involved Zeke jetting off somewhere into potential danger—usually related to a closed case in Chicago involving several evil characters bent on revenge. This trip, however, was her part-time work at the FBI training center at Quantico. Even while still assigned to the Albuquerque field office, Zeke spent several weeks a year teaching.

Her phone buzzed with a text. "Just landed be out soon."

Anne let out the breath she had been holding and started the car. She slowed in the terminal lane and scanned the sidewalk. She spotted Zeke coming out with a carrier bag over her shoulder, a briefcase, and her old backpack. She was as striking as ever with her tall stature, dark eyes, and a touch of gray in her dark brown hair.

Her breath caught, and for just a minute she was transported to the first time she had to take Zeke to the Sunport to return to Chicago.

On three occasions during her medical leave from her last assignment undercover with Chicago's homeless population, they'd bumped into each other near Anne's east mountain home. The third time was on a mountain hiking trail where Zeke fell off a trail and injured her head and leg. Slightly banged up, Zeke needed some nursing care for a head injury. Anne's home health nursing skills helped and an undeniable attraction developed between them. Anne just knew this woman was something special. Now, after ten years together, Anne was even surer. She touched the gold Pegasus necklace Zeke had given her and smiled. Zeke waved and jogged toward the car. After tossing her things in the back seat, she slid in next to Anne and kissed her. "Seeing you as soon as I arrive never gets old."

Anne stroked her face and smiled. "Welcome home. How was your class?" She pulled out and merged with the outgoing traffic.

❧ ❧ ❧ ❧

"Odd group. Much younger and very enthusiastic. They all wanted some assignment with the gang or drug teams. Action." Zeke laughed.

Her years of experience with the Bureau had gradually moved her into administrative work. Her last case chasing the Hussein brothers took her all over the world and finally ended with an assassination outside their family compound in Lebanon. The case caused unimaginable damage physically and mentally, and it had been a long road back. Anne lightly touched her arm.

"What's up? You look sad." Zeke said.

"No, actually I'm relieved and happy to have you home. Even after all these years, I worry until you're back in our home."

Zeke took her hand and kissed the palm. "I'll always come back to you. I promised."

The ride home through the Tijeras canyon was quiet. Spring had finally arrived, and the trees were budding out. Swathes of bright green speckled the hillside among the boulders. Zeke opened her window and took a deep breath.

Anne smiled at the post-trip routine.

"There's a familiar scent underneath the freshness kinda like old wood and stone. It reminds me how old and untouched most of the state is. I feel like we get a real glimpse of the past whenever we take the time to look deeper. It helps me slow down."

"You're certainly poetic today. Any reason?"

"I don't think so. Teaching always puts me in an altered reality—more distant."

Anne pressed the entry code into the driveway gate keypad, and they proceeded up around the curve. She slowed as they reached the newly purchased pasture and barn. The white pipe fencing glistened around the dark green grass and trees. "I still get excited every time I drive up."

Zeke leaned out her window. "Do you think the barn needs painting again?"

"Not really, but we can have Benjamin take a look at it." Anne hired the handyman years ago after watching him help customers at the local hardware store. It seemed like he could figure out just about any problem. The local rumor mill whispered about his service injury and discharge from the Navy, and his engineering degree.

Benjamin was silent when it came to personal revelations. Zeke guessed he was near sixty, but it was hard to tell. His short-cropped hair was nearly black and his soft brown eyes were hidden under large bushy eyebrows. Although he wasn't exceptionally tall, he had a lean, agile style. He lived nearby up the mountain.

Anne opened the new house gate electronically and drove in. Benjamin waved from the nearby barn. "Welcome home, Ms. Cabot."

"Good to be back. And, it's Zeke."

He laughed and shook his head. "Old habits, you know. While you were gone, you had a visitor."

Zeke got out while Anne parked in the garage. "What did they want?"

"Odd. I'm not sure, the guy asked who lived here, and when I asked why he wanted to know, he got nervous. Said he used to know people around here. Then he drove off. Didn't catch all the numbers, but the plate was from Arizona."

"You're right, that is odd. Let me know if you see that guy again." The hair on her neck tingled as she walked to the house. Old agent instincts don't ever fade, just like Benjamin's disciplined military training. She looked back at the locked gate before going into the house. No need to mention it to Anne.

Zeke walked around to the garage, pulled her bags from the back seat of Anne's car, and met Anne in the mudroom. "Hi."

Anne kissed her and said, "I'm going out to the barn for a bit. Text me."

"Okay. I'm going to shower and change."

It was after three when Zeke finished sorting the student papers she had to grade. This term would be over in a few weeks, which would give her a couple of months off. She pulled out her grade book. Everything was up to date, and with this last batch of papers, she'd be able to send the grades in.

Teaching at Quantico was worlds apart from her

duties at the Albuquerque field office. After nearly twenty years as a Special Agent, she closed out her career in the office replacing SAC de la Hoya.

She leaned back in her office chair and put her long legs up on the windowsill. Anne had designed and decorated the small space on the landing of the second floor during their early courtship. Zeke smiled. Anne had surprised her with her own "space" when she returned from her first trip to Chicago. She grabbed her phone and hit Text.

ZCabot: Do you have dinner planned?

Zeke waited. The planner on her desk had "writing" assigned for this afternoon, but she wasn't feeling it. She pulled up the outline for her book and tried to pull some inspiration from the words. Nope.

AReynolds: No, I completely forgot about it. I was trying to balance books. Damn!

ZCabot: Don't fret. I'll find something. I'm a Master chef, remember? XOXO

AReynolds: I <3 U

She sat up, stretched, and slid on her sandals. "Cooking will be far more fun." She jumped up and trotted down the stairs and into the sunny kitchen. Anne had started a shopping list and stuck it on the refrigerator door. The freezer had no inspiration, but there were some skinless chicken breasts in the refrigerator along with an onion, green peppers, and green taco sauce.

Anne had given her a pressure cooker for Christmas right after her doctor had warned her about her creeping cholesterol. Zeke knew the wretched eating habits she acquired over the years were partly to blame, but so were her genetics. Her dad had survived two strokes with some residual loss of function, and her brother had started meds two years ago.

The pantry held the can of green chile and black beans. She lined everything up in order of appearance then started by washing the chicken and peppers, then chopping each along with the onion. This task provided her a pleasant, mindless routine for a while.

Her mind wandered to the beautiful recipes she'd gotten from her grandmother after her mom died a year ago. Her throat tightened. Her passing wasn't a surprise, but the cause of death was a blood clot and not the slow decline of Alzheimer's they had expected for years. Her death about killed her dad, but the doctor assured them she didn't suffer. Once again, Zeke had been out of town. She'd gone to Canada for a two-day workshop. More guilt. When she got the call from her brother, he assured her that it was quick and they'd only held a small memorial service.

The food prepared, she pulled out the pressure cooker, threw in all the ingredients, added a passel of seasoning, water, and taco sauce. She set the timer for "stew" and moved into the family room.

Anne had left the mail on the coffee table, so Zeke picked up the pile and sifted through one piece of junk mail after another, until she held a shiny auto dealer ad with a black SUV. *Didn't Benjamin mention a black SUV and stranger from Arizona?*

She got up and wandered to the front door, and then out to the back deck from habitual wariness.

Her brain was trying hard to find something. *What was it?* Out of nowhere Shayla, their seven-year-old adopted puppy, came flying around the back and up on the porch and into Zeke's lap. "Whoa! Hello to you, too." Shayla snuggled, whimpered, and shared kisses. "Where've you been? You stink of manure."

On most days, both the cat and dog followed Anne around the barn and arena. Shayla had grown into a medium-sized, short-haired, terrier mix— frequently known in New Mexico as "rez-dogs."

They snuggled quietly and watched the shadows grow across the wooded eastern section of their property. Spring birds were out, and it reminded Zeke to buy birdseed. Her cell phone interrupted the moment.

❧❧❧❧

Anne came through the mudroom at the same time Zeke walked in from the deck.

Zeke scooped up the ringing phone. "Hi, Reg. What a nice surprise."

Anne went to the sink and washed up with some special antibacterial soap. Nurse habits. The pressure cooker on the counter showed fifteen minutes left and something smelled terrific.

Zeke reappeared in the family room. "I understand, and I'm sorry for all of you, but I'll need to talk to Anne, and I'll call you back. Love you, too."

"Talk to me about what?" Anne sat on the arm of the couch.

Zeke put her phone on the table and ran both hands through her hair. "My brother. They've got a problem, and he wants our help."

"Well, of course we will if we can." She slid down next to Zeke, facing her. And waited.

"Annie, this feels like it's above my pay grade, but…I've been a pretty poor part of my family for a long time and may need to step up."

"Now you're making me nervous."

Zeke put a hand on her knee and leaned over to kiss her. "I guess I don't need to be all mysterious. They're having trouble with Destiny. That adorable little girl has become a teenage hellion."

Anne laughed. "I'm sure she can't be that bad. All teenagers are rebellious."

Zeke offered a weak smile and swallowed hard. "Well…she's looking at serving time in juvie."

"What?"

"I didn't get the grisly details, but this was a third strike kind of offense that involved a stolen car, alcohol, and personal injury." Zeke pinched the bridge of her nose and sighed.

Anne sat dumbfounded. When they saw her at Christmas four years earlier, she was bright, fun, musical. What on earth could have happened? "Wha… what does he think we can do?"

"He convinced the judge that a couple of months with his aunt would straighten her out—since I'm this tough federal agent. He also suggested that you could probably work some miracle with your horses."

Anne started to laugh then stopped abruptly. "You're serious?"

Zeke nodded.

"Well, why don't we have dinner and maybe sleep on it tonight. I want some more information."

Zeke jumped up. "Yes. I'll shoot him an email and tell him we need her records."

Anne returned her horses to their stalls and left the new bay mare in the arena. Zeke had agreed to wait for the records from Reggie. She'd promised Anne she'd distill some facts before they talked again.

The new horse came to her from Nancy, her training mentor for the equine therapy certification. The mare couldn't work with the men, and since almost all Nancy's clients were cowboys and all military, Nancy needed a home for her. Her name was Dancer, and her original owner thought she looked like Pegasus. From behind the rail, she watched as the horse trotted from one end to the other, tossing her head.

Anne climbed the rails and slowly moved closer. It took a while and some soft talk, but finally Anne got close enough to attach a guide rope. She led the horse to the round pen just outside the door.

"Easy, Dancer. We're going to take this real slow, so you don't have to worry." She led the horse slowly around the ring. At first, Dancer resisted, but after ten minutes she began to tire. Eventually, Anne removed the lead and swung it enough to encourage Dancer to run around the pen. When her gait slowed, Anne stopped and walked over to the rail.

She waited. Peeking over her shoulder she could see Dancer watching her with her ears flicked forward. After several minutes, she returned with the lead and took the new horse back to her stall. Tomorrow was another day.

Once in the stall, she took a brush and began slowly brushing her. When her back leg cocked, Anne smiled.

"That sure looks relaxing. Could I sign up?" Zeke leaned over the stall door.

Anne stopped and squinted at her. "That's a possibility, but you'd have to let me chase you in the round pen with a lead rope."

Zeke cracked up laughing. "Maybe we could come up with something gentler."

Anne put the brush away and went for a hay flake. "Would you grab one for Sunny?"

❦ ❦ ❦ ❦

Zeke wrapped her arm around Anne's shoulders as they returned to the house. Clouds had swept over the mountain, and the wind picked up.

"This wind may have been a trigger for Dancer. She was not ready to settle down today."

"I didn't know horses were so easily spooked."

Anne laughed. "You've been away from your equine therapy, and maybe we should schedule some time for you."

Zeke pulled her closer. She glanced at the gate and fence as they passed. Something was still niggling her. "I think I'll check the security cameras since it's been quite a while."

"You know, I forget about them completely. Are you worried about something?"

"Not especially. But we spent a lot of money, and I should be more diligent or why bother?"

Am I worried? Maybe this was still residual from my PTSD. Anne is right, another session with the horses would be a good thing. "Do you think Nancy would do a session with me?"

"I'm sure she would. Do you want me to call?"

She opened the back door to the mudroom and kicked off her boots.

Zeke followed suit and then hung up her hoodie. "I can call, but I suppose I better wait until we figure this whole thing about Destiny."

Anne dried her hands and put a glass up to the refrigerator water dispenser. "Let's sit a while and see if we can come up with some accommodation."

"Good idea. I'll admit I had trouble getting settled last night. My brain wouldn't shut down."

Anne squeezed her arm. "I know."

"This should be an easy decision. My brother asked me for a favor, and Destiny is family. So why are red lights going off?"

"I'm not worried too much, but I do have several clients lined up for the summer. I'm not sure what your teaching schedule might be. And maybe she's perfectly happy entertaining herself." She curled her legs under her and put her arm on the back of the couch.

Zeke fussed over a broken nail. "I should probably check to see if Reggie sent the paperwork." She stood and headed up to her office. As soon as she got to the top of the stairs, she heard the fax machine.

She gathered the stack of paper—twelve pages from her arrest reports and the Mississippi Department of Children and Family Services. "We have papers. Arrest reports and family services." She held up two sets.

"Let me review the family service reports that's more in my wheelhouse."

Zeke handed her several sheets and sat down beside her. For the next half hour, it was quiet except for the clock near the kitchen.

Zeke set her papers down and went out to the

kitchen for a drink. The stuff she read could not be about that sweet little girl she had known. The description belonged to a druggie or abused kid. How could this have happened? Hopefully, Anne could pull out a few bits of hope. *I sure don't want her to read the arrest reports. Geez.*

"While you're out there, would you please bring me some more water?"

Zeke returned with two full glasses. "Here. Did you find any redeeming factors?"

Anne sighed and put down the papers she held. "Well, I did find some possible warning signs, but I don't know if you'll agree."

"I don't get what you mean."

"According to the social worker who followed up"—she flipped a couple of pages—"on at least five occasions. Destiny started with minor infractions, acting out at school, skipping classes, as well as some minor vandalism."

"Minor infractions! What the hell was she thinking?"

"Believe me; those are minor. The last three visits were for burglary, shoplifting, drugs at school, and car theft."

"I can't believe she's not in prison. My brother is not a disciplinarian, but my sister-in-law sure is. I don't understand. The police reports are no better. Destiny was the very definition of 'resisting arrest' and 'disruptive.' Anyplace else she could have been shot." Unexpected tears welled up and threatened. "If my father hadn't been so friendly with the local cops…"

Anne grimaced. "Honey, let's step back a little. I think therapists made some observations that weren't provided to everyone."

"What am I missing?"

"The abbreviated version is that Destiny was a pawn in a three-way power play with her parents and your dad. She told them that her grandfather was mean to her and punished her for even minor infractions. He had been verbally and emotionally abusive. It got worse when your mom died. Destiny told the social workers she wanted to be in foster care because her parents didn't believe her and punished her for lying."

Zeke fell back on the couch and wiped her eyes. "How the hell did I not hear about this?"

"It sounds like your sister-in-law was just as mean to your brother and niece." She slipped an arm around Zeke. "We'll have to call your brother later."

❧❧❧❧

Anne went out to the kitchen to start dinner and left Zeke with some time alone. That was quite a bombshell her brother dropped. *The child needs some guidance. Better dig out my notes…*

"A horse doesn't care how much you know until he knows how much you care. If your horse says no, you either asked the wrong question, or asked the question wrong…"
~Pat Parelli

She pulled out all her ingredients for a big summer salad and began the ritual washing and chopping while she hummed mindlessly. Zeke's voice? It came from upstairs, and Anne thought it best to give her some space until she wanted to talk. They could probably do this—with some adjustments and a contract of some kind. Maybe her parents' attitude would improve with a break, too.

❧ ❧ ❧ ❧

Zeke rocked in her chair while sifting through the reports. She stopped and tried to imagine her niece getting the same treatment she got from her father. Except now he had no restraints. *Bastard.*

If she closed her eyes, she could still hear his bombastic drawl and see his sneer. She used to look up to him so much when she was little, but he was gentler then. After having a boy, he was delighted at the sweet little girl in his arms.

She heard them talking at night. His inability to achieve higher rank in the military was openly racist. It was back in the sixties, and a black enlisted man would never go far. But he was too proud to complain and just worked harder.

By the time she got to high school, he was an angry man. Zeke didn't understand because he didn't talk, he just yelled orders. That was when her fear started. Any mistake would bring his wrath. Biting, sarcastic, and loud.

She remembered.

The situation with her brother and his wife was unclear, but clearly they weren't supporting Destiny.

She felt they would have to at least try. There wasn't anyone else to help, and they had to see that Zeke's hard work with the horses had saved her life.

A message flashed on her computer screen "Alert, camera-six breach."

She opened the security software on her computer and studied tapes from each camera. When she got to number six, which viewed the south side of the property, she zoomed in. She hit stop when she spotted a dark figure hidden beside a tree outside the fence. It was hard to make out. Could be a person or a downed branch, but if the camera picked it up, there must've been movement.

It moved. It was a tall, thin male.

Zeke jumped up and ran down the stairs and out the front door. She didn't stop when she rounded the barn and hopped the fence.

There was the tree. No car. No person. No movement.

She jogged across the pasture, hoping to find a clue.

"Zeke, are you out there?"

When Zeke heard Anne's voice, she climbed the outer fence and began to jog up the road toward their gate. She did not want Anne to worry about invisible men.

"Hi. Sorry, I didn't tell you I was going to run." She bent over to catch her breath.

"I heard you run down the stairs, but when I finally went out, you were nowhere in sight."

"I should have said something, but I was so angry at my father—"

"Come in. Dinner is ready. After, we can make the call."

Chapter Two

Reggie, I have you on speaker so Anne can participate." Zeke pulled Anne's chair a little closer to her desk.

"Hi, Reggie."

"Hi, Anne. I'm glad you both called. Maura should be back soon. She had to drop Destiny at a youth group meeting."

Zeke nodded and took Anne's hand. "Okay, well we do have some questions for you, but we think we can help. Destiny is certainly welcome here, and Anne is willing to fit in some equine therapy as long as Destiny is willing to work in the barn with the horses."

Anne smiled and nodded.

"Really?" Reg laughed. "I'm not sure she knows what a barn is."

Anne leaned closer. "She will. You might want to consider some work clothes like jeans, boots, and gloves."

"We can do that. Anything else we should bring?"

Zeke whispered, "Manners."

"We can send a note if there's anything else."

"Okay, we need to ask some questions." Zeke sat up and picked up the arrest report.

A knock at the front door interrupted. Anne stood. "It's Benjamin. You go ahead."

Zeke wavered. Benjamin never used the front door. She leaned over to the window but saw no cars.

"Sorry Reg, we don't usually have drop-in visitors. Can you fill me in on what precipitated these reports?" She moved the paper closer and picked up a pen.

Reggie chatted on and briefly sketched out incidents at school and home that resulted in some form of punishment—no phone, no TV, no visitors, early curfew. He believed her angry response to that punishment was out of proportion.

Zeke noted his comments, then asked, "Tell me what has happened with Dad? The social worker's report suggested they were concerned by his behavior and think it affected Destiny."

There was a long pause, and Zeke heard him take a deep breath.

"You know how Dad gets. He thinks he knows better than anyone about discipline. It never happens here, but when Destiny spends any time with him and she comes home in…some kind of state. Angry crying and won't talk." He paused and shuffled the phone. "Maura and I have both tried."

Anne returned and mouthed, "*Benjamin*."

Zeke nodded. "Reg, Anne's back. I think she has some questions."

"The evaluations she's gotten indicate low self-esteem, guilt, and anxiety that result in lashing out."

Reggie laughed. "Low self-esteem? Boy, you'd never guess that when she's on her cocky high-horse telling everybody what to do."

Anne glanced at Zeke with raised eyebrows. "That is pretty typical. If she can manage to reign that in, I think she'll really benefit from working with horses."

"Anne, I trust your judgment, but I sure don't get how that works. Zeke tried to tell me, and I can see what a difference it made for her, but it sounds pretty woo-woo."

Anne smiled at Zeke. "I'll send you some literature."

"Reggie, when do you want her to come, and will one of you bring her?" Zeke asked.

After a pause, Reg said, "It'll be the end of May in a couple of weeks and classes will be finished for my students. Would that work? I'd be able to fly up with her."

Anne nodded, and Zeke looked up at her calendar. "That would work. How long does she need to stay for the court to remove her sentence?"

He was silent for a moment. "Two months."

Zeke covered her mouth and looked at Anne, who merely shrugged.

"Okay, let us know when you have your travel plans."

"Sure. Of course, Maura and I will need to discuss it."

"Umm, that's fine."

"Thank you, guys. You have no idea what a relief this is."

"Oh, I think I can guess."

❧ ❧ ❧ ❧

Anne poured them both coffee and followed Zeke out to the deck.

"Thanks. What did Benjamin want?" Zeke asked.

"He looked at the barn to see if it needed painting. He offered to power wash it. There were a couple of spots that looked rusty."

Zeke's shoulders wilted with relief. "Good idea."

"Do you think we ought to move the exercise

equipment out of the extra room and fix that up for Destiny? It's bigger and has more windows. She could pick out curtains and bedding if she wants, too."

"That's really thoughtful of you. We're volunteering to house a convicted felon, and you want her to decorate her cell." Zeke grinned and poked her shoulder.

"Ass. She's your niece. She's thirteen, and she's suffered the same emotional and verbal abuse you did from your father. Let's try to remember that and cut her some slack. This will not be an easy time for any of us." Anne straightened up. "Oh, and I did warn Benjamin."

Zeke started to laugh. Anne joined her before they both fell silent.

࿇ ࿇ ࿇ ࿇

The two weeks getting everything ready for their young houseguest flew past with plans and rearranging taking place. Then, it was here.

Zeke parked in the cell phone lot at the Albuquerque Sunport. When she rechecked the flight information, their landing was delayed. She texted Anne with the update.

Reggie's emails had been contradictory. First, everyone was excited and shopping; then Destiny pitched a fit and refused to go; then Maura had an attack of mother-guilt and wanted to cancel the plan.

Zeke had her own misgivings. She'd never gotten to know her niece because of her own neglect. The only lawbreakers she'd ever dealt with were criminals, and in her mind Destiny was still a little girl, not evil. And yet...

An unbidden scene popped in her head about her father's reaction when she wanted to quit the basketball team. His rage was unparalleled to anything she'd witnessed. He yelled, belittled her, insulted her, and blamed her. He slammed the book on the floor and towered over as she trembled on her bed. For an hour she endured the torture until her mom came home and stopped him.

It made sense that this current behavior had escalated after his wife's death. He was off the rails now and using a thirteen-year-old girl as his whipping boy.

❧ ❧ ❧ ❧

Anne and Benjamin moved the last two items—a desk and chair—into the new room for Destiny. All the exercise equipment was in the old barn/office/Meka's lair.

"Finished." Anne wiped her hands on her jeans. "Let's get something to drink." She glanced at her watch.

Downstairs, she handed him some iced tea. "Sugar?"

"Yes, ma'am."

"Benjamin, I wanted to give you some information about our guest. Destiny is Zeke's niece. She's only thirteen but has gotten in enough trouble to warrant the juvenile court to intervene."

His eyes were large as he nodded slowly.

"We're hoping some time with her aunt as well as learning to care for the horses and do some real work might help her. But… Here's the thing: I'm not sure how much she can be trusted alone. As long as an adult is watching her, she might toe the line."

"I'll do whatever you need me to, but I don't have experience with kids. My wife couldn't have any."

Anne smiled. "I understand. We haven't either. We'll have to play it by ear." She put their glasses in the sink. "Let's go back out. I need to spend a little time with the new horse."

⚜ ⚜ ⚜ ⚜

Zeke watched as her brother approached the car with the tall, beautiful young lady that was her little niece. "Wow. Look who grew up."

She opened the trunk and waved. "Hi Reggie, Destiny. Gosh, you've sure grown." Standing next to her, Zeke guessed she was at least 5'7".

Her brother hugged her.

"Let's head back. I promised to pick up pizza from the Italian restaurant for supper."

"Great, I love pizza," Destiny said. "But no sausage. Or onions. But extra cheese."

Zeke took a breath. *And so it begins.* She glanced at her silent brother.

"You got it."

When they drove through the community gate, Destiny whistled. "I thought you lived in the desert."

Zeke looked at Reggie. "What do you mean?"

"I thought New Mexico was all flat and dry. These are some big-ass mountains with a ton of trees. How do you have a ranch up here?"

"Well, honey, it's not really a ranch. We only have a few horses for Anne's business and a little bit of land."

"Dad says you expect me to clean the barn. Is

that true?"

"I'm afraid so. We all have to pitch in to take care of the place."

"Seriously? I'm only a kid."

Reggie turned in his seat. "Need I remind you that the judge was angry enough to charge you as an adult?"

"That's just bullshit."

His voice lowered. "Don't make me remind you of our deal, young lady."

Silence.

The gate swung open. "Here we are at Camp Reynolds."

"This is gorgeous, Zeke." Her brother was clearly impressed. In the late afternoon sun, lofty tree shadows stretched across the paddock and gravel pathways to the white house with green trim. The regal brick chimney stretched up toward the tree canopy.

"Is that where the horses are?" Destiny pointed to the original barn that was now the office.

"They used to be, but now it's Anne's office. The riding center and barn are behind it. We'll take a walk later, and I'll show you around."

They parked near the garage as Benjamin walked over. He waved. "Ms. Anne had to run down to the feed store. She'll be back in a while."

"Benjamin, I'd like you to meet my brother Reggie, and my niece Destiny. Benjamin is our foreman, yard man, maintenance man, and general helper. We really depend on him for everything."

"Pleased to meet you all, but I need to get to it." Benjamin nodded and headed toward the riding center.

"You have a lot to take care of. I'm surprised you don't have more help." Reggie took the two rollaboard bags, and Destiny grabbed her backpack.

"We don't really need more help. We can always find someone for extra help if the need arises." She turned to Destiny. "Besides, we have a delightful little helper for the next two months." She and Reggie both laughed.

"Ha ha ha," Destiny said with a sneer.

While Destiny was unpacking in her new quarters, Zeke and Reggie went out on the deck with a beer. He stretched out on a lounge chair. "I can't even tell you how much of a relief it is to know my daughter will be safe with you."

"Hey, don't give us too much credit yet. Neither of us has any idea how this will work out. We're just hoping the change of scenery will give everybody time to reset."

"I get that, and you're probably right, but a man can hope."

"Hang on. I better check on those pizzas in the oven." Zeke hurried into the kitchen and verified that the cheese was not quite melty enough for her taste. She set the timer for another five minutes.

"So, where were we?" Zeke asked, returning to her chair.

"I was about to share the rich and full details of my life."

They clinked bottles and Reggie reported on his teaching job and Maura's midlife crises.

❧ ❧ ❧ ❧

Anne waited while the gate slowly opened. As she drove in, she spotted Shayla racing around from behind the barn. She stopped and got out to avoid hitting her

"Shayla. Come here." The dog disappeared behind the house.

She turned to get back in the car and saw Destiny trotting out from the training barn with a six-foot lunge whip looking for, presumably, Shayla. *What in the world?*

"Hey, Destiny." Anne covered the distance between them in seconds. "Can I ask what you were planning to do with that whip, and with whom?" Virtual steam was building in her head.

The kid laughed. "Oh, nothing, I was just playing with that dog. Then she took off."

"That dog is Shayla, and she is an important member of the family. Whatever games she plays never include any kind of whip. Is that clear and understandable?"

Destiny just looked at her with an incredulous expression. "Geez, bitchy much?" She tossed the whip over her shoulder and strutted toward the house.

Anne gawped wordlessly.

What the hell just happened? Is this what the summer is going to be like? Are we babysitting the spawn of the devil?

Anne drove to the training barn and left the car so Benjamin could unload and stack the bags of oats. She walked back to the house trying to regulate her breathing and control her fury. *I have to be the adult and not get into this child's shit.*

She dropped her things in the kitchen. "Hello?" The scent of garlic and tomato sauce reached her. Zeke must've picked up everyone already, as well as the pizza. The family room was empty, but she heard voices and followed the sounds to the deck.

"Hi, Reggie. I'm sorry I wasn't here to meet you."

He stood and shook her hand. "No problem. Zeke has been a good host."

Zeke stood. "Here, take my chair. Can I get you something?"

"No, thanks. I'm good."

"Reg, do you want to call Destiny to meet Anne?"

"Great idea. I'll run up and see if she's unpacked yet."

Anne fixed a smile and nodded. As soon as the sliding door closed, Anne motioned Zeke closer and quickly told her what happened.

Zeke's jaw tightened. "Unbelievable. We saw Shayla bolt past to the tool shed. She hasn't come out."

Reggie appeared. "She's not upstairs, and she didn't unpack. I tried her cell, but it went to voice mail."

Anne pulled out her cell. "Let me text Benjamin to bring her back or let us know if he's seen her."

Within a minute her phone beeped.

Benj: the kid is in the barn following me around. I'll bring her up.

She read the message. Reggie looked worried, and Zeke chewed the inside of her cheek. That usually wasn't a good "tell." They all headed out the front door in time to see Destiny dragging her feet behind Benjamin. When she spotted the three of them, she stopped.

Reggie walked over. "We need to go back in the house for a minute...to talk."

"Yeah. Whatever."

"I'll get back to feeding the horses." Benjamin

ambled back to the barn.

❧❧❧❧

Zeke put her arm on Anne's shoulder and walked with her to the barn office.

"I am about to explode." Anne turned and closed the door.

"I understand. Let's hope this is just Destiny acting out because she's nervous or scared." Zeke paced. "Maybe we need to set some house rules. We should do it while Reggie is here because he'll have some of his own."

Anne sat at the office desk. "I shouldn't have lost it with her. I knew this was gonna happen, Heaven knows I've taken care of so many kids acting out for one reason or another. What every one of them wants is to have some attention."

"You're right. We haven't been very welcoming, but she makes it hard." Zeke walked to the window. "Anne, if you have any reservations, tell me now and I'll get her a ticket and send her right back with Reggie."

Anne looked up at her for what seemed like a full minute.

"We can't do that. We made a deal, and I know we can help if she will just trust us."

Chapter Three

Food's ready." Anne set out the pizzas and a salad on the counter. "Just get your food and take it in the dining room."

The flap on the dog door opened and Shayla ran directly to her bowl. She stopped when she saw Destiny. Her ears were flattened and her tail was curled between her legs.

Anne sighed and knelt down beside her. "I know you're a little scared with new people, but, no one is going hurt you." She stroked Shayla's head and looked up at Destiny.

"I didn't mean to scare her. We were just playing."

"We only use whips while training horses. Never for games. After dinner we can show you some of the things Shayla likes to play with."

Reggie moved behind Destiny. "Go ahead. I'm sure you're starving."

She took two pieces of the cheese pizza and a tablespoon of salad. Reggie shrugged and followed her into the dining room. Zeke and Anne trailed right behind. The food went quickly, including seconds.

Destiny started to get up and Zeke stopped her. "Hold up. We have some house rules to review first."

"Seriously?" She smirked. "House rules like camp or something?"

Zeke leaned back and pointed to the chair. "Yeah, like that. Do you know why we're doing that?"

Anne took the empty plates to the kitchen and brought a notepad and pen. "All set. Reggie, please feel free to add ideas."

"You have the whole ranch to explore—but only if there's an adult nearby and they know where you're going."

Destiny rolled her eyes.

Anne wrote the suggestions down, including all their cell phone numbers. "I'd like to add some time for your chores." She finished writing. "Tomorrow, I'll spend some time teaching you about the Equine-Assisted Therapy program I teach. Zeke can fill you in on her experience."

They spent the next hour suggesting, revising, and listening to Destiny argue.

"Reggie, if you'd help me for a few minutes, Zeke and Destiny can have a chance to tour the ranch."

"Sure, I'd be glad to."

❧❧❧❧

"Let's go meet the horses. When I first came out to New Mexico, I was afraid of horses." She turned to Destiny. "You know what it's like where we grew up; there are trees, sand, and the Gulf. I never had any pets and certainly never spent any time with horses or cows or any other creatures."

"So how'd you end up here?"

Zeke laughed. "Good story. I was hiking on a trail higher up near the crest when I crossed paths with a huge rattlesnake. I jumped, fell over backward and down the hill. When I gathered my senses, I heard something crashing through the bushes and I was convinced it was either a bear or a mountain lion."

Destiny's eyes were huge. "Oh my god, what did you do?"

"I pulled my service weapon and waited. When I finally spotted something, it was a horse. Then I passed out."

"But were you okay?"

"The good news was that it was a nurse on a horse. She was able to get me off the mountain and to the hospital."

"Wow. That was lucky."

"It was more than that, it was serendipity. That nurse was Anne, and here we are all these years later." Zeke opened the barn door.

"This is Shadow, the horse that rescued me." She patted his neck. "You can touch him, but first move close enough so he can get your scent."

"They don't bite or anything, do they?"

"Not usually. Horses are prey animals so they're very wary of strangers or anything sneaking up on them."

Shadow sniffed and flicked his ears back and forth.

"Okay, pat his neck. Don't go for his face."

"Wow. His hair is wiry."

Zeke handed her a cup with oats. "Pour this in that box inside the door. You'll be his friend now."

"Man, these are huge animals."

"This lovely lady is Sunny. Let her sniff, then offer her some oats."

Destiny moved very slowly. "She's pretty. Are there any more?"

"Just one and she's new, so I think we'll wait until she's more comfortable." Zeke took Destiny around and showed her the tack room, the tools and supplies, and the hay bales. "Every morning they need to have their stalls mucked out and the water changed. I'll show you tomorrow. It's not hard, and it's a good way for them to learn to trust you."

"It sounds disgusting."

"Remember, horses eat hay and oats. No animal products so it isn't so bad."

"What do I do the rest of the time?"

Zeke smiled. "We have a very extensive library along with some great movies. When I'm free we'll do some touring around the area. There are some haunted ruins we can explore."

"Haunted? No way!"

"I have a book you can borrow that I read before I did my horsemanship training. It was really surprising to find out all the things I didn't realize about horses. They're amazingly intuitive. If they trust you, you won't find a better friend. They don't lie, cheat, steal, betray, or desert you."

"Sounds like you got over being scared of them."

"It took a long time and a lot of hard work, mainly because I didn't want to believe they could help. Boy, was I wrong. We'll talk about that some other time. Right now, I want some ice cream. How 'bout you?"

"Totes!"

The last rays of sun disappeared behind the mountain as pink and purple painted the sky. Crickets and night birds began their songs.

"Zeke, are there dangerous animals out there?" She pointed to the forest above.

"I suppose some, but they don't come down unless they're really hungry. They don't like hanging around humans."

"I don't blame them."

Zeke laughed.

❧ ❧ ❧ ❧

Anne and Reggie were in the family room having coffee.

"Hi guys. We thought ice cream would be a good idea. Anyone else?" Zeke said.

Reggie brought his coffee cup out to the sink. "I'll have to pass. I've had a long day and I'm going to head up to bed." He stopped. "Destiny, I expect you to get that room squared away before you go to bed."

"You know you sound just like Grandpa when you say stuff like that." Destiny banged down the dessert bowl and ran up to her room.

"I'm sorry about that. I'm sure you both must be tired, too. I'll check in on her, but thank you both for everything. I really appreciate it." He turned and climbed up the stairs.

Zeke continued to dish out some ice cream and then followed Anne into the family room. She curled up on the couch.

Anne whispered, "You know, the fact that she responds to your brother that way probably means she associates those comments with your father. Maybe things will smooth out when he's not here."

Zeke took another bite of the mint chocolate chip and held the spoon in her mouth for a moment. "I can certainly understand how she feels. My father was a bully before it was popular. He can still make me feel like a six-year-old."

Anne leaned over and kissed her cheek. "I'm sure it's been very difficult for her."

Zeke finished her ice cream and headed for the

kitchen. "I think we need a more detailed schedule for Destiny. It's going to be hard to keep her occupied, especially if we both have to work." She retrieved her iPad from a briefcase.

Anne grabbed her planner from her desk. "We should probably work out a reward system for good behavior. I don't know what she's interested in or if she's even reward-motivated."

"One way to find out. My next teaching gig will be the second week in June, and while I'm gone she might be more motivated to please you."

"That should be okay, I don't have any clients scheduled." She made a few notes and looked up. "If Destiny still shows some interest, that might be a good time to do some work with her."

Zeke smiled. "That would be wonderful. Especially if she has the same result I did."

Loud voices echoed down from upstairs. "Why don't we take Shayla for a walk?"

Anne nodded. Zeke grabbed the leash and they slipped out the back door. Shayla ran up from her hiding place in the tool shed. "How about some quality time with our best girl?" Shayla wiggled and whimpered with excitement.

The solar lights and the covered barn light revealed the path to the gate. Zeke clicked it open. "Let's run for it."

Anne giggled and they took off. The half moon had risen over the eastern plains and was peeking through a couple of lonely clouds. It was more than enough to light the road in front of them. In the distance they could hear a dog bark a reply to a couple of coyotes. Shayla perked up her ears and issued a low growl. "Good girl."

Anne slipped her arm around Zeke's waist. "We haven't done this in a while. I miss our walks. In fact, I miss being alone with you."

Zeke stopped and pulled Anne into an embrace, and then put her hand on Anne's neck, pulling her close enough to kiss.

Anne melted into her embrace and moaned softly. "You know, I had almost forgotten your magical mouth, and I like the new addition."

Zeke pulled back. "What new addition?"

Anne ran her tongue across Zeke's lower lip. "The mint ice cream."

"Okay, then." Zeke pulled her in again for an encore. Shayla whined.

"Busted."

They continued to walk around the loop until they were back at the gate. As they walked up to the back door Anne said, "You know, we're probably not going to have as much time alone. Maybe none."

Zeke stopped walking. "Oh, that would not be good. In fact, that would be bad. What do we do?

Anne leaned over and unclipped Shayla's leash. "I don't know, honey. But if it's actually two and a half months, I'm going to be real cranky."

Zeke snickered. "We'll think of something. I promise."

When they got to the back door. Anne stopped. "Would you mind if I talk to Susan about keeping an eye on Destiny? I think we may need another pair of adult eyes."

"Actually, that's a good idea. Susan is a pretty good watchdog."

Once inside, Shayla took off for her bed in the family room and Zeke hung up the leash. "Did you notice Destiny's light is still on?"

"Yes. I suppose kids stay up late and sleep late."

Zeke laughed. "Well, I have to take Reggie to the airport by seven, so she'll need to get up if she wants to say goodbye to her dad."

"If I recall, you had some trouble adjusting to the regimented schedule when you began equine treatment at the Tucson ranch."

"No kidding. First barn work, then breakfast, then group therapy. Maybe we could adopt a similar plan."

They proceeded to lock up, shut off lights, set the alarm, and head up to bed. All was quiet. The light shone under the door at the end of the hall and snoring could be heard across from their room.

Once they were getting ready for bed, Anne asked, "Did you leave your desk chair pulled out?"

"I don't think so, but I'd better start locking my desk."

"Not a bad idea. Where are you keeping your weapon now?" Anne slipped under the covers.

"Hmm. In the gun safe in the closet." She turned off the light and slid next to Anne. "Move it?"

"Be a good idea."

Zeke curled behind her. "I love you."

Anne murmured, "I love you, too."

"What you're doing for me and my family is really above and beyond. I'll never be able to repay you for your kindness and generosity. I hope Destiny will realize how lucky she is to be in a loving home with people who care instead of alone in lockup." She kissed the back of her neck and heard soft snoring. She giggled. "Good night, my love."

Chapter Four

Anne was coming in from the barn when Zeke came down with her jacket. "Good morning. Sorry I faded last night."

Zeke kissed her and went for the coffee. "No worries. I crashed right away."

Anne refilled her cup. "Anyone else up?"

"I heard Reggie's razor. Nothing from the princess."

"Will she want to go with you guys?"

"That would be nice."

Reggie set down his bag. "Good morning ladies."

"Coffee?"

"Thanks."

"Help yourself, and if you want a bagel, they're in the bag." Anne pointed.

"Did you sleep all right?"

"Oh, yes." Reggie opened the bag. "It was so quiet and the cool night air was glorious. No wonder you love it here."

"Is Destiny coming with us?"

Reggie sipped his coffee. "Not sure. I asked her to come, and she growled at me."

Zeke put down her cup. "I'll go ask."

Reggie leaned forward. "Anne, you are amazing, and I'm so grateful Zeke found you. She's never looked happier."

"I'm pretty happy I found her, as well. And

please don't worry about your daughter. We will do everything in our power to get her on a good path."

"She growled at me, too," Zeke said. "She's 'too tired.' Right. She doesn't even know tired yet."

They all laughed as Zeke headed to the garage.

"Take care, Reggie." Anne hugged him.

"Thanks again, we'll be in touch. Please call anytime."

❧❧❧❧

Anne waved as Zeke backed out. "Let the games begin." She walked out and called Shayla. "Come on, sweetie. Let's enjoy some peace and quiet."

The kitchen was cleaned, laundry started, and her clients confirmed when Destiny dragged her pitiful self to the kitchen.

Anne looked up and smiled.

"I'm hungry, is there any of the pizza left?"

Why not? Nobody else wants plain cheese pizza. "Sure, do you want it heated or cold?"

"Cold. Do you have any Coke?"

"Sorry. I thought we could shop after you got here. I had no idea what you might want." She set the pizza box on the counter. "Milk?"

"Okay."

Anne watched her. She had her aunt's beautiful eyes and short curly hair. She would be a beautiful woman, one day. Hopefully.

"I know it's your first day, but since Zeke took your dad to the airport, I could use a little help this morning. Just for a little while, then you can do whatever."

Destiny sighed the apathetic, dramatic poor—me

sigh of adolescence. "I'll probably go back to bed."

"Oh, couldn't you sleep?"

"I can't go to sleep until real late. So it's weird to get up early."

"I understand. Well, after you help me, you can do that. When you're up to it, we'll go shopping and see what you like. So think about dinner."

"I like pizza."

"So do we, but not all the time."

❧ ❧ ❧ ❧

By eight thirty, Destiny clomped downstairs in some baggy jeans, a work shirt, and some work-ready western boots.

"You look perfect. Let's go."

They walked out the back door, and Shayla trailed along behind them.

"Do you think she's still mad at me?"

Anne looked over her shoulder and shrugged. "Don't know." She dug in her pocket and handed Destiny a dog treat. Call her softly and offer the treat."

"Come here, Shayla. I have a treat."

"Just wait."

Finally, Shayla inched forward next to Anne and gently took the treat. "Tell her she's a good girl."

"That's a good girl."

Shayla wagged her tail.

"Seems like feeding animals is the way to get them to like you."

Anne smiled. "It sort of is the best way." They took a few more steps, and Anne said, "So, did you like the pizza?"

"Yeah." She stopped and smiled at Anne. "I get

it."

Anne put an arm around her shoulder. "Excellent student. You're going to do very well."

Once in the barn, Anne quizzed her on what Zeke had shown her. She remembered where everything was as well as the horse's names. She showed surprising interest in the workings of the operation when she asked why the horses mostly got hay and oats very rarely. Anne explained that hay was a good food source, but horses sometimes needed added calories and nutrients. Destiny nodded sagely. Once the horses were brushed and out in the paddock, Anne taught her the easiest way to muck the stalls and refill the water buckets.

"Boy, you're fast. This would take me forever."

"Keep in mind, I've had these two horses for ten years. We have a routine. Ask your aunt how long it took her to learn the routine." Anne laughed. "Okay, I'm going to spend some time getting the new horse acclimated. If you want to go back to bed, you can."

"Could I just watch you?"

The wonder of wonders. "Sure, if you want to."

❧❧❧❧

Zeke pulled into the garage and then checked her text messages.

AReynolds: Destiny and I are working with Dancer. She asked if she could!! Be in later.

She walked into the house, laughing. "My God, this kid is an enigma." Since Destiny wanted to work in the barn, she had time to do some writing. With a water bottle in hand, she headed up to her mini office on the landing. From that vantage, she could see much of the downstairs and the front yard.

"And speaking of improved visibility." Zeke booted her laptop and opened her surveillance program. Each camera had a list of "incidents" and whether they were intrusions. There were always wildlife intrusions, and sometimes even the weather triggered a recording.

The cameras on the front of the house "recognized" her, Benjamin, and Anne. *Probably ought to log Destiny into the program.* She stopped and said aloud, "On second thought, it might be good to know when she comes and goes."

She scrolled backward through the digital recording twenty-four hours to the time they returned from the airport. The tape moved quickly as her car pulled in and everyone went into the house. Soon after, Destiny was crossing the yard from the front door. She looked around and headed toward the arena. Shayla could be spotted following her.

"Smart dog."

Sometime later, Anne drove in, and Shayla ran past with Destiny chasing her with a whip. Anne stopped her.

Zeke leaned back, weighing her responsibility regarding Destiny's right to privacy. She decided Destiny gave up her rights when she sneaked out and went after the dog.

The other cameras showed pretty usual footage, with animals and an occasional neighbor walking their property or on the road. She was growing bored when a black SUV cruised by slowly on the screen. She checked the time stamp. It was last night, just before they went for a walk. *Damn.* Making a note of that vehicle, she looked for any other occurrences. There were four. The other two were a night over a week ago—while she was at Quantico. "Shit."

"Okay. There's no point in getting crazy-paranoid." She shoved back her chair and stood. Her whole body trembled. "I need to get a plate number and call Mike Donovan."

After returning from the bathroom, Zeke set the parameters to search for all angles of the black SUV, and hit Enter.

It took about a minute while she spun in her office chair making up possible scenarios. How badly did she want to bother Mike after all these years?

The ding provided a list of photos—all pretty poor quality. A plate was visible in six of the fifteen.

Her phone beeped.

AReynolds: Don't know if you're back yet, but we're craving Big Burgers from Eddie.

ZCabot: Just working in my office, I'll run out in about twenty. Send me the order.

She magnified the pictures and got some hazy possibilities. What was clear were the Arizona colors: blue, white, yellow, purple, like a sunset. AX was visible in two, A clear in three, A1917 in one, 17 in four.

Her new file labeled Destiny's Child now held the photos and possible license plate number combinations. She hit Save and closed it up. As an afterthought, she put her laptop in the drawer and locked her desk. It was difficult to admit not trusting her own niece, but until she proved herself more reliable and trustworthy, they would need to be vigilant.

Zeke grabbed her keys and wallet and trotted downstairs.

⚘ ⚘ ⚘ ⚘

Anne took a deep breath and leaned against the wall of the round pen. This horse was exhausting every trick she knew. *No wonder Nancy got rid of her.* This was either the most neurotic animal she'd ever worked with, or the most stubborn. She rubbed her neck.

"Okay, Dancer, we're both tired, but if I stop now, you'll have won."

Swinging the lead rope over her head, she repeated, "Keep going, go on, Dancer, run." The horse was cantering around in a circle shaking her head and snorting. Whenever she slowed, Anne changed direction and ran her in the other.

Both horse and trainer glistened with sweat. Anne's long-sleeved shirt and vest had been draped on the rail. Her navy tank top was soaked.

"Can I go back to the house?" Destiny called out.

"Sure, go ahead. Let Zeke know we're having a standoff."

Dancer slowed, and Anne went over and picked up the lunge whip. "Again, girl, get moving." She snapped it behind the horse. Dancer's ears turned, and she jumped. Five long minutes and the horse slowed. Clearly they were both exhausted.

Beaten, Anne walked to the rail for her water. "Shit." She draped both arms over the railing and pulled the shirt over to wipe her face. The sound of blowing breath stopped, and she turned. Dancer stood behind her.

Carefully, Anne turned away and walked slowly

across the center of the ring—Dancer followed behind. Anne stopped and smiled. *Victory.* "You ready to work with me now?"

Dancer flicked her ears forward and allowed Anne to stroke her neck. Anne retrieved the lead rope and harness as Dancer followed. With slow, easy moves, Anne slipped the halter up and over her ears, attached the lead, and walked her back to the barn. She set out fresh water and tied the horse between the crossties in the aisle.

While the horse drank, Anne splashed the fresh water on her head, neck, and shoulders. It was chilly in the barn, but she didn't care.

"You're going to get a special treat for supper, but first a good brushing."

"Just when I think I've seen you at your sexiest."

Zeke's sexy drawl made her smile then laugh. She turned as Zeke wandered over and gave her a kiss.

"Oh please, I am so sweaty and gross. I can't wait for a shower." She laughed as Zeke kissed her neck. "Wait, where's Destiny?"

"I left her in front of the TV with her giant cheeseburger."

"That sounds heavenly. Let me finish brushing Dancer. Would you get her blanket and some oats?"

"Special occasion?"

"Yes. A major breakthrough. I think we've reached an agreement." She rubbed Dancer's forehead.

"Let me help you." Zeke grabbed a brush. "You're both soaked. Why don't you run ahead and jump in the shower, and I'll finish here and heat up our supper?"

"That sounds divine." She kissed Zeke and jogged out of the barn.

When she walked into the mudroom, she kicked

off her boots and wet clothes, which went in the washer. She listened and heard the TV blaring, so she snuck through the dining room and upstairs in her underwear. Once in the shower, she slid down on the small teak bench and let the water from two faucets drench her. She felt alive and invigorated. If she had given up, Dancer might never be able to have the life she deserved. This was one of the two great joys she garnered from her work. The other was the remarkable growth her clients could achieve when they broke through.

She was a little sorry Destiny didn't see it, but thirteen-year-olds had the attention spans of a mayfly. She did stay longer than Anne expected. Maybe there was hope for her, too.

After what seemed like too long— in truth, about fifteen minutes—Anne stepped out into her steamy bathroom and slipped into the decadently thick Turkish bathrobe Zeke had splurged on at Christmas.

She was drying her hair when Zeke came in.

"Thought I better at least change clothes before we eat. You smell wonderful." She nuzzled Anne's neck.

"Stop. We never know when Destiny will pop up."

"She's in her room with music playing." Zeke threw her jeans and shirt in the laundry and slipped into her favorite eggplant-colored warmup suit.

"I thought she was still watching TV when I came in."

"Nope, she left her dirty dishes so she could practice her music appreciation skills."

They both laughed.

Anne donned flannel lounge pants and a hoodie. "Let's go eat that obscenely good burger."

They both prepared plates and some iced tea and settled in the family room for the news.

Anne replayed the morning with Destiny and her exhausting work with Dancer.

"You know I was afraid she wouldn't make the cut. You are quite the horse whisperer," Zeke said.

"What were you working on this afternoon?"

Zeke paused to wipe her mouth. "I did some rereading and research for the book. I thought about what you said and locked my desk with the computer in it."

"Probably a good idea."

As it got later, Zeke said, "I'm going to fix ice cream. Do you want some?"

"I'm full. Why don't you ask Destiny? She missed out because of her tantrum."

"Good plan." Zeke trotted upstairs calling Destiny.

"Anne, she's not there, and her phone is on the bed. The radio is on, but she's not anywhere upstairs."

"Okay. Let's not panic. There's probably a reason we've missed, so let's split up. I'll check the barns and arena. You check the back, and then we'll get the cars out if need be."

"All right. Why don't I call the Godfreys, another two helping to search?"

"Good idea." Zeke hurried out to the garage for the large beam lights. She called Shayla. "Girl, I don't know what kind of tracker you are, but let's give it a try." She grabbed the sweatshirt Destiny had borrowed earlier.

"Don't forget phones and flashlights. Please keep in touch," Anne called after her, then picked up her phone.

"Hello, Jim. This is Anne next door. I hate to

bother you, but we have a problem."

"Sure, Anne. We're always here to help. What's goin' on over there?"

"We're watching Zeke's thirteen-year-old niece for a couple of months. Her dad dropped her off yesterday, and all was well until this evening. She's disappeared."

"All right, I'll get my ATV out and drive around. Let me put Susan on the phone for some details. What's her name?"

"Destiny. Thanks, Jim."

She heard him brief Susan.

"I'm sorry. That's just horrible. Don't you worry, we'll find the kid. How long you figure she's been gone?"

Anne felt choked up. "We're not sure. She was watching TV and having supper while Zeke and I settled a new horse. We thought she was in her room, but when we looked she was nowhere to be found, and she left her phone."

"I'll get my car and notify the neighbors. Keep your cell phone handy."

"Thanks, Susan." Anne hung up and started to cry. How could this happen without them knowing?

Chapter Five

Zeke walked the perimeter of the eastern part of the property, which was mostly wooded on a steep slope. It was slow going with the uneven ground. Shayla's collar jingled her location. She could hear Anne's tense voice calling out from up the hill.

The moon was up and helped light the area. "Shayla, I sure wish I had some night vision goggles." From below, only the muffled sounds of traffic on the highway reached her ears. She tried to use her profiler skills to figure out what possessed Destiny to take off. She didn't seem upset about her father leaving, and there hadn't been any sort of blowup. Zeke felt sure Destiny was happy with her dinner.

Zeke tripped over a large branch and almost fell. She smiled as she grabbed a branch and thought about having to call Anne to come rescue her...again. No, not funny.

Within view of the eastern fence, Zeke headed north. "Shayla, come here." Crashing through the leaves, Shayla bounded up having the time of her life. "I'll bet this is fun for you, huh, girl?" She bent down and hugged her. "Let's not forget what we're doing." She stuck the sweatshirt in front. "Destiny. Find her, girl."

They started again, looking for any clue. If it had been daylight and Destiny determined, she might have found the overgrown deer path down to the highway.

But there was no sign.

Susan drove to the new arena and found Anne inside searching every corner.

"Need some help?"

"Boy, am I glad to see you." Anne almost wept with joy. "I'm driving myself crazy. I was sure this would be the logical place to hide out."

Susan looked around. It was an enormous area with corners and bleachers galore. "I agree…if she wanted to hide out."

Anne stopped. "What do you mean?"

"I don't know the child, but she's only been here a short time, and she has plenty of room and freedom, so what would make her run off?"

Anne slumped against the bench near the door. She took a drink from her water bottle. "I didn't think this through. When we found her gone, I just went into full panic mode." She laughed. "And this from a professional nurse." They both laughed, but Susan was right. What was going through that kid's mind?

Susan's phone rang. "Hey, Jim. Any sign?"

Anne watched for any indication as Susan nodded and muttered uh-huh.

"Sorry. Jim's covered the trails in a one mile perimeter. Said we better call the police."

"I guess he's right. I just thought it would be safer if we found her before authorities were contacted."

"Why's that?"

"Let's take a walk around the paddock."

As they walked, Anne relayed some of Destiny's history and the reason she was staying with them.

If there was a police report, it might mean her third strike.

⚘⚘⚘

Zeke was fading fast. It'd been a long day, and this was not how she wanted to end it. As she neared the house, the yard lights and decorative twinkle lights welcomed her back. *I wonder if those lights might have had the same effect on Destiny? Maybe she went for a walk and got lost.*

As Zeke turned toward the house, Shayla took off barking. "Great. Shayla, come." The barking sounded like it came from Jim and Susan's house.

She turned toward the barking. "Damn it. We can't lose a dog and a kid at the same time. "Shayla! Come back here. Shayla." There was a small worn path between the two houses that Anne and Susan had used for years for coffee klatches. Apparently, this was a lifeline during Anne's divorce.

At their house, the lights were all on but the truck and ATV were still missing—as was Shayla. "Come on, girl. Time to go home and get cookies," she shouted.

Shayla ran out of the shadows from behind the barn looking uninjured, and not a bit guilty. No sign of damage to wildlife. "Good girl," she petted her. "Eww, you smell funny…"

Shayla yanked the sweatshirt out of Zeke's hand and ran off. "Damn, now you think it's play time."

Zeke ran after her and into the barn. "Okay, that's it. Game over. Let's go."

She wagged her tail, whimpered, and walked backward.

"I'm getting a little pissed," Zeke said through

gritted teeth until the ceiling light shone on a pile in the feed stall.

"Holy shit!" she ran over and peeled back the red hoodie. Destiny was sound asleep, snoring and reeking of stale wine. Beside her was a half-empty bottle of expensive Bordeaux.

Zeke checked her pulse, kissed Shayla, and called Anne.

"I found her. Well, Shayla did. She's okay. I'll bring her home."

Shayla you will get the biggest prize ever. I love you, sweet little orphan-pup.

With some effort, Zeke was able to rouse Destiny to her feet and half drag her home.

꧁꧂꧁꧂

Anne, Susan, and Jim were waiting outside when Zeke came out of the trees by the garage.

Jim hurried over. "Here let me help you." With one swift movement, he swept the half-conscious juvenile into his arms and carried her in through the garage.

Anne hurried ahead. "Let's put her in the family room for now." She went to the kitchen and retrieved some ibuprofen and a large glass of water.

Everyone was standing watch over the bleary-eyed kid, who looked confused.

"Can I get you guys something to drink?" Anne said.

"No, thanks. I think it's best if we head home. You have your hands full."

Anne hugged them both. "We owe you big time. Let's plan a night out."

"I'll walk out with you," Zeke said.

Anne sat next to Destiny and wiped her face with a damp towel. The idea crossed her mind to take a picture to remind her of this adventure, but at the moment she was just glad to see she was safe and uninjured.

"Here's some water, and I want you to take these pills."

Destiny obeyed. Silently.

"Are you hurt anywhere?"

She shook her head.

"Good. When your aunt comes back you need to thank her—and Shayla—for finding you before it got any colder."

"Shayla?"

"Yes."

Anne heard Zeke come back. "Drink the rest of this water and don't move."

Zeke looked exhausted. "Honey, are you okay?"

"I will be. I think it's best we all get some sleep before we talk about all this."

Anne recognized the conflicting feelings. "You're probably right. Why don't you go up and I'll get her to bed?"

"I will. But first, I promised Shayla a treat." Shayla's ears perked up from her bed by the heat duct.

Zeke took some ground beef out of the freezer and defrosted it. "If not for this dog's tracking and persistence in getting me to follow her, we might have had a much worse outcome." The bell rang, and Zeke tore the fresh ground beef apart and gave it to Shayla, who sat politely with her tail beating a steady rhythm.

Anne poured another cup when Zeke walked in. "Good morning."

Zeke put her arms around Anne and hugged her close. "You are the most wonderful human being on this planet, and I adore you."

Anne returned the caress and kissed her. "You're very sweet. I thought you might still be upset after last night."

Zeke added cream to her cup. "Oh, I'm still upset, just not homicidal."

Anne snickered. "You didn't sleep too well. Was that it?"

"Partly, but my back hurt."

"Did you lift something or get hurt last night?"

Zeke's eyes lit up. "Yes, that's it. I tripped over a branch and caught myself with one arm. Then I used the same arm to drag home the drunk. Completely slipped my mind."

"I can certainly see why. Let's work on that later." Anne sat at the breakfast table. "How do you want to handle this thing with Destiny? Do you think we need to call Reggie?"

Zeke set down her coffee cup and a plate with some toast. "I'm not really sure. I do not want to parrot the same scolding she's gotten before."

"I agree. Destiny has already built up her defenses for punitive reactions. We need something else."

Zeke smiled. "If she pulls this shit to get a reaction, why give her one?"

"You mean ignore the whole thing, but—"

"Hear me out. I don't intend to let it pass. I just want her to be waiting for the shoe to drop. Let's proceed calmly and put her to work. No time for mischief. Each of us needs to make a list of chores, simple or time-consuming, to fill her day and exhaust her."

Anne leaned back. "Genius. That could work. I also want her to do some work for Susan and Jim as compensation."

"Excellent. Let's start with the barn work while I figure some house chores or errands…then back to the barn."

Anne got up. "Sure doesn't leave time for a hangover."

"I'll go wake her with the schedule for breakfast—which she might miss."

❧ ❧ ❧ ❧

Zeke knocked. No answer. Again. Faint groaning. Zeke opened the door. "Destiny, you need to get up. It's late. If you're not ready in ten minutes, you'll miss breakfast."

She cracked one eye. "But, I can't. I don't feel good."

Zeke bit her tongue. "Look, it's a busy day, and you need to do your part. Get up. Now."

Destiny looked up at the sound of the soft threat. "Now."

Destiny swung her legs over and stood.

"Ten. Minutes." Zeke walked down to her office and listened from the landing. The toilet flushed. Water running. Quiet. Then she heard the door open.

Anne called up the stairs. "I'm going down to the barn. Send her down as soon as she's ready. There's cereal on the counter." She winked.

"Okay. I think she'll be ready soon," Zeke said a little louder than necessary and unlocked her desk.

She had a hunch about the video surveillance. If she was correct, the garage camera might have caught last night's little caper. Four minutes.

She opened the app. Then shut it. *Might be better if she didn't know we had this capability.*

Destiny came down the hall in her work gear. But that was the only thing that looked normal. "Good girl. There's some cereal on the counter, and you've got about three minutes to gobble that and get to the barn."

"Auntie…"

"You really need to hustle." She smiled.

⁂

Anne got out the extra broom for floor scrubbing. In the half hour she'd been working she had shed a shirt and scarf. Mornings were still brisk, but once the sun hit the slope, temps rose rapidly. She needed to maintain the trust with Dancer garnered by yesterday's Olympic workout, but she also needed to keep a tight rein on Destiny. Her behavior the night before could not continue. Zeke had rightly decided they needed a velvet glove technique. Too harsh would just reinforce Destiny's belief that adults were all mean and abusive.

She filled a pail with Lysol and water. Her professional work had always meant dealing with adults in need of her care. This child didn't even know she needed help.

Destiny schlepped into the barn looking like death warmed over. Anne bit her lip to avoid pitying the poor soul. This probably wasn't the ideal time to tell the tale of her own alcohol problem and its cause.

"Hi, Destiny. Did you get to eat?"

"Yeah, I had some cereal." Her color was gaunt.

"Good." She handed her a bottle of water from a tall cooler and started walking toward the paddock. "I'm sorry you had to leave yesterday because not long after that Dancer came to her senses. She quit fighting me, and I think we can begin work."

Destiny thought a moment then said, "What do you mean, 'quit fighting'?"

They stood at the door of the paddock. "What do you notice that might have been different yesterday?"

After a while, Destiny said, "Well, they're all standing together down there eating grass."

"Why do you suppose that's different?"

"Maybe Dancer didn't like Sunny and Shadow? Or maybe they didn't like her."

Anne smiled. "You're right. I think Dancer didn't feel like she could trust anyone. When I asked her to trust me, she refused. And believe me, I was exhausted from trying to help her." Anne leaned back on the rail. "But then, like trying to work a padlock, the tumblers clicked into place and the lock opened."

Destiny looked skeptical. "What do you mean?"

"Dancer got that I was not going to hurt her, and she relaxed enough to trust me. She let me close enough to put on a halter and lead."

"Oh."

"So, today I hope to build on that and maybe get a saddle on her. Maybe." Anne turned back indoors. "I fed them and turned them out early because we need to do a good cleaning. Whenever a new horse joins us, we need to be very careful."

Anne walked to the end of the stalls. "Each stall needs to be swept out. When all the straw is gone, we'll brush and hose the floor. Then, let it dry before putting down new bedding. Got it?"

Destiny looked gobsmacked. "All that in one day?"

Anne laughed. "With the stalls empty, it won't take any time at all. Sweep each stall, and I'll help you get it out and to the dump pile. When Benjamin comes, he'll move the pile with the tractor."

"Do I really have to do this?" *The whining begins.*

"Yes. It takes a village to run this place, and we all have to earn our keep. That's the deal." Anne held out the push broom. "I'll be in the round pen with Dancer if you have questions." She turned and made her exit without waiting for any more excuses.

As she crossed the paddock to get Dancer, she texted Zeke the details and plan.

Seeing the horses standing near each other, it was clear that Sunny and Shadow were both more filled out with shiny coats. By comparison, Dancer looked less vibrant. But at the moment, she was calm and eating. She didn't have that worried, frightened look. Baby steps.

Anne approached her horses first and offered pats and small carrots. As she spoke softly to each of her horses, she watched Dancer from the corner of her eye. It didn't take long to get her attention. She was watching from about ten feet away. Her ears moved forward.

"Hi, Dancer. Would you like some of these carrots? Sunny and Shadow seem to think they're good."

Dancer took a step and waited.

Anne continued talking and stroking the other two. Several minutes passed with one or two steps. Then a few more. When she was close enough to touch, Anne put her hand out with a carrot. Dancer sniffed, then stepped closer and looked Anne in the eyes.

Anne's breath caught as she seemed to see deep into the soul of this poor horse. They stood that way for what seemed like a long time. Neither moved. Anne could almost feel the fine silver thread connect them. As soon as she recognized that, Dancer reached forward and gently took the carrot.

The tears came unbidden. It was not something she could ever explain. The connection. When it happened between a horse and a client, she knew instantly because the client glowed with a new sensation.

She gave out a few more carrots to all three and thanked them, then she stroked Dancer's neck and slipped the harness and lead rope on. Without hesitation, the horse followed her out of the paddock to the round pen.

❧ ❧❧ ❧

Zeke looked out the window and couldn't quite see the paddock, but smiled. This would be the time when horse and trainer breached free.

Her time at the Arizona Equine Center broke her just as Anne did with new horses…and clients. Her time there was make or break; her career was at stake. If the program hadn't worked, she might have lost her job. If only they could provide the same breakthrough for Destiny, even if she could just make a connection between a fearful distrusting horse and her own fear and distrust.

Zeke sat back down at her desk. She'd checked the surveillance and watched Destiny sneak out of the garage. It followed her as she walked right to the tool shed, sat on the upturned wheelbarrow, and started sipping the wine. The time stamp indicated eighteen thirty hours, and it was still light out.

That was the when she and Anne were still in the barn. *Wow. Never even knew.*

She moved the record forward and almost missed it. Destiny looked up at the house and hurried into the trees on the lot line. She was barely visible walking toward the neighbor's barn—unless you knew what to look for. Zeke did. She saved it.

The cursor blinked, and she vacillated between "call Mike" and "don't call Mike." After excruciating minutes, Zeke pulled out her phone and dialed Mike's cell phone.

"Donovan."

"Hi, Mike. Is this a good time to talk?"

"Hi, Zeke. It's a perfect time. I'm choking on monthly reports. What's up?"

"I know how you've missed my paranoid rambling the past couple of years, so I thought I might try one out on you."

Mike laughed out loud. "You crack me up. Are you serious?"

"Afraid so."

"Let's hear it."

"Remember the exotic and expensive surveillance system I installed?"

"Oh, yeah. Awesome technology."

"Well, a few days ago Benjamin reported a black SUV trolling around. When he asked what he wanted, the guy asked who lived here now. He told him to get lost but noticed part of an Arizona plate. I didn't think anymore about it until later, and then checked the tapes. There were four appearances in the past two months. One sighting of a male outside the south fence."

"That's weird. Probably nothing. What are you thinking? And don't tell me that the Hussein brothers might be zombies."

Zeke had to laugh. "Well, I didn't, but now that you mention it…Seriously, I don't know what to make of it, except we've dealt with those bad actors in Arizona and I'm not sure those creeps are still in prison, or out and pissed."

"That's a possibility—remote—but I can do some checking. Do you have the partials?"

Zeke read him what she had. "I can send the screenshots if it will help."

"May as well. I'll see what I can find."

"Thanks, Mike, I appreciate it."

"Take care…and don't worry!"

Zeke thought she better check in.

ZCabot: Is all well??? Should I get some lunch ready? ETA?

AReynolds: All is good. Great—I think we're both starved. I<3U

Zeke trotted downstairs and had just opened the refrigerator when her phone rang.

"Hello?"

"Hi, sis. I just wanted to know how things were going."

She closed the door and walked to the sink. *Uh-oh.* "Hi, Reg. I guess you made it home okay. Have you talked to Destiny yet?" That might give her an idea of how much she needed to say.

"No. I tried a couple of times, but it went to voice

mail. I guess she's still pissed. I can understand that. Or maybe she's just having too much fun with you guys." He laughed.

"Matter of fact, she's out in the arena with Anne right now. Sounds like she's engaged a little bit into the whole horse business."

"That's great. I won't keep you, but let me know if you need anything."

"Right. I will."

She slid the phone into her pocket. Her brother had a right to know what was happening, but he had put a lot of faith in them to manifest a miracle. A drunken escape might not soothe his conscience.

Once she'd gotten out the leftover spaghetti and garlic bread, she chopped up some lettuce and tomato for a salad. With the food in a lidded casserole dish, she stuck it in the microwave. Anne would hate that. She'd much prefer proper re-heating.

While she waited, she went out on the deck. The warm sun was directly overhead, but she was still glad she wore a hoodie. She whistled, and Shayla came flying up the hill, ears flapping and tail wagging.

"Hey girl, whatcha been up to?" She leaned over and rubbed her belly. "Looks like you might need another bath. Hmm, I wonder if the kid could be trusted to do that."

Her phone beeped with a text.

AReynolds: On the way.

Time to warm up the food and get the plates out.

Anne walked up the aisle in the barn, inspecting the cleaning job. "This looks good for a first effort. Congratulations. Benjamin can help you bring in clean hay after lunch. Then set a flake of alfalfa in each of their feed boxes and fill up their water buckets." She stopped. "Did I tell you to wash those out?"

Destiny threw her hands in the air. "Are you frickin' kidding me?"

Anne took a step toward her. "Excuse me?"

The youthful glow on her latte complexion paled. She did not respond.

Anne took a deep breath. "I think we'll go back to the house to wash up for lunch. Is *that* alright with you?"

"Yeah."

Anne led them out of the barn at a very brisk pace.

Chapter Six

Zeke, do I really have to go over there?" Destiny was whining pathetically. "I don't know those people."

"Well, they know you. They were kind enough to drop everything and drive all over looking for you. Plus, you chose their barn to hide out in and consume half a bottle of expensive stolen wine."

Zeke cleared the dishes and put them in the dishwasher. She tossed a dishrag to Destiny. "Would you please wipe the counters?"

Destiny grumbled while she carefully wiped the counter and table.

"When Anne comes down, I'd really like you to make an effort to be cooperative and pleasant because I'd really like to take you on a getaway. That hinges on today. Got it?"

❧❧❧❧

Anne called Susan and asked if they could stop by, then she changed clothes and brushed her hair, which helped her haggard appearance. Still, she did not enjoy playing Bad Cop. Right now, it was important for Zeke to be her protective aunt.

"Shall we go? I need to get back to work, and you have a few things to do."

"Okay, I'm ready." She glanced over her shoulder

at Zeke.

Daylight made the path more visible, and Anne hoped Destiny would recognize it. "Susan and Jim have been my neighbors and friends since I moved here almost fifteen years ago. I don't think I would have managed my divorce without them."

"You were married? To a guy?"

Anne laughed. "Hard to believe, I know. It was a different time."

Destiny went silent, and Anne guessed she was trying to sort this out. More explanations would have to wait. Today was the start of her accountability.

Anne knocked on the sliding door to the family room, and Susan opened it.

"Hi, neighbor. Come on in. Hello, Destiny."

"Hello, Mrs. Godfrey."

"Can I offer you something to drink?"

"That's not necessary, we just finished lunch and I need to get back to work, but I wanted you to meet Zeke's niece formally."

Susan smiled.

Anne nodded.

"I apologize for causing so much trouble for you and Mr. Godfrey. It was dumb, and it won't happen again."

"Thank you. You know, honey, we were all pretty scared for you. Lots of bad things can happen out here and no one would know. You should probably remember to carry your cell phone at all times so if you have an accident, we can find you."

"Yes, ma'am."

"Since this little adventure inconvenienced you folks, Destiny would like to offer you some help if you need it."

"That's awfully nice. If something comes up, I'll let you know."

Anne put her hand on Destiny's shoulder. "We need to get back, but I'll call you."

"Thanks for coming by."

She waved as Anne steered them back to the path.

"You did a nice job, thank you."

"She seems like a nice person."

"One of the best. Ready to get back to work?"

"Can I ask you something? Do you guys work all the time?"

Anne cracked up. "Sure seems like it. No, we don't. When I don't have clients and Zeke isn't teaching, we entertain, see friends, go out to dinner. Sometimes, we just sit around and watch TV."

"Right."

"After we get the stalls set up, would you like to learn about riding?"

"The horses?" Destiny stopped.

"Well, yes."

"I dunno, they're pretty huge. Do you have any little ones?"

"Like a pony? Afraid not. But you're pretty tall and would have no trouble with Sunny."

They got to the barn and began hauling clean straw and fresh hay. The scent of Lysol lingered but smelled fresh and clean. Together they were able to finish quickly. Everything looked neat and tidy.

"Looks like we finished and there is still time for me to work. Thank you, Destiny. You may want to check and see if Zeke has anything. If not, maybe a nap." She winked.

"Okay." Destiny turned and jogged out of the barn.

Anne shot Zeke a text and warned her, then rolled up her sleeves and went to spend some time with Dancer because she didn't want to lose the ground they'd gained.

※ ※ ※ ※

Zeke read the texted note and finished the section of her manuscript about the interstate smuggling ring.

Whenever she discussed details of her past cases—without identifying markers—the details popped into her consciousness. Although she still had all her field notebooks, she rarely needed them. This was enough for today. Maybe she and Destiny could grocery shop and get a few things that would make her feel more at home.

The back door slammed, and Destiny straggled up the stairs. "Hiya, ranch hand."

Startled, Destiny looked up. "Is that what I am?"

"When you're not an honored guest, my favorite niece, or trouble…yeah."

"I'm exhausted. This is not a fun vacation." She collapsed on the top step.

"Is that what your dad promised you?"

"Well, he thought it would be an exciting adventure to see you and where you lived."

Zeke smiled. "Right. In that case, why don't you change and I'll show you some local color."

"Does that include ice cream?"

Zeke laughed. "You know, it might, but don't tell."

Destiny jumped up and ran to her room. Zeke backed up her work, saved it to her flash drive, and shut down her computer. With a scratch pad in hand, she began a list of staples they needed. Milk, bread, coffee, salad fixings, chicken, ground beef. *Oh, don't forget more dog treats.* She folded and stuck it in her pocket.

Destiny appeared just as she locked her laptop in the desk. "Why do you lock up your computer?"

"Habit mostly. I had to do it for work." She grabbed her keys, and they headed down to the garage.

"But didn't you, like, work for the FBI?"

"Yes, but we had a lot of confidential information on our cases."

Destiny laughed. "That's weird. I mean don't you trust the people you work with?"

"The short answer is yes. But, there are laws about documentation and chain of evidence. We each had responsibility for some pretty serious information."

"Like what?" Destiny asked, buckling her seat belt.

Very sincerely, Zeke said, "If I told you, I'd have to kill you."

Destiny's jaw dropped. "Auntie!"

Zeke shrugged and pulled out of the driveway. She honked as she drove by the paddock and round pen.

Dark clouds rolled in over the mountain along with quickly cooling temperatures, not uncommon for spring and certainly welcome. They'd been enduring a drought for almost a decade which caused myriad difficulties, not the least of which was fires. Living in the forest on the green side of the mountain was beautiful, but also prone to lightning. The changes disrupted the wildlife and bears, mountain lions, coyotes, and other small animals came down closer to civilization for food or water.

Zeke explained this as they drove down to the market. "When we shop, I want you to tell me what kinds of things you normally like to eat. And I don't mean snacks or junk. Like favorite dishes your family eats."

"Can you make red beans and rice? And…fried chicken with sweet potatoes?"

Zeke smiled with the memory. "I think I can if you help me remember. What do you usually eat for breakfast, and do you take lunch to school?"

"Sometimes scrambled eggs with crumbled sausage, and maybe peanut butter toast. I really like French toast a lot."

"What about lunches?"

"Mostly sandwiches or wraps, you know. And chips."

Zeke parked. "Okay. I'll take the cart for the stuff on my list, and you track down things you think would be good and bring them to the cart."

Destiny jumped out and ran into the store. Zeke followed and got a cart. This was a small neighborhood store, but they had a great bakery, meat department, and an excellent wine selection. *Maybe I should let Destiny pick out a bottle; she seems to have good taste.* She chuckled to herself.

One item after another was checked off her list. In between, Destiny ran up with her choices. Most were good; a few got the thumbs down and the sulk. The shelled peanuts and potato chips were fine, but Zeke held a line on too many sweets. She agreed to the Coke once a day and let her pick out some ice cream. She chose an Oregon brand Marionberry she'd never seen.

Zeke passed quickly on the wine. Beer was only an

occasional thing and mostly for company. Anne didn't drink any longer, so why put it out as a temptation? The deli offered some delicious-looking meatloaf. Zeke stood weighing the choice when Destiny dropped a jar of baby gherkins in the cart. "Do you like meatloaf?"

"I love it. Especially the kind grandma used to make." Her eyes welled up with tears.

Zeke put an arm around her, pulled her close, and whispered, "I know. I miss her, too. A lot." Zeke ordered the meatloaf, and the clerk packed and weighed it.

"We'll get some fresh green beans and twice-baked potatoes. Should go great with the ice cream you picked."

They checked out and carried the bags to the car. Destiny was quiet the whole way home. Zeke wanted to ask why but didn't. Destiny would open up when she was ready.

They pulled in the garage to unload, and Destiny asked, "Can I go and lie down?"

"Sure, just help me get these bags inside, and I'll put stuff away."

Anne walked in while Zeke washed the potatoes and soaked the beans. "Where's mother's little helper?" She slipped her arm around Zeke's waist and propped her chin on Zeke's shoulder.

"She went shopping with me and when we got home asked if she could go to her room. I *think* she's up there."

"Want me to go check?"

"Nah. I think she's okay." She retold the scene at the store when Destiny teared up talking about her grandmother. "I hadn't thought about how Mom must've been a buffer for Destiny between her and

Dad. No wonder she misses her."

"Plus, that might have been her first real loss," Anne added.

Zeke dried her hands. "There's probably a lot going on in that adolescent cranium. I hope in time she feels safe enough to trust us."

She put the potatoes in the oven and set the timer. "Let's go sit outside and enjoy the evening. I was afraid we were going to get rain all night."

"Let me grab a jacket. You want one?"

Zeke nodded.

❧❧❧❧

Anne stretched her tired legs out on the patio table and zipped up her jacket.

Zeke stepped out and closed the sliding door. "You look comfortable." She sat next to her and took her hand. "I peeked in on Destiny, she's curled up with a stuffed bear sound asleep."

"Good. She's undoubtedly tired. I worked her pretty hard."

"How's it going with the new horse?"

"Better than expected, but it's still push-pull. That mare just trembled when we started, then suddenly did a complete one-eighty. Then today she's just spotty. It's like she's reacting to extraterrestrial signals that I can't see or hear."

"Will you be able to use her for working with clients?"

Anne scrubbed her face and turned her head back and forth to loosen the muscles. "I'm not sure yet. I need to see if she'll let me ride her, but I'd like you there if I try."

Anne's racing mind finally slowed, and she leaned on Zeke's shoulder and watched the sun slip away through the trees.

⚜ ⚜ ⚜ ⚜

Destiny looked better except for the puffy eyes, and was eating like she'd been starved. Zeke put another piece on meatloaf on her plate while she buttered another roll. "Should we check the meal off as a success?"

"Oh yeah." Destiny garbled with a mouth full. "I could eat this anytime. These cheesy potatoes are boss."

"Glad to hear it." Zeke cleared her throat. "So, Anne thought tomorrow might be a good day for us to go on a little road trip—after chores."

"Really? Where would we go?"

"Up the Turquoise Trail." She set a well-worn travel book on the table. "When I moved here, this was one of the first things I did because everyone I talked to said I would enjoy it. And I did. That's why the map is so marked up."

Destiny picked it up and opened it.

"Maybe you could go through it before bed, and we could talk about it in the car."

Destiny carefully removed more of the baked potato and pushed it around her plate. "Sure."

Anne winked at Zeke. "This is a great dinner. Thanks. Maybe tomorrow night we could do tacos and burritos."

"I love tacos."

Zeke nodded "Good to know."

Anne stood. "Destiny would you help me clear—"

"Yeah, and don't forget the ice cream."

❧❧❧❧

Anne put her spoon down. "This has been lovely. Thank you both for a good day and a lovely meal." She paused and folded her hands in front of her. "Destiny, I am very impressed with how quickly you learn things and pitch in to help. So, it puzzles me why you'd act out the way you did last night. Did something happen that ticked you off?"

Destiny sat stock-still, listening. She looked furtively between Anne and Zeke like she was ready to bolt.

Zeke calmly sat forward and said, "I'm not sure you get how scared we were. I mean, we were just getting to know you, and you took off. We want you to feel safe here. But, not knowing where you are or being able to contact you is not okay."

"Can you help us understand what happened?" Anne asked.

After an interminable silence with Destiny twisting her napkin, she whispered, "I don't know. I was pissed off." Her anger was palpable.

"At whom?" Anne said.

"Everybody."

Zeke leaned forward. "Can you tell me why you think your dad brought you here?"

"Because they don't have time for me. Mom and Dad are busy fighting and doing their own stuff. I'm not allowed to do anything anymore."

"I'm not sure—"

"Wait, Zeke. Destiny is telling us her side of the story, which is her truth."

Zeke did a double take, then acquiesced.

Anne slowly tried a new tack. "That's terrible, and I understand, now, why you're angry. I think it's important to distinguish who you are angry with and not just act out. Your aunt and I offered to have you come visit because we wanted to get to know you better." She glanced at Zeke. "Do you think we deserved to be disrespected by you?"

Destiny looked up, and a series of emotional reactions flashed across her face. "No."

Chapter Seven

This road is called the Turquoise Trail, mainly because the area has so many turquoise deposits, or it used to. It's about fifty-three miles and runs to Santa Fe. I think it's got the best variety of scenery anywhere."

Destiny looked out the window then back at the book. "It sure is brown and empty,"

Zeke laughed. "You're not the first to notice that. I think there are two groups of people: those that love the desolate scenery and those who think it should be green and full of people and houses. Personally, I like the wide openness."

"Will there be someplace to eat?"

"Hmm. Sure, we'll go through Madrid and on to Cerrillos, then on the way back we'll walk around and eat something at the Mine Shaft. They have great food, especially their cheeseburgers."

Destiny nodded, pulled out her earbuds, and closed her eyes.

Guess the guided tour is over. On the other hand, Zeke thought it was okay to have some quiet after a couple of crazy days. Some fresh air blew through the open window carrying with it the faint but distinctive smells of the desert. This section of highway came out of the hills, and the vast central prairie opened up all the way to the horizon and, north of it, mountains that belonged to the tail end of the Rockies.

Desolate beauty that soothed the soul with its timeless endurance.

She glanced at Destiny. Her head against the window and her mouth slightly open suggested she was asleep. Undoubtedly, the whole ordeal had taken a toll on her as well.

Zeke hoped they could bond enough to earn her trust.

***

At first, Anne walked Dancer around the round pen on a lead. Then she walked beside the mare, tossing the lead rope across her back hoping to get her used to having something touching her. When they stopped for a break, Anne brought some water for her and went to the barn for a saddle blanket.

She glanced at her watch and wondered how the tour was going. Zeke really wanted to get to know her niece, but thirteen-year-old girls were difficult under optimal circumstances. This little girl had some demons, and she was really too young to understand.

Benjamin parked his truck near the round pen, and stood and watched as Anne tried to introduce the blanket. She waved. Dancer had some real issues with being touched, and after several tries, Anne backed up and let her out into the paddock.

"How's it going, Benjamin?" Anne pulled off her gloves and shoved them in her back pocket.

"I borrowed Susan's ATV to check the fences and found three areas that need repair."

"Normal wear and tear, or do they need to be replaced?" Anne removed her hat and wiped her forehead with a folded bandana.

"The two down near the road can be reinforced, but the one over there on the Bascoms' side looks to be cut."

"Cut? Why don't you take me over there? We should be able to get to it in the truck." She followed him to his truck and got in. "Why would anyone cut the fence? I've always gotten along with Roger and Denise. I think they would have called me." They bounced over the uneven ground along the paddock fence until he stopped on the south side of their newly added piece of property.

Anne walked closer and was incredulous when she saw all four strands of barbwire cut along the post. As she looked around, she saw no tire tracks or other damage. "Can you fix it?"

Benjamin rubbed his chin, which was his sign of thinking. "I think I'll need to run new wire because the posts slipped a bit."

"I can see that. Do whatever you need. I'll check with Zeke to see if the security cameras cover this area." She walked a short way in both directions looking for other damage, then looked back toward the house.

Knowing how paranoid Zeke could be, Anne thought hard about what to say to her. She waited as Benjamin tacked up some temporary snow fencing.

"I'll take you back and go down to the hardware store." Benjamin started the truck, and they bounced through the tall grass to the barn.

"While you're there, would you see if Dick has any fly masks? I just got an idea that might help Dancer."

He pulled up next to the new barn. Anne said, "Would you mind dropping me at the house instead?"

She waved as Benjamin headed out the gate. The

time had flown by, and it was past time to eat. "If I'd gone on the tour, I could be sitting down with a Mine Shaft cheeseburger."

In the end, she settled for a peanut butter sandwich and grapes. Once consumed, she stretched out on the sun-warmed couch in the family room and closed her eyes…just for a minute.

Her cell phone rang. Anne startled out of sleep, and she fumbled the phone. "Hello."

"Hi, babe. Did I catch you at a bad time?"

"No, I came in to eat something. Everything okay?"

"Sure. We stopped in Cerrillos for a few minutes, then headed back to Madrid. Destiny slept most of the way up here. I guess I can understand why," Zeke said.

"Where is she now?" Anne sat up and shook her head to dispel the cobwebs.

"I dropped her off to go to the bathroom while I parked the car, which is in some tiny extra parking area behind the Mine Shaft. I'm waiting for her in front."

"Would you think I was crazy if I asked you to bring me a cheeseburger?"

"Yes, and I'd do it." Zeke laughed. "In fact, I'll give you Destiny's if she doesn't hurry up."

"I was going to make tacos, but maybe I better try for taco salad. Have you noticed our eating habits are going downhill fast?"

"Yes. But I remind myself we're caring for a child, and trying to make her happy."

"Right. Zeke, what am I going to do while you're gone teaching?" Anne wandered to the kitchen and got a bottle of water.

"Are you that worried? I could try to get a sub for my week."

"No. I'm sure we'll be okay."

"You can always call Reggie and tell him to plan a visit…"

Anne leaned on the sink. "I'm sure it will be okay. Susan and Jim are next door. I also thought about asking Benjamin to stay in the office. That couch pulls out."

"That's not a bad idea."

"That reminds me, he checked the fences today, and there are a few spots that need repair. Then he drove me to the south lot line with the Bascom's where a section was cut. He went to get new wire."

Silence.

"Zeke? Are you still there?'

"Yes. I was looking for Destiny, but I heard you. That's very odd. Did you call them to see if they have any ideas?"

"Yes, but they haven't called back. I'll try later, but I need to get back to work. When will you be back?"

"Shouldn't be too long. We'll eat and head back. She's not very interested."

"Okay, hurry home. I miss you."

"I love you, later."

Anne finished her glass of water and headed to the barn. "Get ready, Dancer, it's show time."

※ ※ ※ ※

Zeke rechecked her watch it had been twenty-five minutes. She looked up and saw Destiny coming down the side of the street waving.

"Hey, guess what? There's this really cool Western boot store, and they have millions of crazy wild western boots. Can I get some? They're awesome."

Zeke took a breath. "I'm glad you're okay, but why didn't you text me? I've been waiting for almost half an hour."

"I'm sorry. I didn't know it was so long. But—"

"Let's go in and eat. We can talk about it later." Zeke hurried her in the door and found a crowd waiting to be seated. *Great.* Her mind was ruminating about the cut fence spurring her to get home to check the surveillance. She gave her name and turned to see a gnarly dude cozying up to Destiny. He was way too close to her. She pushed her way back through the irritable throng of hungry diners just in time to see him put his hand on her lower back.

Pushing one couple out of the way, she charged him. She grabbed his shirt and vest and slammed him against the wall.

She kept her voice low, but the menacing guttural sound was evidence of her anger. "I am a Federal law enforcement officer." She shoved her badge and ID in his face with the other hand. "And I want you to get your filthy, pervy paws off that child."

He raised his hands. "Hey, I wasn't doing anything wrong. Ask her."

People moved back from the scene.

"Show me some ID."

"Hey, look—"

She gripped tighter and pushed her elbow into his neck. "ID. Now."

He reached back and produced a large leather and chain number.

"Open it."

"Look, Agent Cabot, you got this all wrong. We was just talkin'."

"No, Delmar. I watched you put your hands on

this child, and that's molesting a juvenile. But, I'm going to cut you some slack. Turn around and walk out of here and you won't be arrested."

"You can't arrest me."

"Oh." She turned to the pale-faced hostess. "Miss, could you call nine-one-one?"

"Okay, okay, I'm leaving. Geez, what a bitch." He grabbed his wallet and pulled away toward the door.

"You'd be wise not to come back, Delmar Bauggins."

He scurried out while several people clapped. "Thanks, lady."

"We need more cops like you."

The hostess came over. "Your table is ready."

Zeke opened her menu and took a deep breath. She looked up at Destiny who was a bit pale. "You okay?"

She nodded.

"What did he say to you?"

She swallowed hard and sipped some water. "Not much, the guy said I was pretty and reminded him of his daughter."

Zeke gripped her napkin under the table. "Has that happened to you before?"

Destiny tipped her head and muttered, "I don't know."

"I didn't mean to scare you. It's just a reaction because I've been trained to act quickly. How about we order food to take home? I'll order something for Anne, too."

"Yeah, that's a good idea."

Zeke carefully put the bags in the trunk and went to unlock the passenger door. Destiny still looked shell-shocked. Zeke suspected it was her reaction as much as the stranger.

"Can I give you a hug?"

Destiny clung to her and trembled.

"Honey, I didn't mean to scare you."

"I know."

❧ ❧ ❧ ❧

Anne finished chopping the lettuce and tomatoes when she heard the garage door. She wiped her hands and went to the back door as Destiny ran in.

"Gotta pee."

"Okay. Wash up."

Zeke had called and told her they were bringing home supper. "Can I give you a hand?"

"Yes, and then you can give me a hug." She handed her one of the paper bags, they hugged, and walked into the kitchen. Shayla trotted over, tail wagging. "Hi, girl." Zeke ruffled her fur.

Anne placed the bags in the warmed oven.

Zeke went behind her and opened the refrigerator. "Do we have any beer?"

"Sure, bottom shelf." Anne laughed. "Was she that bad?"

"Let's go outside." Zeke twisted off the cap.

Once outside, Anne slipped her arms around Zeke's waist and kissed her cheek. "Better?"

"Much." She took a swallow of beer and sat down with Anne. "Here's the short version." She hurried through the episode at the restaurant while waiting for a table.

"That must have been terrifying. No wonder she looked so pale. Wasn't that overreacting a bit?"

"Boy, I sure didn't plan it. I saw the guy put his

hand on her and some primal rage took over. That was my niece, and it was not okay. I'm going to check his record and then notify the state cops."

Anne took her hand. They both remembered their assault when Zeke first arrived in New Mexico. She snuggled closer. "Honey, you're both okay, but I'm sure that wasn't easy for you, either."

Zeke kissed her temple. "No. It was a total flashback."

"Do me a favor, would you call Robin Taylor tomorrow and tell her what's going on?"

"I'm not sure that's necessary."

"Maybe not so much for you, but I thought she might have some ideas about Destiny. And it certainly won't hurt for you to talk, too."

Zeke nodded. "You're right. Actually, I did think about that before she arrived."

"Why don't you finish your beer and I'll check and see if she's ready to eat."

Anne knocked softly on Destiny's door.

"Come in."

"Are you hungry yet?" She sat on the desk chair. "Your aunt told me you had a scare at the restaurant."

Destiny sat up and pulled her knees close. "Yeah, she kinda freaked."

"Can I tell you a little story? When Zeke came here to visit, we took a long ride up to northern New Mexico to see the Enchanted Circle. We turned onto a side road by mistake, and two men followed us. They attacked both of us..." Her voice caught. "They left, but Zeke was hurt. It took a long time for her to get over it because she thought she should have been better prepared. Anyway, when she saw the man with you, it was like a bad dream, and she got mad."

"Yeah, she was scary mad."

Anne smiled. "I know, she has quite a temper. It's usually because she hates injustice and gets very angry when she sees it. It's her job, but it's also her nature. She can't stand to see someone in pain or danger, and she can't help trying to protect them. It might be good if you told her you were okay."

"All right."

"You brought us a wonderful dinner. Are you ready to eat?"

"I'm starving, but I wanted to get out of there, too."

"I understand. Come on down, and we'll eat and maybe watch a movie."

⁂

Zeke finished the beer and stretched her arms and shoulders to relieve the tension. Her hand was sore from gripping the guy's shirt so tightly. She went in and tossed her bottle in the recycling bin as Anne came in.

"She'll be down in a few minutes. I think she's okay, but you certainly put the fear of God in her."

Zeke cringed. "Wasn't my goal."

"I did give her a sanitized version of our encounter with those two men when you arrived out here. I explained that you are trained to be very protective."

"Okay. Thanks."

Anne set the table in the kitchen, and Zeke brought out the salad and then the burgers.

"That smells so good." Destiny came in and sat down.

"I agree," Anne said, setting down the ketchup

and mustard.

Nobody spoke while they devoured their meals. Zeke finished first and folded her napkin.

"I need to answer some email. Destiny, would you please help Anne clean up for me?"

Destiny started to say something, stopped, and said, "Sure, I can do that."

Once her computer booted up, Zeke opened her FBI port. She typed in the name of the guy at the restaurant and waited. Finally, a hit. She read his report. He had previous convictions for assault and battery and larceny, had two outstanding warrants, and he was a registered sex offender. Last known address was Arizona. *Gotcha.* She copied the information and picked up her phone. She called the State Police and asked for Sam Harkins office.

They met when she and Anne had that harrowing assault. He was amazingly patient and kind, and she told him she hoped to return the favor.

"Harkins."

"Sam, it's Zeke Cabot. I don't know if you remember me, but I told you I owed you a favor about nine, ten years ago."

"Cabot, Cabot. Wasn't that the Enchanted Circle case? You're FBI?"

"Good memory. I'm mostly retired but doing some teaching at Quantico."

"Good to hear from you. What can I do for you?"

"I had an encounter this afternoon in Madrid. I was at the Mine Shaft with my thirteen-year-old niece, and some dirtbag put his hands on her. I lost it. I let loose and scared him. But I got his name off a New Mexico driver's license and checked him out. A registered sex offender who last checked in two years ago in Arizona and has a few outstanding warrants."

"What's his name?"

"Delmar Bauggins, the address was in Santa Fe."

"Just a minute…got him. Damn! The local guys were looking for him in connection with a stalking complaint. Glad you called. We'll have a talk with him. Hope your niece is okay."

"Thanks, Sam. I think she will be, and I think we'll both sleep better."

"Take care."

Zeke hung up and pulled up her security program. She started to open it when she heard Destiny coming. She closed the computer lid.

"Thanks for helping out," Zeke said.

"I think I'm gonna go to bed early. Anne has a huge list of things she wants to do tomorrow. Thanks for the adventure," she said seriously.

"Good night."

Zeke waited a minute but then thought she'd have to try later. She locked the desk drawer and went back downstairs. She found Anne in the family room with the remote in hand.

"How about some mindless entertainment fluff?"

Zeke flopped down and propped her foot on the coffee table. "Can we watch *Real Housewives*?"

Anne collapsed, laughing.

Chapter Eight

After breakfast, Zeke listened from her desk on the landing as Anne described the plan for the day. She sounded excited about trying something new with her horse.

Destiny, on the other hand, sounded bored.

She smiled and went back to scrolling through surveillance footage. It had been a while, so there was an abundance of nature and wildlife sightings. It was too dark to see the details of the eastern fence, but the area on the Bascom's southern border now had a large piece of orange snow fence. Easily identified.

She leaned closer. Was that the same place she spotted the male figure? It took a minute to find the attachments she sent to Mike.

It was hard to tell, but the time stamp for both was close, and so was the angle.

She leaned back.

If this is the same spot, and if someone is standing there watching, why cut the fence? It's easy enough to get over.

The Google map of the area showed its relationship to the buildings. Nothing much jumped out. Could they reinforce it? Electrify it? There wasn't too much she could do but wait to hear from Mike.

Boots, came to her in a sudden thought. The fabulous boots Anne gave her replaced some she'd bought when she arrived. Maybe the older pair would fit Destiny.

After checking her closet, she looked in the guest room, and finally the exercise room that they had converted to serve as Destiny's room. "More than likely, Anne tossed them." She laughed, thinking of more than one heated discussion on the value of keeping old stuff.

Several lidded file boxes lined the top shelf of the closet. She stepped over all of Destiny's clothes piled on the floor. Box three was her stuff and the boots. *Bingo.* She tossed them toward the bed and put the box back. It was tempting to throw all the clothes on the bed and let Destiny sort them out, but it would look like she was spying on her niece.

One of the boots had slipped under the bed with her errant toss. As she crouched to reach the rogue boot, she spotted a leather bracelet with silver and turquoise features. *What in the world?* She reached under and pulled it out. It seemed brand new, with a price sticker on the back: $210.

Zeke sat hard on the bed. She recognized the price sticker as coming from the Boot Ranch in Madrid.

❧❧❧❧

Anne hurried Destiny through the barn chores, anxious to get to work with Dancer. They mucked and cleaned, added straw and fresh water. Destiny worked right alongside her, and Benjamin loaded up the truck with the manure without complaint.

They brushed all three horses and led Shadow and Sunny into the arena. Anne hurried back for Dancer and applied the fly mask before walking her to the arena. At first, she was resistant, but after a few minutes, she relaxed. With the halter and lead rope on, Anne walked her into the arena with Shadow and Sunny and took off the lead.

"Destiny, will you help me?"

The teen nodded and walked over to Anne.

"I just want you to attach the lead to Sunny's halter and walk her around the arena."

"By myself?"

"Yes, she won't be a problem. She's done this a hundred times."

Anne stepped back to the rail and watched Dancer's reaction. After the second circuit, Shadow stepped out and followed Sunny. Anne covered her mouth to keep from laughing. Destiny looked like the pied piper. Dancer stood alert and watching.

"Are we done yet?" Destiny called from the far end.

Anne put her finger to her lips.

She carefully clipped the lead to Dancer's halter, and when the small parade passed them, she led Dancer behind Shadow. After several minutes, she laid the lead rope across her back and continued to walk beside her. As she suspected, with fewer distractions, Dancer felt safer and was more willing to be part of the pack. It was vital for her to recognize her two stablemates as related to her.

She saw Zeke sneak in and sit in the bleachers, and smiled.

"Okay, Destiny, take off the lead rope and just let them do what they're doing."

Sunny walked a bit then wandered over to the water trough. The other two followed.

"Looks like a team of well-trained horses," Zeke said.

"Ha!" Anne laughed. "But we're making headway. Thanks, Destiny."

"I thought it might be time for lunch and I was thinking about those tacos you mentioned."

"That's a great idea," Destiny shouted.

All three horses turned.

"Oops."

⁂

Zeke put away the taco mix and repackaged the unused shells.

"I hate to eat and run, but I want to get back to Dancer before she learns any bad habits." Anne took her plate to the sink and rinsed her hands.

"You go ahead, Destiny and I are going to run an errand. Anything you need?"

"I'll text you if I think of anything."

They cleaned up the kitchen and started out of the garage.

"Where are we going?" Destiny buckled her seat belt.

"We're going back to Madrid."

Pause. "How come?"

"I need to return something, or I should say you need to return something."

"Like what?"

Zeke pulled the bracelet from her shirt pocket and held it up. "Recognize this?"

Pause. "No. Why, should I?"

Sarcasm wasn't smart. "Because I found it under your bed and I'm quite sure you didn't pay for it because I called to ask."

"I don't know what you're talking about." She

crossed her arms defiantly.

Zeke let that hang for a couple of beats. "I'm pretty sure I don't need to remind you that I am a federal agent of a major law enforcement agency. It is my job to arrest and jail people who break the law."

Destiny was fidgeting and looking out the window.

"Given that information, could you explain why you, of all people, thought you could get away with shoplifting?" *Don't raise your voice. Stay calm.*

Zeke passed a bread truck and accelerated. They drove in silence for several minutes until Zeke muttered, "You have the right to remain silent."

Destiny started to cry.

There was no more talking until they slowed down and parked across the street from the boot store. "Here's what we're going to do. We'll go in and ask for Maria, the manager. Give her the bracelet and apologize for what you did. Ask if you owe her anything else and we leave. Got it?"

Destiny nodded. Her jaw was tight and her eyes dark.

A bell rang as they entered. Luckily for Destiny, there were no customers. A woman came to the register. "Hello, may I help you?"

Zeke bit her tongue. She was as nervous as her niece.

"I need to talk to Maria."

"That's me."

Destiny turned, and Zeke handed her the bracelet. Their eyes met, and Zeke could see the fear. *Stay strong. She has to do this.*

"I took this the other day, and I'm sorry. Do I owe you anything?" The words rushed out like a small geyser.

Maria took the bracelet. "This is a trendy piece. If you couldn't afford it, you could ask to see something less expensive. We have an extensive backstock."

Before Destiny could start bartering, Zeke jumped in. "I think what she really has her heart set on is some new boots, so time to start saving money. Isn't that right, honey?"

Destiny nodded.

"Thank you, Maria. This won't happen again. Right?"

"No, it won't."

They waved and walked out. Instead of going to the car, Zeke turned the other way. "There's a shop with excellent ice cream across the street."

They sat on a log bench with ice cream cones. "Think you could tell me why, if you liked those boots, you took a rather expensive bracelet?"

"No."

"Try."

"I knew there was no chance to get the boots and it made me mad. I never get what I want."

Zeke took a breath. The dark chocolate-lemon combination was outstanding, but she had to address this now. "Destiny, I'm sure this seems to happen to other people, but we never get everything we want. Sometimes if we wait or save or barter we might be lucky. Mostly it leaves us feeling sad and frustrated." She took another bite of her ice cream and wiped her chin. "It's hard when you're young and you don't have your own money. But maybe we can do something about that. Would that help?"

"I guess. What do you mean?"

"Well, you know you have to help out. What if

we assigned points or dollar value to things and you could do as much or as little extra work as you want— provided you did the basics. What do you think?"

She shrugged. "I guess."

They got back in the car and started home.

"Are you going to tell Anne?"

"Anne and I are partners in everything. We don't have secrets. That's why our relationship works. So yes, I am going to tell her. However, it might be a new start if you tell her."

They drove for a while without talking. Zeke finally cleared her throat. "Before you arrived, I read your arrest reports and notes from the social workers. Did any of those people ever take you to see lockup?"

"Not really. They just called my parents and got me in tons of trouble."

Zeke took a mental step back. "Oh. Really." *Time for another field trip, chickie.*

Once in the garage, Zeke said, "Why don't you go on up to your room until dinner? It might be a good idea to review what happened today and yesterday. By the way, the pervy guy at the restaurant is a convicted felon and a registered sex offender."

"Fine. Whatever."

"Leave the attitude when you come to dinner or don't bother."

Zeke went out on the deck and texted Anne.

ZCabot: Will you be finished soon?

AReynolds: 5 min. <3

It was so hard to keep from going all in and fighting with Destiny, but she knew it was pointless.

She went through her cell phone messages and stopped at the one from Mike.

MDono: Do you have time for lunch or coffee Friday?

ZCabot: Sure do, let me know what time works best. Do you have connections at the juvenile detention?

If the time worked out, they could go by the juvenile detention center downtown. Welcome to New Mexico Scared Straight.

Zeke went in and met Anne at the fridge. She gave her a hug and a kiss. "Would you hand me a beer?"

"Uh-oh. Looks like we're having a talk." She grabbed a water and a beer, the latter of which she handed to Zeke. "Our office?"

They got comfortable outside, and Zeke looked over her shoulder. "You may hear more of this later, but I found something this morning, and that was the reason for the quick trip." She turned to face Anne.

For the next half hour, she relayed what had happened with the bracelet, then a more detailed story of the guy from the restaurant.

"My god, what have we gotten ourselves into?"

"Hold on. What I suggested was a little quid pro quo. We assign monetary figures to any task or chore. She'll need to do the basic barn or house jobs, but can opt to earn money doing extra work to buy stuff."

"I need to think about that. Zeke, the nice approach doesn't seem to be working. Please call Robin." She pushed her hair back and sighed. "I've got a client day after tomorrow. I won't be able to watch her."

"Let's play it by ear. Okay?"

"Okay." Anne sighed heavily. "Would you mind making something to eat? I'm not hungry, and I just want to take a shower and lie down."

"Of course." She leaned over, stroked her cheek, and kissed her.

Anne went into the house while Zeke slumped back on the porch chaise. *What the hell can I do to fix this?* She clenched her fists and took a breath. *Maybe Mike and I could meet at the gun range.* She shot him a text.

She picked up her cell and dialed her brother's number. *Don't scare him.*

"Hello."

"Hi Reg, is this a good time?"

"Sure, is anything wrong?"

"Boy, you sure have been primed. We're okay. As expected, Destiny is pushing boundaries but also being quite pleasant. She's a very bright girl. I'm still trying to get a handle on what's making her so scared and distrustful."

"You saw the social workers' comments. They think it has a lot to do with Mom's passing and the way Dad treats her. It's frustrating, I know."

"That makes sense. She's had a few good moments with Anne and the horses, so we'll see if that's a good avenue."

"Zeke, are you being straight with me? Has she done something?"

She took a breath. "Well, yeah. I took her to Madrid yesterday, and she pocketed a bracelet. I made her return it, and we're going to set up a plan for her to earn her own spending money."

"Oh, shit."

She heard him hit something. "Reg, I can handle this. We're planning a field trip to the Bernalillo Juvenile Detention Center."

"Seriously?"

"Yup. She said nobody ever talked to her about what lockup was like."

Pause. "Yeah, well, Maura didn't want to frighten her."

"I think now might be a good time. If Destiny has no fear of stealing while living with a federal officer, she needs some reality work. She evidently doesn't think there are consequences to any of her behavior."

"I am so sorry. We have completely dropped the ball on that front. We've been so busy worrying about our own relationship that she's been ignored too much."

Zeke covered her mouth to keep from saying something she'd regret. "I hope you are at least in couples counseling."

"Oh, right. We've definitely talked about that."

"Reggie, you are going to lose custody of your daughter if you two don't get your shit together!" Immediately she regretted her outburst.

The silence on the other end was deafening.

"Zeke, Maura just got home. I'll hafta call you back later."

"Reg...?" *Too late. Shouldn't have gone off on him. Shit.*

Chapter Nine

Benjamin knocked on the office door.

Anne waved him in. "Good morning. Would you like some coffee?" She indicated the carafe.

"No thanks, I just finished some. The barbwire is in the ATV. I came back because I needed a couple more tools to keep it tight." He walked back into the former stable where Destiny was filing old forms and invoices.

Anne stood at the door and asked, "Could you use another pair of hands?"

Benjamin smiled. "That would sure make it go quicker."

"What do you say, Destiny, do you want to learn some fencing repair?"

She shrugged. "Sure. It's gotta be more interesting than filing."

Both Benjamin and Anne laughed. "I don't think he'd agree with you."

Anne gave Destiny an extra pair of leather gloves. "Why don't you hang on to these while you're here. It's always important to protect your hands, but especially on a ranch or farm. I don't suppose you know if you've had a tetanus shot?"

"I don't get shots." She took the gloves. "These are cool. I'll be careful."

Benjamin loaded the tools in the back seat and Destiny climbed in.

Anne waved. "Note to self, check on medical records."

She saw Zeke coming from the house with a covered plate. "Hi, you. What a nice surprise."

"Freshly baked chocolate chip cookies. An enormous peace offering for both of you." She set the plate on Anne's desk. "Where's the kid?"

"I sent her off to mend fences with Benjamin." She paused. "I hope she doesn't scare him."

"I wouldn't worry. Benjamin is unflappable. Excellent choice." Zeke gave her a kiss and took a cookie before perching on the corner of the desk.

"What have you been working on?" Anne helped herself. "Ooh, and they're warm."

"I made some changes to my book outline, shortened my teaching schedule, and called Robin."

"Great, what did she say?"

"That she does work with kids and that thirteen-year-olds are impossible to reason with. Before we do any more, she wants me to come in."

"Why does she want to see you?"

"Because the heart of Destiny's problem is my parents, same as for me. From what I told her, she's concerned that Destiny will trigger stuff for me."

"I hadn't thought of that. We can't let that happen. I think I better start getting Destiny close to the horses so they can get to know each other."

"Boy, it sure would be great if she could have the same kind of response." Zeke snatched a cookie.

Anne nodded slowly. "Oh! I just remembered what I wanted to ask. Did you get a chance to look at the fence surveillance?"

"Right. The eastern cameras are obstructed by the trees so I may get the company to lower them. The south view was clear, but I only went back a few days before I was interrupted." Zeke walked over to the open door. "Here's what I'm trying to figure out. To get to the house, why cut the barbwire? It would be much easier to go in near the garage. If it's just trespassing or vandalism, it's easy to hop that fence." She turned around. "If it were to steal equipment or something larger, they'd have to drive all the way across the paddock and pasture, which is difficult at best."

"Not to mention the chance of being seen by someone," Anne said.

"Exactly. I'll finish reviewing the tapes then call the security company. We didn't pay all that money for weak areas."

"Well, I'm going to take Dancer back to the round pen. Thanks for the cookies. Destiny and Benjamin will be thrilled."

❧❧❧❧

Zeke walked out of the office and out to the front gate. She stood looking at every potential point of entry. They installed the security system after they each had been kidnapped. Happily, they'd never had a problem after that. Well, except for the terrified bear cub—whose mom rescued him.

The gate was secure and well lit. Even entry to Susan and Jim's was a locked gate. The only way would be the Bascom's. They had no security fence or gate, just a long driveway because their house was set back in the trees.

As she returned to her office, the one question bothering her was "who." Hopefully, Mike would have an answer soon. Before sitting down to write, she checked to be sure her weapon was safe and ready. Then she peeked into Destiny's room. Still a mess. "One problem at a time." She closed the door and went over to open her laptop.

The novel she was working on loosely followed her career with some significant changes in details. The first sections were finished, covering her time at Quantico and Washington, DC. The next chapter was Chicago. It would be hard to disguise the details of the megalomaniac doctor decapitating homeless people for medical research. Even harder would be her involvement.

She reviewed her outline and started typing. The words flowed as the memory came alive in her mind. At the time, she was in peak physical and mental condition, and fresh off some victories and awards in Washington.

The weeks undercover hunting down the perpetrator who was terrorizing the homeless population wore her down mentally, physically, and emotionally. It was shortly after that assignment concluded that she took medical leave and fled to New Mexico and met Anne, without whom she might not have recovered at all.

She leaned back and looked around while salty tears rolled down her face. She was so lucky. And she could not let her niece slip into the dark place she'd been in.

※ ※ ※ ※

Anne worked and got Dancer to take the saddle blanket, finally. Now it was time to see if she could just get on bareback. For that, Anne walked Dancer to the mounting steps near the wall. Once Dancer stopped shifting, Anne leaned over her back gently until she had her full weight on. She whispered, "Good girl, you can do this. There's nothing to worry about." After about a minute, she pushed herself up and put one leg over. With no resistance, she sat on her back.

Dancer flicked her ears and shifted. "Okay, you want to move now, take it slow." She tightened her knees and right heel, causing the horse to flinch, but she started to walk. Anne held the looped lead rope loosely and continued to quietly encourage her.

They made one circuit in the round pen, and Anne heard the distant sound of the ATV. She pulled the horse up and slid off before the noise scared her.

"Good job." She rubbed her forehead and patted her neck. They walked to the paddock gate while Anne removed the lead rope. "Go on, burn off some energy." She patted her rump and Dancer took off.

Not knowing which Destiny might appear, she wanted to protect the vulnerable horse.

Benjamin pulled up to the barn and Anne walked over to meet them.

"How did it go?"

He'd loaded Destiny with tools to take inside. "Real good. That kid is stronger than she looks. We got all three areas secured and put an extra post where the cut wire was." He wiped his forehead and pointed to the south fence. "Might be worth putting in a metal post with a cement base. Just extra security."

"That sounds like a good idea. Get whatever you need."

Destiny returned smiling. "We did a great job."

Anne and Benjamin both laughed. Benjamin patted her back. "You sure did."

Anne pointed. "If you go by the office, there's a plate of fresh cookies."

Destiny took off in a run while Benjamin spun the ATV around. He won.

❧❧❧❧

"Zeke?" Anne called from the kitchen.

"Up here." Zeke stood up and waved as Anne came into the hall.

"I'm going to run over to the feed store to see if they have some tack for Dancer. Might be time."

"Congratulations. Okay, I'll be down in a few minutes. Where's Destiny?"

"She's finishing up the chores she left when she began her new career as a fence-mender. Be back soon."

Zeke smiled and got back to writing. Sometimes the words just flew out of her head, and this was one of them, so she didn't want to stop while she had a full head of steam and enthusiasm. She typed for at least half an hour before she remembered she had to take the chicken out of the freezer for stir-fry.

She got everything put away and hurried downstairs to defrost the chicken and clean the vegetables. She texted Destiny to come in to help with dinner. After fifteen minutes, Destiny was still MIA. She was tempted to go after her but decided it was better to get the food ready, so she sent another text.

A few minutes later Destiny burst through the back door out of breath. "Sorry."

"Is anything wrong?"

"No, I was just busy with the horses. It's cool. They're all fed and happy."

"Wash up, change, and help me chop this stuff."

She heard the garage door. *Darn. Not quick enough.*

"Zeke! Come help me!"

She dropped everything and raced out the door and into the driveway. Anne was running toward the front gate. All three horses were trotting around the yard loose.

"What can I do?"

"Grab three halters and ropes."

Zeke raced to the barn and found all three stall doors standing open. She gathered the equipment and ran out to meet Anne. Sunny was standing by the fence, and Zeke looped her lead rope over her neck and tied it to the fence.

"Thanks. Dancer is freaked out. Would you keep an eye on her and I'll get Shadow and Sunny tied up?"

Zeke walked slowly toward Dancer, who trotted away around the house. "Shit. Please don't go down in the woods." She followed slowly behind her.

Anne caught up with her carrying a pail of oats. "What the heck happened?"

"I don't know. I texted her to come in, and she didn't show up for about twenty minutes."

"Why don't you go down the hill and herd Dancer back up the hill to the barn?"

It took a while, but they got all three horses back into their stalls.

"I'll get to work on dinner if you'd go find out just what the hell Destiny was trying to do," Anne said.

❧ ❧ ❧ ❧

"She's not in her room." Zeke stood in the doorway.

Anne felt the tremor in her gut. It was hot and painful. Her vision blurred red and she gripped the cutting board. She briefly closed her eyes and hurled the cutting board laden with chopped vegetables across the room, striking the refrigerator.

She didn't hear the scream but felt it, and she slid to the floor, grabbing her knees to her chest to stop the shaking.

The kitchen was totally silent. Even the usual hum of the freezer stopped.

Zeke moved slowly, sat across from her, and waited.

"I can't do this. I just can't," Anne whispered.

"I know."

"Come in the other room." Zeke stood and put her hand out.

With no answer, Anne followed her into the family room and sat on the couch. Zeke brought her some tea.

"I'm going to go look around. I don't know how we missed her." She set Anne's cell phone on the table.

After a few minutes, the trembling stopped and she could sip the tea without spilling it. It was hard to even remember the last time she'd gone off so horribly. "Oh, Zeke. I'm so sorry. You must be scared to death, and now there's was a huge mess in the kitchen." She began to cry.

Her phone vibrated then she heard Zeke's ringtone, "Dixie."

"Did you find her?"

"Well, the county sheriff did, and I'm on my way to get her. She's okay."

Anne pushed on her chest and felt her heart pounding. She took a few deep breaths and finished her tea. They had to find some way to manage this kid. As angry as she was, sending a thirteen-year-old to jail was not the answer.

But after tonight, she honestly didn't trust her alone with the horses.

Her phone rang again.

"Zeke? Everything okay?"

"Yes. We're on the way back soon. Could you call Benjamin and see if he could come over?"

"Sure." *What does she want Benjamin for?*

Chapter Ten

Yes, I'm her aunt, Zeke Cabot." She flipped open her bureau ID. Destiny was seated, handcuffed, on a curb by the air pump at a gas station/convenience store. Next door was the Laughing Lizard Bar and Grill.

The county sheriff was even taller than Zeke with cropped steel-gray hair and mustache. His uniform fit tight over his broad shoulders. His tag read "Lafferty," and his stripes indicated long service. "So here's what I got from the manager here. At approximately eighteen fifty hours, Ms. Cabot pulled in on that ATV. She parked on the median and went into the bar—where they threw her out. She pitched a fit and the manager called us." He flipped a page in his notebook. "When I got here, the young lady in question became a little belligerent and refused to provide her information. She had no ID. She finally gave us your name and number."

Zeke covered her mouth to keep from screaming. She glanced at Destiny and motioned to the sheriff, and they walked down the driveway. She gave him a quick summary of Destiny's situation, then said, "Right now I'm angry and frustrated. I think a night in lockup might wake her up. However, her situation is precarious in Mississippi. It's a three-strike situation, and my brother convinced the judge to give her two months here to get her act together."

He smiled, "Between you and me, I've got a

fourteen-year-old grandson dealing drugs. I stuck him in a holding cell for twenty-four hours, and it scared the crap out of him. Completely off the books. Not the first time we've had to help out." He cinched up his duty belt and glanced over at her.

Zeke thought hard about what she was going to do. Then she thought about Anne and her reaction. "Okay, can we say twelve hours? I'll just tell her there was no choice."

"Is that your ATV?" he asked.

Zeke turned, and the light bulb went on in her head. She smiled. "Why no, it isn't. It belongs to the Godfreys, our next-door neighbors."

"Stolen property, got it." He handed her his card. "I'll be on duty till eight a.m."

"Thank you, Sheriff. I'll go break the bad news." She walked over and knelt next to Destiny. "I tried, but you're going to have to go with the sheriff. This is grand theft, and until I can square it with the Godfreys, you'll be in juvenile lockup."

Tears ran down her face, and her eyes got huge. "What? Jail? You're sending me to jail? Why—"

"I'm not doing anything, Destiny. This is all on you, the horses, taking the ATV, and driving on state roads without a license. This is big trouble, Destiny. I'm going to have to tell your dad, and you may be headed home." Zeke stood. "I love you, and I really thought we could work something out." She turned to her car and winked at the sheriff.

"Wait! Please take me with you. Please..."

Zeke drove off without looking back. Tears ran down her face knowing how frightened her niece must be. Maybe this was a huge mistake, and then she thought about the pain she saw on Anne's face. She wiped her eyes as she pulled in and saw Benjamin's truck in front. Anne was talking to him.

"Thanks for coming over. Benjamin. Let me quickly fill you both in. Destiny stole the ATV and drove down to the convenience store across from the turn up to Cedar Crest. The manager of the bar called the cops. She got belligerent and was cuffed. The sheriff and I talked and...he's taking her in for the night."

"Zeke! What were you thinking? She can't go to jail." Anne was screaming.

"Stop. It's not an official arrest. It's a wake-up call. I explained it was because she stole the ATV, and I'd have to convince the Godfreys not to press charges."

"But she didn't steal it, I borrowed it with Susan's permission," Benjamin pleaded.

"I know, I know. I'll go pick her up first thing in the morning. The sheriff said they do this sometimes to help kids. It won't be on the books." She took a breath. "Annie, please go in and relax. Benjamin, can we get the ATV in your truck?"

"Sure, with the ramp. I'll go hook it up." He got in and drove to the barn.

Zeke put her arm around Anne and walked her back to the house. "Please trust me on this. Honestly, it broke my heart to leave her and drive away." Tears started again, and her voice cracked. "But I'm praying this will wake her up. Either that or she will hate me the rest of her life."

Anne hugged her tight. "What have we gotten ourselves into?"

❧❧❧❧

Zeke led Benjamin to the convenience store and

mercifully the sheriff had gone. They managed to steer the ATV up the ramp into the truck bed and strapped it down.

"Good job. If you don't want to mess with it tonight, we can do it tomorrow morning," Zeke said.

"Thanks. I'm pretty beat. Don't worry, it'll be safe in my garage till tomorrow."

"I really appreciate your help. Always." She slipped him two twenties and got in her car. Now, she needed to get home, help Anne clean up that mess, and try to forget what she had voluntarily done to her only niece. This could easily destroy any relationships she had worked to build with her family. Her father would be furious. Reggie and Maura would never trust her.

She wiped her eyes and pulled into the garage. *Deep breath.*

The kitchen was clean and empty. A wineglass sat on the counter. That might take the edge off her hunger, but first, she needed to check on Anne. Only one light on in the hall.

"Hi." She found Anne in bed, reading.

"Hey, you. Are you okay?" Anne patted the bed. "Come talk to me."

Zeke sat on the edge and looked into Anne's breathtaking blue eyes filled with nothing but love. She curled up with her head in Anne's lap and sighed. "I'm not sure. I'm angry and scared that what I did is the right thing. And I'm worried about the fallout when my family finds out."

Anne stroked her hair from her forehead. "I agree. Maybe we don't tell them."

Zeke sat straight up. "What?"

Anne shrugged. "We deny the whole thing, tell them she made it all up."

Zeke was incredulous until she saw the twinkle in Anne's eyes. Then they both started to laugh and continued until they were convulsed and utterly exhausted.

From the floor where she slid, Zeke said, "I love you so much, Anne Reynolds."

Anne stopped laughing. "I love you, too, and I do understand why you made that choice. After you left, I went in and tried to be logical about it. It really was the best idea. What else could we have done here other than scream and fight with her?"

Zeke stood up. "That helps a lot. But, I'm starving, and I'd really like some wine. You can read or go to sleep, I don't blame you, but I'm too wound up to sleep."

"Of course, go ahead. Do you want me to fix something?"

"No, I'm okay." She leaned over and kissed her.

In the dark kitchen framed by the refrigerator light, she pulled out a piece of leftover pizza with nothing but cheese that Destiny just had to have. A half-full bottle of Riesling lay on the top shelf. She grabbed the wine, the glass, and a paper towel for the pizza.

Without turning on the light in the family room, she turned on the TV to the east coast news channel. Catastrophic earthquakes and hurricanes plagued people all over the world. But, right here in the mountains of central New Mexico, a thirteen-year-old kid was spending her night in a jail cell. Hopefully, Sheriff Lafferty was providing her with some sage advice.

Anne yawned and poured some coffee. Zeke hadn't slept and wanted to be at the sheriff's office as soon as possible, and she wanted to be sure to get a report from Sheriff Lafferty. Sadly, there wasn't much they could do until the real Destiny either appeared or sunk into her black hole.

One thing Anne knew for sure, she wanted her horses cared for before there was any trouble. In fact, she thought it might be good to be sure Destiny's chores happened when the horses were out of the barn.

The other chore would be talking to Susan about the ATV. If it had been damaged, they'd have to replace it, and an allowance of any size would not cover that expense.

After rinsing her cup, Anne ran up and dressed quickly while checking her phone repeatedly in case Zeke might want to talk to her.

Shayla followed behind her to the barn. In the daylight, she could see the glaring evidence that three horses had been running loose. Divots, prints, and manure. With luck, her client would drive directly back to the arena. The barn was warm and the horses were waiting for the lady with the food.

"I'll hurry. Promise." She brought a flake of hay to each horse, greeted them, and then gathered their individual tack.

Soon they finished eating and were escorted to the pasture. In spite of the late afternoon romp the day before, they raced out and took long turns around the area. She never tired of watching them out of the confines of the barn.

Her dream was still to get a place with acres of land to roam. Adding the extra acres to their property helped a great deal, but enough for just three horses.

"Come on, Shayla. Let's get back to work for a while." For a very brief moment, she thought there might be a couple of those cookies left. Then she laughed.

⁂

Finding the sheriff's office was a little tricky. It was south of the interstate on a side road that could be easily missed. Once she'd parked, she noticed the sheriff's car was parked in front. She took a breath to ease the feeling of throwing up. *Stop it.*

The front door had a buzzer, and a young man in a brand-new uniform answered. "Good morning. How can I help you?

"Good morning. I'm Zeke Cabot, and I'm here to pick up my niece."

"Sure thing. The sheriff said it might be you. Come on back." He used his ID badge to open the door to a hallway.

She could see offices on the right side and windows along the other wall. Behind them were individual cells. She swallowed hard. What in the hell had she been thinking sending her thirteen-year-old niece to jail?

"Right in here." The young man held open the door. Zeke stopped in the doorway.

Destiny and the sheriff were eating burritos.

"Good morning, Agent Cabot. I figured you'd be in early, so I thought I'd better get the inmate ready." He laughed. And so did Destiny. "Have some coffee with us."

Destiny waved and kept eating.

"You run a very hospitable unit." The deputy handed her a mug and left.

"We had a talk this morning, didn't we?"

Destiny stopped chewing and nodded.

He raised an eyebrow.

She looked up reluctantly. "I've been a real jerk, and I'm sorry. You guys have been so nice, and I never should have run away like that. Or any of the other bad stuff." Tears welled up in her eyes. "I was scared last night, and I don't ever want to do that again, Auntie. Can I come home?"

Zeke gulped when Destiny walked over and flung her arms around her. "I'm sorry, too, honey. I just didn't have a choice. And of course, you can come back." She stood. "Thank you, Sheriff, for your understanding."

He grinned. "Serve and protect, ma'am."

"Next time, maybe we can just get a beer instead of going through all this."

Destiny turned. "Thank you."

They buckled their seat belts and Destiny said, "You know what the sheriff told me?"

Zeke contained her smile. "What?"

"He told me you were kind of a hero in the Albuquerque Field Office. You got some bad dudes off the street even though you got hurt." She smiled.

How in the world would he know about all that? Never underestimate the grapevine, especially in law enforcement. "Yeah, in my younger days I was badass."

"You're pretty badass now," Destiny cracked sarcastically.

Zeke looked at her. "We can kid around, but I take your behavior very seriously. When we get home, you need to make amends to Anne for destroying her yard, hurting her business, and scaring her to death. I fully expect you to jump through whatever hoops you have to regain her trust. Can you do that?"

Destiny nodded. "I will."

Zeke pulled into the garage. "I'm going to shower and change. You might want to do the same. Then we better see what we can do to repair the yard."

"Okay. Can I get my phone back?"

"Let's see how today goes."

Destiny's eyes darkened momentarily then she smiled and ran upstairs.

Zeke started the coffee pot, then followed her upstairs for the promise of a hot shower. She could hear music, so she hurried to get her share of hot water. As she waited, she looked at the scars on her chest from the gunshots she sustained when she was being "badass." Damn lucky, but they would always be there to remind her.

The steam and hot water brought thoughts of both relaxing and restoring. The scent of the shampoo was fresh and brought a vision of Anne. A wave of desire flooded her thinking about the woman who had rescued her more than once and wholly owned her heart. *We need some quality time alone. Soon.*

She rinsed and stepped out. The lure of a nap pulled her, but right now, she needed to keep Destiny on track.

A clean, long-sleeved T-shirt and jeans with new socks and short boots felt good. She ran her fingers through the unruly damp waves of her hair and shrugged.

❧ ❧ ❧ ❧

Anne poured a cup of the fresh coffee, grateful

for Zeke's thoughtfulness.

"Hey, whaddaya doin' with my coffee?" Zeke whined as she entered the kitchen.

Anne turned and laughed. "And I thought you did this just for me."

Zeke enveloped her and provided a make-up-for-lost-time kiss. Anne put the cup down and eagerly responded. "I've missed you," she murmured.

Zeke's kisses grew stronger and more passionate. "Let's go upstairs."

Anne stopped, took a breath. "Isn't Destiny upstairs?"

"I don't care. Besides, the princess is in the shower, and we can be extremely quiet and really quick." She grabbed Anne's hand, and they ran up two steps at a time.

Music still blared from Destiny's closed door. Zeke locked their door and made good on her promise to be quick.

By the time they heard the music stop, they were lying still and breathing hard.

"Hurry up and get down there, you randy devil," Anne said. "I'll be right down."

"Cruel, cruel mistress," Zeke muttered as she pulled her clothes on and slipped into her boots.

Anne flopped back on the bed and smiled. Really smiled. How did they manage to get so caught up with life that they forgot the essence of their relationship? It was the fierce chemistry they'd had from the very beginning. Their sexual appetites had always been in sync.

She dressed and promised not to let this flame weaken—even with the new demands on their time.

The kitchen was empty when she got downstairs,

but there was still some coffee. She popped some bread in the toaster and got out the peanut butter and jam. When the sandwich was ready, she wrapped it in a paper towel, grabbed a bottle of water, and headed out to see how the repairs were going. Smiling.

Destiny was raking divots in the grass while Zeke and Benjamin were huddled over the ATV. Uh-oh. "Please let nothing be broken."

"What's the verdict, Benjamin?" Anne asked. He was half under the ATV sitting on the ramp.

He scooted back and sat up. "Not bad. Must've run over a couple of curbs and through bushes. Minor scratches I can buff out. I was about to take it out and run it."

"Well, that's good news. Go ahead."

He backed the machine down and drove slowly toward the pasture.

"I'm afraid your horses weren't as careful." Zeke pointed to the side of the house.

They walked around, and Anne stopped. There was a slight incline falling away from the foundation which revealed several long sliding ruts. "One of them nearly took a bad fall. That would have been catastrophic." Her hands trembled slightly thinking about broken legs or necks. "Has Destiny seen this one?"

"Not yet. We started with the easy fixes. When the ATV is cleared, we'll have to attach a wagon with some topsoil and seed. I'm not sure where all they ran," Zeke said.

"I had no idea. No wonder they were so excited about hitting the paddock today. Running is fun." Anne shook her head. "My client will be here soon, but it shouldn't be too long. Can you wrangle these folks?"

"Yes ma'am, but I will need my Stetson for this…" Zeke smiled broadly.

Anne took a step forward. "In my opinion, you don't need a thing."

Zeke actually blushed enough to cause her tawny skin color to glow. "Shucks."

They walked back around front when Anne stopped and laughed. "Do you remember the night of your birthday when you wore your sexy new Lucchese boots to bed?"

Zeke smiled. "Vividly. But I don't remember that as funny. They were incredibly comfortable."

Anne chuckled, remembering Zeke's raggedy T-shirt and bare behind marching to the bathroom in her new boots, and she waved as she continued to the arena.

⚘⚘⚘⚘

Zeke's phone buzzed. Mike. "Hi, Mike. What's up?"

"I've got some info about your…project. Can you do lunch tomorrow?"

"Sure. Usual place at eleven?"

"Perfect."

That would work fine. Zeke had an appointment with Robin at nine thirty. She walked to the front yard where Destiny was still massaging the dirt with her rake. She was another one in the house she cherished. There were too many people at stake to risk allowing any kind of outside threat. Hopefully, Mike could disabuse her of her paranoia.

Chapter Eleven

The yard looks really nice, thank you. Where are you off to?" Anne poured milk on her cereal.

"I'm meeting Robin Taylor this morning and then a quick lunch with Mike." Zeke got up and rinsed her coffee cup and plate. "Before I go, I want to set up a daily chore list, starting with her bedroom. Summer camp is over. I thought she could repaint the landscape rock that got dirty."

"Good idea."

"How was your client yesterday?"

"Interesting. I felt comfortable with all three horses in the arena since Beth has been working for a while. I expected Shadow to recognize her, which he did, and Dancer followed suit and started to approach her then turned back. I was surprised she went that close; I was sure she'd stay far away." She cleared her space and loaded the dishwasher. "I'm off to get the feeding done. Send Destiny out as soon as she's ready."

Zeke kissed her, then kissed her again. "Love you."

"Text me when you leave."

❧❧❧❧

Zeke walked upstairs with a water bottle and knocked on Destiny's door. "Time to get up and get going."

She went to her desk and got out her laptop. While it warmed up, she jotted a note with chores.

1. Clean up the kitchen after eating.
2. Check with Anne about barn chores.
3. Ask Benjamin for a brush and the white exterior landscape paint.
4. Repaint the landscape stones in front.
I'll be back after lunch.

Ten minutes later, Destiny stumbled out in her work jeans, T-shirt, and work boots. "Morning."

"Did you sleep okay?"

"Heck ya. It's way quieter than the jail and has a much better bed." She grinned.

"Well, that's good to know. I have a couple of errands to run, but I made you a list. Check in with Anne after you eat something." She handed her the list. "And Destiny, please try hard."

"I will." She trotted down the stairs.

Zeke pulled up her surveillance program and watched last night's films. The new fence repair on the south side was holding. She flipped back to the day before and focused on the front cameras. She watched Anne drive out, and then Destiny leave the house. She stopped when she found the office door locked. What would Destiny be after in there? Instead, she went back to the new barn.

Benjamin packed up his truck and drove out. After about ten minutes the horses walked out one by one. Sunny headed back to her old pen followed by Shadow. Dancer bolted out the door and ran straight toward the house and north fence, turned, and raced past the front and around the side. Soon each of them was making loops from front to back.

Zeke shook her head. "Sure looks like they enjoyed themselves." She checked messages and shut down the computer, then locked up everything.

❧ ❧ ❧ ❧

Anne laid out the saddles and bridles along the stall doors. It had been ages since she had given the tack a good cleaning. It seemed like a useful task to do with Destiny so they could talk. Zeke had gone the extra mile, and now Anne had to step up. It was hard to keep the anger in check when she watched her horses, but fortunately none of them were hurt.

She started back to the house and saw Destiny talking with Benjamin. The paper she held looked like Zeke's work. She chuckled.

Benjamin was pointing to the areas where the landscape stones needed paint.

"Hi, Anne. I was just coming to the barn to get started."

"Good morning. Go ahead and start with the stalls and I'll be right back. I thought we might do something fun with the horses later."

Destiny looked confused, but nodded and started for the barn.

Benjamin laughed. "That kid is a handful."

"What was she asking?"

"Zeke told her to ask me for white paint and a brush to clean up those rocks. Probably a good idea. I'm guessing there might be a little Tom Sawyer action at some point."

Anne nodded. "I'll bet you're right."

❧❧❧❧

Dr. Robin Taylor crossed her legs. "Let me see if I've got this right: you offered to look after your thirteen-year-old niece to hopefully keep her out of jail. Within an abbreviated period she's run away and gotten drunk, shoplifted a bracelet, turned out Anne's horses—with attendant damage, then stole an ATV, tried to get into a bar, mouthed off to the sheriff, and ended up in jail. Did I forget anything?"

Zeke shook her head. As her primary therapist, Robin Taylor had been instrumental during her struggle with PTSD. She'd even worked with Anne on her drinking. Robin knew their family well. "Did I mention she's a sassy, smart-mouthed know-it-all?"

"No, but I just tossed that in as well."

"Robin, it took a while to see how much like me she was. I felt the same way but never had the guts to act out like this. She's got the same issues with my overbearing, abusive father and by extension, any authority. She's furious and scared."

"And you can't control her. Right?"

"You guessed it. We haven't got much time and then Destiny's fate may be up to the courts."

"Has Anne tried working with her?"

"Briefly. But after the problem with the horses, even Anne's afraid to trust her."

"Can't say I blame her, but unless I'm mistaken, horses are a much better judge of character than we are. That would be my recommendation. Now, you mentioned something else."

Zeke took a deep breath and relayed the information she had about the black SUV, Arizona plates, and the cut fence.

"I haven't mentioned it to Anne because it may be nothing, but it's bringing up a lot of anxiety and fear about anything happening to Destiny."

"I understand that. What steps have you taken so far? Because I know you have." Robin smiled warmly.

"Well, yes. I sent the information to a friend at the FBI, and I'm meeting with him after this. I also asked the security company to come out and make some adjustments."

"Perfect. I gather there's something else going on or you would probably have called the local police."

Zeke felt the cold sweat between her shoulder blades. "It was the black SUV with Arizona plates that started the attacks from Hussein."

"I remember now. That was very difficult, but didn't you tell me that both of the brothers were killed?"

She twisted the plastic bottle in her hands and felt her chest tighten. Her vision darkened and her hearing was fading.

"Zeke. Listen to me and take a breath. Breathe now."

She fought back and gasped. *Shit. This can't be happening.* "Okay."

"Look at me. Are you all right?" Robin was kneeling beside her.

"Yes. I don't know what happened."

Robin returned to her chair after handing Zeke another water bottle. "Are you sleeping all right?"

"Not since Destiny arrived."

"Okay. That needs to stop. Since you refuse medications, I want you to try some diphenhydramine. Anne will know. Sadly, time's up, but I want you to try the medicine, and hopefully you'll get some helpful information today. If not, I want to see you again."

"Thanks, Robin." Zeke gave her a hug.

❧❧❧❧

"Don't these saddles look wonderful?" Anne held up Shadow's old saddle.

"They do look like new." Destiny wiped her hands on her jeans and helped carry the bridles to the tack room.

"Do you think you might like to learn to ride sometime?" Anne asked.

"I'm not sure…maybe sometime."

"Tell you what we can do. Let's go out to the arena. Bring your water." Anne led her down the aisle. The last task had gone well, so maybe it would be a good time to talk about the advantages of working with animals.

"Let's sit in the bleachers." Anne pointed. All three horses were just outside in the paddock and clearly visible through the wide-open doors.

"Since you've been caring for them, they recognize your scent. It's important to remember that although horses are very large, they are prey animals and very fearful of the unknown. The thing that makes them so unique—and has for centuries—is that they are incredibly empathic."

"What does that mean?"

Anne smiled.

❧❧❧❧

Zeke drove north on Wyoming Blvd. toward the coffee shop to meet Mike. She had to admit that, although she was still worried, her sense of relief was enormous after talking to Robin. Just being able to verbalize her concerns diminished their power. It probably would have short-circuited some of her anxiety to have shared some of it with Anne, but until she knew the details, it was safer to wait.

Mike was waiting when she drove up. She got out and waved.

He stood and gave her a hug. "Long time, no see, Cabot."

"Too long. Have you ordered?"

They walked inside and brought their drinks back to the table. "I'm gonna have to get back, so let's get to it. First, here's the phone tracking chip you asked for. If you want to hook it into the national lost children database, there are instructions in there."

"That's perfect. I'll send you a check."

"Okay, so here's what I've got on the car." He pulled out an envelope.

A waitress brought the tray with their order. "More iced tea?"

"No thanks, we're good," Mike said. "First, let me say this very clearly. I found no connection with the Husseins, alive or dead. Their reign of terror in Chicago set medical research back twenty years, and in case you don't recall they were blown to smithereens in Lebanon."

Zeke laughed but also sighed with relief. "Thank you."

"Second, the car was a rental, and the reservation was the most convoluted thing you ever saw. It's due to be returned tomorrow. Supposedly a family touring the southwest from Phoenix." He took a bite of his sandwich, chewed, and continued. "Here's the weird part. The address they gave was two doors from that rug merchant in Arizona or whatever he was. The one we busted."

"That's quite a coincidence."

"I agree, so I asked the Phoenix boys to do some snooping, nothing official."

"Thanks."

"Worst case, somebody's still holding a grudge. The guys we convicted could be out by now."

"Mike, here's my concern. Why cut a section of barbwire from the farthest point from the house?"

"That is weird."

"It made me think someone planned to steal something big. But it's gated community with several eyes and ears."

"That's good. I say, put out a detailed flyer with pictures and plates. Get every one of your neighbors worried. Also, tell the local cops." He finished his food.

Zeke laughed. "Oh, the sheriff and I are on good terms." She briefly relayed Destiny's run-in and its consequences.

"Whoa. You are wicked. But it's good we have him in the loop. Fill him in on this. The local guys like a little espionage."

"Mike, I really appreciate you helping out. This whole thing is making me crazy."

"Listen, if you're up for it, maybe I could bring the girls out to 'see the horses' on Sunday." He made air-quotes. "And we could take a look at the fence."

"That's a great idea. I'll check with Anne, but it sounds great."

"Okay." He looked at his watch. "Crap, I gotta go."

"I've got this. I'll call you later. Thanks."

Mike jogged off to his car. Zeke hadn't noticed

before that her old partner was getting gray. She felt a little melancholy about her days with the bureau, missed the camaraderie and the adrenaline kicks. But she also liked teaching the newbies and remembering her fresh-out-of-Quantico days and what a high that was. She'd lived on the excitement and the patriotism while living and working in Washington, DC.

She left a generous tip and walked back to her car.

As much as part of her pined for the active-duty days, she really loved her life with Anne and their small circle of close friends. With her pension, savings, and token salary, they had no worries. Plus, Anne's reputation was bringing more and more clients just by word of mouth.

She steered back toward home. Now, back to life as the evil aunt.

⁂

Anne had Destiny stand in one spot in the near end of the arena and do multiplication tables in her head. One by one she brought the horses into the arena.

"Just keep focusing on numbers until I tell you to stop."

All three horses hung around the open doors even though there was a barrier across it.

"Okay. Stop and tell me what you're feeling in your gut."

"I don't know. Nervous?"

"That's fine. Are you worried about anything?"

"Yeah. Whether Aunt Zeke is gonna send me to jail again."

Anne let her sit with that. "Just breathe. And stay still."

It only took a couple of minutes, and then Dancer walked over and stood behind her.

Destiny opened her eyes. "Somebody's behind me."

"It's okay. It's Dancer. Does she make you feel better or worse?"

Destiny screwed up her face in thought. "I think better."

Interesting. "What feels better?"

"I think she likes me."

"I think she does, too. I'd like you to close your eyes and turn around to face her."

It took a minute, but she did. Anne waited and walked a little closer. Dancer was standing very still, watching. When Destiny turned around, Dancer moved very close and bent her head to Destiny's chest.

Neither moved. Finally, Destiny started to cry. Dancer stood still and then shook her head and ran off to the other end of the ring.

Anne moved up behind her. "How do you feel now?"

Destiny wiped her face with her sleeve and then smiled. "I don't know." She laughed. "I feel happy and kinda light."

"That's good. That's exactly how you should feel."

"Wow, that was totally weird. Why did Dancer run off?"

"I'll tell you more about that later. What do you say we get the horses back in their stalls then go in the house and make a surprise dessert?

"Like what?"

"Zeke's very favorite pie."

Chapter Twelve

Zeke entered the house from the front door. She heard voices in the kitchen and hurried upstairs before Destiny came up. The GPS chip shouldn't be hard to install, and it would provide a modicum of security.

The laughter stopped her in her tracks. Destiny laughing?

She unlocked her desk, got Destiny's phone, and took it into the bedroom. The instructions were straightforward, and she got the tiny chip connected. It was nearly invisible, but Zeke doubted Destiny would even look.

The voices still traveled up upstairs as she went into Destiny's room. It looked better. The junk was on the chair or desk, the bed was half made, and the dresser drawers sat open. She was figuring out a place she could leave the phone, and then she stopped. A white pharmacy cap poked out from under some socks that caught her eye. Red warning lights flashed in her brain as her trembling hand hovered over the drawer. This act could make or break the tentative truce they had.

The label listed the med as diazepam ten milligrams, for spasms. The patient was Robert Cabot. There were ten tablets in the bottle. Did he give them to her, or did she take them? This was not a conversation for right now. Zeke put the bottle back, then retrieved it and removed one tablet and stuck it in her shirt pocket. If the topic came up and she denied it, Zeke had proof. Emboldened, the special agent carefully searched through the rest of the drawer and found nothing.

After closing the door, she crept back to her desk and set about installing the locator app. It took only minutes and seemed to work. Now to deliver it with praise for doing such good work, which she had. And an especially good job on the bright white rocks out front. But first, she went back into their room and messed the bed up, then went down to the kitchen.

"Hey, what's the racket?" she said from the door.

"Zeke, when did you get home?"

"A while ago. I was beat and took a little nap." She yawned.

Destiny pointed at their project. "We made a blueberry pie." Her enthusiasm was endearing despite what Zeke had just discovered in her drawer.

"Looks yummy." She leaned over and sniffed. "Oh, boy."

Anne wiped off the counter and cutting board. "Thought you'd like that. Destiny and I have to feed the horses, but we'll be back to start dinner. The vote was for spaghetti." She turned. "Destiny, go ahead. I'll be right out."

When the back door slammed, Anne asked, "How were your meetings?"

Zeke looked toward the back door. "Both good. I asked Mike to check the surveillance tapes, and he reassured me the car is registered to a family of tourists from Arizona." Mostly true. "Like me, he had no clue about the cut fence but suggested he bring the girls to see the horses and he and I can take a look."

"It would be fun to see them again. The girls must be so big by now. How about Robin?"

"She was great. Can we talk about that later, alone?"

"Of course." She hugged Zeke and hung up her towel. "I'll be back soon."

❧❧❧

Destiny had cut free several flakes from the new bale of hay and carried one down to Shadow.

"Good job." Anne grabbed another and took it to Sunny, on purpose. She watched for a reaction between Dancer and Destiny.

"Here you go, enjoy your supper."

Dancer moved forward and brought her large head out the stall door. Destiny looked at Anne quizzically.

"Go ahead and rub her forehead." *Score.* "That's good. Horses have few ways to communicate. Trust and closeness are significant."

They swept up and headed back to the house.

"Do you think Auntie is still angry at me?"

"No. I think Zeke has a lot on her mind. She has to teach next week, and I think she wants you settled in and on a good schedule."

"Because she still doesn't trust me. Dancer does."

Anne laughed. A fair point. "You're right, and that surprised me because Dancer's been very slow letting go of her anxiety and fear."

"Maybe Auntie needs to go work with Dancer?" Destiny said very earnestly.

"You may be right." She struggled to keep a straight face.

Anne smiled. "Well, how did it go?"

Zeke went to the walk-in closet and changed into her favorite lounge pants and T-shirt. "Pretty good. Guess we'll see. After washing up and brushing her teeth, she hit the light and crawled into bed with a satisfied sigh.

"Tell me again why you needed another GPS chip? Aren't all smartphones equipped with GPS?"

"Yes, but kids often disconnect the 'share my location' feature specifically to keep their parents from tracking their movement." She stretched her arms behind her head. "This way we can have an idea where she is around here. I'll add the app to your phone as well. I'll feel better not losing track of her."

Anne turned out her light and snuggled closer. "Can we talk about your visit with Robin?"

"Sure. When I described everything out loud, it was a clear connection to my fear and anxiety after the assault, your kidnapping, and my father. Feeling powerless is debilitating. And that's what happens when Destiny flips out and is uncontrollable. I get the same feeling."

Anne gently rubbed her arm and put her head down on her shoulder. "That must feel awful after all this time. I wish you'd told me because I thought you were just angry."

"I was angry. Angry that my niece could trigger this panicky feeling. But I didn't get it until Robin laid it all out."

"Of course. It's been years since another confrontation like that. I'm sorry. We probably shouldn't have agreed to do this."

"No, it's okay, and I think Destiny is doing better. Between whatever magic Sheriff Lafferty pulled and the work you did with Dancer today, she's better."

Anne wrapped her arm over Zeke. "You wore your cologne today. I love that scent. What's the name?"

Zeke smiled, "Vetiver. I bought more after I ran out, just for you."

They were both quiet for a while until Anne asked, "Honey, are you worried about leaving next week?"

"Maybe a little."

"I did talk to Benjamin, and he agreed to stay. We'll pay him, of course. And Susan said Jim will be around because their boys will be home from school. I'll plan to keep her busy."

"I guess it should be okay." Zeke yawned.

Anne kissed her. "Good night, sweetheart."

✿ ✿ ✿ ✿

Mike and his girls showed up to great fanfare. The toddlers were now seven and eleven, but still remembered the horses. Anne walked Becky and the girls to the barn with Destiny while Zeke took Mike over to see the fence repairs on the ATV.

"Wait, can I go with Auntie?"

"Destiny is more interested in the ATV." Zeke pulled her aside, "I need to talk to Mike about a case. We can take it out some other time. Stay with Anne. She may need you to help."

Mike followed Zeke to the barn for the ATV. "Does your niece share your love for basketball?"

"I'm not sure, but I doubt it. My brother and

sister-in-law aren't into sports, and the only thing my father watches is boxing."

"Seriously?"

"Yup. I never could figure that out." Zeke backed out the machine and Mike got aboard.

"Hey, why not start up here and follow the fence to the side." He pointed to the white pipe fence beside the barn.

Seeing it through his eyes, Zeke realized that although it was attractive and kept the horses in, it was simple to breach. "Boy, that's an invitation isn't it?"

He nodded. "Exactly what I was thinking."

She drove solely looking for marks on the fence, tamped-down grass, or other signs of attempted entrance or surveillance. Mike pointed at one area with some tire tracks, and she nodded and made a mental note. There were a few others tracks, but they could be from cars trying to pass one another on the narrow lane.

At the corner, she stopped. "This is where the Bascoms' property begins." The roadside border was wide with bushes and a decorative post-and-chain border. Two tall stone gate posts flanked the driveway which wound through trees to the elegant three-story brick home. She slowed as they turned the corner.

"Let's walk this stretch." Mike got out, looked around, then turned toward their house. It was up a slope, and this was a perfect view. "Did you bring binoculars?"

Zeke handed him a pair and wished she'd thought of that sooner. Glancing around, a spot in the Bascoms' trees would be invisible from almost anywhere. *But why?*

They continued to walk the fence line until they

could no longer see the house. He walked deep into the pasture and tall grass area just before the trees, and asked where the cameras were. "You've got a good setup, and I agree that those cameras could be lower."

They turned and started back to the ATV. "Any suggestions?"

"I think, if I were you, I'd ask the surveillance company to monitor the cameras for a few weeks. I know you do, but I'm guessing it's hours or days later. If, and that's big 'if,' there was any concern at all, it would need to be identified and addressed right away." He looked around. "The good news is that if the local cops got a call, I'll bet they could get here quicker than anybody could get out."

They drove down the hill before turning up toward the house.

"You guys have a beautiful place here. I can see why you love it and why you want to protect it. More importantly, I trust your instincts over any logic."

"Thanks, Mike. I appreciate your help, and we do love the place. I think my apprehension comes from the fact that one week a month I'm at Quantico. I don't know how long someone may have been watching. If more than a couple of months, they know I'm gone, and Anne is alone with my niece."

"Tell you what, when I get back to the office I'll dig a little deeper. That SUV license search dead-ended, but I don't know anything about the driver. It may be completely unrelated, but even if it was a horse thief, I don't think they'd be spying. Probably show up at night and walk out the front gate to a trailer. You'd probably sleep right through it."

Zeke couldn't help laughing at the absurdity, even though it might be right. "Well, I'm heading out tomorrow and asked Benjamin to stay on site while I'm gone."

"Great idea. I'll give Anne a call to check in every day or so."

They drove up just when Anne, Becky, and the girls came out of the barn. Zeke pulled up and stopped. "Perfect timing."

"We got a call from our neighbor. The dog got out, and she can't catch him," Becky said.

Mike smiled. "Guess we have to run. I'll keep in touch. Thanks, Anne. This place is so beautiful."

They all waved as Mike drove off. Destiny was sitting on the ATV. "Can I take it for a ride?"

Zeke looked at Anne and shook her head. "Seriously?"

"What do you say we go make lunch?" Anne said.

"Let me know when you're ready. I need to make some notes." Zeke hurried upstairs as soon as they got in the door. She pulled out her laptop and opened a blank document before she forgot the things Mike told her. *Maybe have Anne ask Benjamin to install heavy-gauge wire fence along the pipe fence.* It pissed her off she hadn't thought of that first.

When the surveillance program opened on her laptop, she went through a series with each location, primarily the ones she'd ignored. She'd always assumed the front was most vulnerable. And yet, she'd settled for pipe fence.

She shot an email to Davis at the surveillance company and asked him to make the camera changes and add office monitoring for the next sixty days. She hit Send and leaned back. *I know this is just paranoia, but I can't squelch the niggling feelings.*

Since she had a pretty early flight, she went

through her briefcase and then went to check her carry-on. The Quantico schedule was lighter this week. The co-teaching Field Counselor was from Los Angeles and had a lot of exciting field experience to share. Zeke was happy to play second fiddle and enjoyed his stories. So did the students.

All to-do boxes checked, she went down to find food. Happily, Anne was busy making grilled cheese sandwiches while Destiny stirred some homemade tomato soup. "I'm sorry I wasn't here to help. I'll clean up, okay?"

Anne smiled. "You'll get no argument from me. Did you finish your checklist?"

"Yes, ma'am." No secrets from this one. Anne paid attention with a capital A, and Zeke only wished she could teach that quality. It could sometimes be the difference between life and death.

Destiny was unusually quiet during lunch. Anne talked about the way the girls reacted to seeing the horses again. She and Becky were going to arrange some time for riding lessons.

Knowing full well what the answer would be, Zeke asked Destiny, "Is something wrong with your lunch?"

"No. It's fine."

"Ah, then it must be that you are still mad I wouldn't let you drive the ATV."

Silence. Anne winked at her.

"Maybe you'd like me to tell you why." Zeke wiped her mouth with the napkin, folded it, and set it next to her plate. "First, it does not belong to us. Although that didn't seem to bother you when you boosted it. Second, you were nearly arrested and charged with some felony counts, which would have gone right to juvenile court in Biloxi. Third, you have mistreated the dog and the horses. Not to mention how you've disrespected Anne and me. Fourth, you are not legally old enough to drive it." Zeke took a breath and leaned forward. "And finally, you still have not convinced me that you can be trusted." She leaned back. "Do you understand, now?"

Destiny said nothing then jumped up, knocking over her chair, and ran out the back door.

Anne stood, and Zeke put her hand up. "Let her go." She pulled out her cell phone and tapped the Monitor tab. "Watch this." Anne came around and stood over her shoulder, watching. When the GPS screen stabilized and zoomed in, a flashing green spot was moving away from them to the southwest.

"Looks like she's going to the barn," Anne said. "Do you think she's going for the ATV?"

"Probably. But I have the keys. We'd better make sure we know who has them at all times." Zeke stood. "I'd better go after her."

"No, you stay here. I'll head out to the barn and see if Destiny wants to talk."

Zeke cleared the dishes. "Do you think I was too hard on her?"

"Actually, no. You never raised your voice, you were factual, and best of all, honey, you never lost your temper." Anne kissed her. "I'm proud of you. And I'll have a whole week to get her off the ceiling."

Zeke laughed at the image as she rinsed the dishes and loaded the dishwasher. "It's true I was calm."

⁂

Anne walked in the barn with the pretense of working with Dancer. She gathered her halter and lead rope, then walked through the barn. No sign of Destiny. The arena was empty. She walked out to the paddock and spotted Destiny sitting under a tree across on the far side. All three horses were hanging around her. "I can't imagine her mood is that attractive, but maybe they're worried."

Destiny didn't see her, so Anne slipped back inside the arena and watched. As sensitive as horses were to negative energy, it was odd they chose to be with her. It was puzzling. Unless she wasn't angry at all. What if it was fear or loneliness, or a real sense of abandonment? If that were the case, the horses would be tuned in, not turned off.

Anne walked back to the barn and sat on one of the bales. That was enough invitation for their vigilant barn cat to appear. Once called Meka, they renamed her Morticia for her evil behavior toward Shayla.

If her assessment was accurate, they would need a new care plan. If Destiny had been scarred somehow by her grandfather's foul temper, it was possible that Zeke was a frightening reminder.

Probably better to save that notion until Zeke got back from Quantico. But Anne had a whole week to work on her theory.

Chapter Thirteen

Her flight landed on time, and a shuttle van pulled up to the marked staging area. Zeke moved toward the navy-blue van with her carry-on. A young marine standing at the van door eagerly moved to help. "Welcome back."

"Thank you, Mendoza." She read from his name flap. She took a seat near the back and nodded at another marine and two civilian contractors. Just before they pulled out, another man jumped on. He was tall, stocky, and had a gray buzz-cut and huge smile that could only belong to one man. He stopped halfway down the aisle. "Cabot?"

Zeke laughed. "Yup. What are you doing here, Agent Rick?"

He folded himself into the seat next to her. "Special call. I need to meet with some kid at the OTD for training. After that, who knows? What are you doing here? Secretary Ryerson call you back?" He laughed.

After her protection detail seven years earlier with the Undersecretary of Agriculture, word had spread that she was a particular favorite of the Secretary. It didn't hurt her reputation, and it was true. They formed a bond, and it was because of that bond that Zeke accepted her need for therapy to alleviate her PTSD symptoms. In a way, Secretary Ryerson saved her life.

"Matter of fact, I retired after working as Supervisory Special Agent in Charge of the Albuquerque field office. And a week later, I got a call asking me to participate in the Training Division as a field counselor."

"Sounds perfect for an agent with your great experience." He loosened his tie and put his head back.

"Seems to me you were talking about retiring when we met. What happened?" Zeke asked.

"Long story, but my son-in-law got shot in a drive-by in Chicago, so my daughter and her two kids came to live with us. Needed the money and the insurance."

"Got it."

❧❧❧❧

With Zeke away, Anne needed Destiny to step up. Anne left her to clean the kitchen while she and Benjamin measured for fencing to replace the pipe fence. His two cousins were between jobs and were willing to install it off-book.

"Mind if I ask a question?" Benjamin rewound the measuring tape.

"Never a problem."

"Is there something worrying Ms. Cabot about these fences?"

How to answer that? "We had some grave trouble several years ago because of a case she was working. She takes security very seriously now. And the black SUV you mentioned was recorded on surveillance. So she had her former partner do some checking." She wrote down the numbers Benjamin gave her for the fencing. "It worries me since this is a gated community."

"Well, that makes sense. I'd worry, too."

They walked a little farther and set the tape. "Mind if I ask a question?"

He laughed and said, "Okay."

"Are you comfortable staying here overnight?"

He stopped walking. "I don't mind, and since you told me how worried Ms. Cabot is, I'm glad if it helps. Besides, the food is much better than what I cook."

Anne sighed with relief. She hated thinking they were taking advantage. Benjamin had been on his own since his wife left him ten years earlier. When Anne met him five years ago, it was a perfect match for them. He lived close by and had years of ranch experience. And she was pretty flexible when he needed time off.

When they finished, Benjamin took the note with the measurements to the farm and feed store for materials. Hopefully, they'd start soon. Anne returned to the house to see how Destiny was faring.

Music was the first thing she noticed when she came in the mudroom and kicked off her boots. It was their soundtrack from *Mamma Mia.*

The family room resembled a bomb zone with all the furniture in the middle of the room with Destiny washing the windows—and doing a good job.

Anne slipped into the sparkling clean kitchen from the back entry. "The kid has talent."

She opened the fridge for some water, then sat down at the table when Shayla came in through the doggie door. She scratched her behind the ears while she thought about what to fix this week that would both satisfy hungry people and leave leftovers.

"Hi, sweetie. Got any ideas for dinner?" Shayla barked. "I know what you want." A list would be a good idea. As she retrieved a pad and pen, Destiny breezed in singing. Anne applauded. "You have a great voice."

"I didn't know you were here. I wanted to get a soda." Destiny looked stunned.

"It's perfectly okay. I was making a list for the store. I want to make some big dishes like chili, so we'll all have stuff to eat without fussing. If there's anything special, you need to jot it down on here." Anne turned in her chair. "I have to ask, are the songs of *Mamma Mia* special to you?"

Destiny dried her hands and opened the soda. She hoisted herself up on the counter. "Yeah, that's Mom's favorite. When Dad's not around, she plays it constantly. So I guess it's the soundtrack of my life."

"I love it, too. Zeke…not so much. But when I'm in a bad mood or cleaning house, I always put it on. Way back in the day, I used Donna Summer's music to clean house."

"Mom likes her, too. I even think Dad does."

"Have you talked to your folks lately?"

Destiny fiddled with the tab on the soda can. "Well, no. I didn't have my phone and then…well, I don't have much to say, and I don't want to answer a million questions."

"Perfectly understandable." Anne stood up and tossed her water bottle in the recycling bin. "You're doing a terrific job, and when you're about finished, you could clean up and go to the store with me"

"Okay. I'll be out in a few."

Anne slipped her boots on and headed out to the barn. On the way, she sent Zeke a text.

AReynolds: Destiny is deep cleaning the family room while listening to Mamma Mia. <3

She headed out in the paddock to bring in the horses. Usually, she'd leave them out while she went to the store, but she and Zeke agreed to be extra careful for a while. There was no reason to think her horses were a target, but better safe than sorry.

It took some time to get each horse back in their stall. Anne glanced at her watch. Benjamin would probably be back soon, but, she locked the arena doors and the barn door.

ZCabot: Are you joking or doing a few lines with Destiny??

AReynolds: Gods truth! Says her mom loves the soundtrack. Dad…No.

ZCabot: Classes are good and relatively lite. Miss you. We're halfway.

AReynolds: Miss you too. Hurry home.

Benjamin slowly drove through the gate with his truck's bed full of fencing supplies. Behind him followed another pickup with two more rolls of fencing. She waved, and they drove back behind the barn near the fence. When Benjamin got out, she met him.

"I wasn't sure how long you'd be, so I locked the arena, barn, and office. You have those keys don't you?"

"Yes, ma'am." He pulled out a key ring.

"The ATV keys are on my desk if you need them. Destiny and I are going to the store. We'll be back a little later."

"I think we'll start back near Bascom's and move

up to the gate." He pointed back over his shoulder.

"Sounds good. See you guys later." She turned back toward the house just as Destiny came out. "You ready to go?"

"Yup. All cleaned up."

✥✥✥✥

Zeke sat on the desk in front of a small group of students. Her teaching partner took a handful of students outside to learn some martial arts tricks he'd mastered. The group that stayed were mostly female and wanted to know how the Bureau had changed since Zeke started. They all had questions.

She pointed to a young woman from Pocatello, Idaho. "Heidi?"

"So, you came from Mississippi, what drew you to law enforcement and the FBI?"

"Good question. You know I'm not certain. My dad was in the military his whole career, and I knew I didn't want to do that. I got a bachelor's degree in statistics, but my family wanted me to go for a Ph.D. I wanted to play basketball." She stood and walked around. "Around that time a recruiter came through to talk about government careers. I read about all of them, and a swell of patriotism pushed me to serve. The FBI offered the classes I wanted. Josh?"

"What was the worst experience you've had?"

Her brain began to reel with memories about Chicago and the undercover case of the decapitated homeless victims. But she didn't want to open that door. Then she remembered.

"I guess it would have to be when I was shot."

The gasp from the students was audible.

It took a minute while her muscle memory did a flashback and she instantly regretted the choice. She swallowed the bile in her throat, and she started almost whispering. "I planned a meet with an informant. I chose a small area in downtown that had good visibility, and I had another agent parked nearby watching." Her throat tightened, and she tried to summon saliva.

"The informant showed up, we sat at a small picnic table, and within minutes a low rider slowed around the curve behind us. I saw the gun ..."

"Agent Cabot?"

"Ma'am, are you okay?"

"Go get her some water."

"Should we call someone?"

She put up her hand. "I'm okay. Just a little blank spot. Where was I?"

A small voice said, "You saw the gun."

She cleared her throat. "Right. The informant was the target and had his back to them. He took the brunt of the shots, but two hit me. My vest saved me. But that whole thing haunted me for a long time."

"Did he die?"

"Not at the time. The informant had a long recovery, and then when his brother came to take him home to Mexico, their private plane was blown up. They closed the case."

"Wow, that's incredible."

"Guys, remember that those kind of experiences are not the norm. I can honestly tell you that eighty percent of the work is investigation and paperwork."

They began to joke with each other, so Zeke put her hand up. "The reason I told you that particular story was a lesson. What did I do wrong that might have prevented that drive-by?"

They each took a shot at some general ideas: a different location, more agents, more vests, video cameras. They spent some time discussing options until Zeke stopped them. "What I feel was my critical error was not paying attention to my environment. That low-rider drove past coming from the opposite direction, and I saw it but didn't register it until after it passed again. Then it was too late. Ten to twenty seconds and I would have had him on the ground and me firing back. Hindsight."

No comments came from the gallery.

"I think that'll do it for today. Do the readings for tomorrow, and we'll be talking about field office assignments."

They filed out, and Zeke put her class notes in her briefcase. She had time for a run before dinner. For old time's sake, she went over to the course where they all trained. With luck, there wouldn't be many there to watch the old retired agent running. Admittedly, forty-nine was not that old, but it sure felt like it after spending time with the new class.

She changed clothes into shorts and a T-shirt. It was a beautiful warm evening with a light breeze. Some people were out walking, biking, or running. Partial memories of her time as a recruit flickered through her mind. It had been a very satisfying career, and she went out on top when she was ready. There was a long period when she was sure the PTSD would cut short her ability to function, but happily, Robin and the Equine Therapy in Arizona pulled her back from probable ruin. That and Annie, of course. She smiled.

When Anne and Destiny returned from the store, Anne made a point of watching the electronic gate opening and closing. It was slow enough to allow another car to enter. She'd been working on the neighborhood flyer and promised to talk with Susan about distribution. Maybe later.

"How come you're going so slow?"

Anne laughed. "Sorry, I was thinking about stuff I have to do and worrying about that gate being so slow."

"Yeah, anyone could walk through that. Do you guys worry about bad people getting in?"

Anne thought about that. "Actually, yes. A long time ago Zeke had a case that was a nightmare, and the bad guy did all kinds of stuff to harass us."

"Well if it was a long time ago…"

"It was, and he's gone, but every once in a while, strange cars show up, and if it's more than once, it's worrying."

After a prolonged pause, Destiny said, "Are we safe?"

"Oh, yes, honey, I don't want you to worry. But that's why your aunt was so worried when you took off and we couldn't find you."

The garage door went up, and Anne parked the car. "Let's get the groceries in before the ice cream melts and the ribs get cold."

On impulse, Anne decided to stop at The BBQ for the best ribs and chicken. She got enough for leftovers that might last a couple of days until Zeke got home. She sent a text to Benjamin to let him know dinner would be ready soon.

Destiny took armloads of canned and dry goods to the pantry while Anne washed and bagged the fresh produce. Destiny took the empty bags to the recycling bin and then plopped down on the desk by the refrigerator.

"You know, I get upset because everyone treats me like a baby. I'm not. I'm even in accelerated classes at school, but nobody ever wants to talk about that."

Anne hoisted up by the sink. "You're right. That's disrespectful, and I apologize." She waited, hoping Destiny might engage. Nope. "We don't have to do anything right now, but if you feel like talking about your plans or anything else, let's do it. Okay?"

"Sure. Can we eat now?"

"Yup, let's."

They each filled a plate with ribs, chicken, coleslaw and potato salad. As soon as they sat down, Benjamin knocked.

"Come in. We started without you."

He grabbed a plate and filled it up. "This looks wonderful."

Anne stared. She divorced so long ago she had forgotten how much men ate. She was grateful she bought extra.

"How's the fence going?"

He chewed and swallowed before answering. "We got as far as the barn, and I think we can finish by tomorrow. I think you'll be pleased with it."

"Any problems?" Anne looked at him, hoping he understood her question.

He looked up. "Nope, everything looks good. No problems."

"Good, thanks. Destiny, I'll clean up if you want to watch a movie or go upstairs."

"Thanks." She jumped and ran into the family room.

Anne waited for the TV to start and watched Benjamin go for seconds. For a moment, she felt content. Everyone in her domain was safe and fed.

When the food was stored away, Benjamin took some reheated coffee with him and said good night. Anne ran to her room, changed into lounge pants and a long-sleeved shirt, then she joined Destiny watching *The Avengers*. She looked over at Destiny chewing a fingernail, wholly absorbed in the film, and wondered what her life was like at home that triggered her wild behavior. Reggie seemed so laid back, and while she'd never met Maura, Zeke seemed to think she was a delightful, loving woman. That left only one wild card—Master Sergeant Robert Cabot. How could she find out?

When her phone rang, she hoped it would be Zeke.

"Hello."

"Hi, Anne, it's Susan. Is this a good time?"

"Sure, just watching TV. Do you want to run over? We can sit on the deck, and I think there may be some Riesling."

Susan laughed. "On my way."

"Susan is coming over, and we'll be out on the deck if you need anything."

"Okay"

Anne poured Susan some wine and went out on the deck, turned on the twinkle lights along the railing, and shortly heard the "yoo-hoo."

"I'm here."

Susan came up the steps with a dish in her hand. "I had to make brownies for the boys, and stole a few quick."

Anne smiled at her neighbor's thoughtfulness.

"Why don't you stick your head in the door and give them to Destiny."

Susan slid open the door. "Do you want to take these, hon? Fresh out of the oven."

"Thanks."

Anne smiled. "I think I've discovered the way to her heart…food!" She pointed to the wineglass.

"Thanks. I sure need this. Honestly, those men at my house have driven me to drink."

"Your boys are so sweet."

"Ha! You haven't seen them lately."

"But I'll bet you're glad they're home safely."

"Of course I am. But I called about your neighborhood memo. It looks fine, but I'm curious about who brought this to you. Is there something going on?"

Anne sat up and lowered her voice. "If you remember a few years ago, we had some trouble with one of Zeke's cases."

"My God, of course I do. It was terrifying. That's why you put in all that security equipment. Is there something that caused you guys to issue this neighborhood watch?"

"Benjamin reported a black SUV coming by and asking him who lived there."

"Huh. I've seen that car."

"My motivation is based on how they got into the subdivision, and more than once. I hope that involving the whole neighborhood will add to the number of eyes and ears."

"Do you think those guys are casing the houses?"

Susan sounded worried, and Anne enjoyed her dramatic take on the situation. It was hard to impart a level of seriousness without whipping up a frenzy.

"I'm not sure there's a cause for fear, but we do have a locked gate to prevent street traffic from using our lane. I guess I feel like most of us have lived here so long that we take our security for granted."

Susan took another swallow and nodded. "I can't disagree with that. We're not as neighborly as we once were."

"I feel bad about that. We used to have some fun potlucks."

Susan set her glass down. "I think the flyer is a great idea. I'll take them around tomorrow if you'd like."

"I'd appreciate it. I've got a plateful this week while Zeke is gone." Anne nodded toward the family room.

"Good night, thanks for the wine."

"Thanks, Susan."

Anne washed and dried the wineglass. It was almost ten, and that meant midnight in Washington. Maybe she could catch Zeke in the morning. She went out and called Shayla, who came tearing around the corner of the garage.

"What have you been up to? You're all dirty. Tomorrow is going to be bath day. Maybe we can interest Destiny in being a dog hairdresser." She put two large biscuits in Shayla's bed. "I think it's about time to turn in."

She turned off the lights, locked the doors, and set the alarms, chores that Zeke always managed to do.

The movie was long over, and Destiny was curled up with a blanket sleeping with an angelic expression. "Time for bed, sweetie." She gently removed the blanket and pulled Destiny to a sitting position.

"Can't I just stay here?"

"Nope. It gets chilly down here. Just brush your teeth and go right back to sleep."

When they got to the stairs, Anne heard a knock on the patio door. "Susan must have forgotten something." She turned on the back deck lights, but no one was there. "Maybe she thought we were asleep. I'll call her tomorrow. Let's get to bed."

Chapter Fourteen

Zeke tried again, but Anne's phone went to voice mail. *Maybe she's talking to Susan. That usually takes a while.* She continued eating her breakfast and went back to her room to change. Today would be the last class for them, and if she ended early, she could make the early flight home.

"Agent Cabot?'

"Yes." She couldn't remember the student's name.

"May I ask a question?"

"Sure. Walk with me." They headed toward the building housing her classroom.

"You mentioned working in Albuquerque, and I wondered if you'd recommend that for a first assignment."

"Are you from the area?"

"No. The Midwest, but my grandmother lives there, and she's getting older. Well, I'd like to spend some time with her before." He blushed. "You know."

"Yes, I do. Where does your grandmother live?"

"In Los Lunas."

"I enjoyed my time—for the most part. I'd worked in big cities most of my career and liked the small-town feel and the variety of characters I ran into. I'm not sure you'll get too much choice for your first assignment, but it wouldn't hurt to ask."

"Um, how's the office about discrimination and

inclusivity?"

She wasn't sure where he was going with that, but guessed he was gay. He didn't appear to have a racial profile. "Well, I didn't have any trouble except for being a woman."

He laughed awkwardly. "You also had a rock-solid rep."

"Thanks. Let me know if you get assigned to Albuquerque."

He looked puzzled. "How would I—"

"If you're in the field office, someone will know." She winked.

"Oh yeah. Right." After finishing with the student, Zeke gathered her teaching materials and laptop, and caught a ride to the airport. "Anne? I've been trying to call you. Is everything okay?"

"Hi. We're fine. My phone was dead, and I had no idea why. You know, I always charge it before bed. Oh well, it seems to be fine now. Are you on the way home?"

"Yup, I'm on my way to the airport. I should be home by eight or so."

"Great. I'll wait till you're home to eat."

"Can't wait. I love you, hon."

"Love you, too. Be safe."

❧❧❧❧

Benjamin walked down the fence line from the gate. Anne followed, examining the new security fencing. He pointed to the heavy-duty wire mesh fence. "This is very hard to cut. And I think it will be a good warning."

"Why did you leave the small gap at the bottom?"

"Mostly to allow small creatures to escape when the horses are out running. Also, when we have heavy rains, the debris won't pile up on the fence."

"You really put some thought into this." She stepped back and pointed. "It's not that obvious. I was afraid it would look like chain link. It's doesn't. You guys did a great job."

"It's been quiet lately, not much traffic. I've been checking the fences more often since I've been staying here." They walked a bit more. "It may not be my place, but I think using the Godfreys' ATV has been really helpful to me for checking more of the property. I feel bad using the Godfreys' all the time." He stopped and turned. "If you'd be okay with it, I could look around for a used model or one to fix up."

"That's not a bad idea. Let me talk to Zeke, but I don't want to abuse the Godfreys' generosity, either."

"I don't mean to be costing you money, but doing these fence repairs was a whole lot quicker with the ATV because the terrain is kinda rough. I also thought we might do some trimming to prevent the chances of fire. That could be a real problem."

Anne stopped and thought about the forest fire they'd survived several years earlier. She'd been terrified that her horses would be lost. The Godfreys had saved them.

"Benjamin, thanks for being proactive about our safety."

Through his ruddy complexion Anne could see a blush forming. In spite of the graying temples, the man was still in his physical prime, and it saddened her that he had not remarried.

She went back to the barn and found Destiny busily cleaning up after mucking the stalls. "Good job.

You might have a new career opportunity."

Destiny laughed. "Like I want to do barn work for a living. Seriously?"

"Well, just a thought. Did you have breakfast?"

"I had some toast and a Coke."

"I didn't have much and thought I'd make some egg salad. You could have some eggs if you felt like it."

She shrugged. "Maybe in a tortilla with cheese?"

Anne threw an arm around her shoulders. "I'm sure we can do that. And remind me to call Susan after we eat."

❧ ❧ ❧ ❧

The luggage carousel rumbled by empty and the metal sheaves scraped each other as they circled. Tired conversations lent a background to the hum of the Sunport. Finally, her flight number flashed on the board, and the conveyor belt from the back jerked and bags emerged.

Luggage in hand, she headed to the car lot shuttle, and within twenty minutes of landing Zeke was back in her comfortable car, windows open and music playing. It was always nice to have Anne waiting, but their "houseguest" took priority.

Coming home after a week of teaching was becoming more and more pleasurable. The teaching was okay, but the travel was becoming grueling. She steered onto I-40 east and began to ruminate about teaching opportunities in Albuquerque. Her thoughts morphed into teaching children, and from there to her niece. *Oh yeah, Destiny.*

Being engaged with students in law enforcement distracted her from the problem at home. Anne hadn't said anything negative, but Zeke suspected she was waiting until she got home. *Deep breath. Enjoy springtime sights and smells of the mountains.* She took a deep breath and embraced the rich scent of pine and juniper.

As she rounded the curve in the subdivision, she spotted the Bascom property and then the sizeable shiny mesh on the white pipe fence. It evoked a palpable feeling of security. It certainly wouldn't prevent a determined felon, but it sent a message, and she liked it.

Anne stood in the kitchen door smiling as Zeke pulled into the garage.

"Here, let me help you." Anne took her jacket and briefcase, then kissed her.

"It's so good to be home. Everything okay?"

"Yes, fine. I'm sure you saw the fence. Benjamin did a great job."

"Yeah, it looks perfect." She took her suitcase in and stopped. "I think I'll change. Where's Destiny?"

"In her room. We just had lunch. Can I make you a sandwich?"

"Sounds wonderful. I'm starving."

She got to the top of the stairs and heard music. Should she say anything or wait? Wait. Once changed and refreshed, she laid her briefcase on her desk and hurried down to spend a few minutes with Anne.

The table had a placemat, a sandwich, chips, and a brownie. "Wow, this looks terrific. So, catch me up on what I missed."

Anne joined her with her own glass of iced tea. "You won't believe me, but it was a peaceful week, and Destiny was fine. She did what I asked with only minor resistance, no hysteria."

"You're right. I don't believe you." She winked.

"Tell me about your week. I feel like we didn't have much time to catch up."

Zeke wiped her mouth with the napkin and took a drink. "You know, it was good. Good group of kids, interesting questions, and it's a nice time of year to be at Quantico. I even took a run on the old trail. But I skipped all the obstacles." She took her plate to the sink and rinsed it. "On the way home, I was thinking about it and realized I like to teach, but I don't want to do the travel."

"I wish you didn't have to travel so far, either."

"Do you think there is any way to teach law enforcement without a teaching degree?"

"I'm not sure. It would have to be something private. You could check with the office." Anne took a bowl from the refrigerator to the sink and rinsed some strawberries, which she proceeded to slice. "Susan came over last night to discuss the neighborhood flyer."

"Oh, good. Will she help?"

"Yes, she thinks it sounds like a good idea. She remembered back to the time when the neighbors used to be more social. It was nice."

"I guess that was before my time. I'm not sure I've even met everyone."

"Maybe we should plan a barbeque to get everyone together. It might encourage people to be more watchful."

"Oddly, after she left and we were heading to bed, I heard a knock on the patio door. I thought Susan came back because she forgot something, but when I called today, she said she didn't. It was strange. I went over to turn on the lights, and no one was there." She laughed.

Zeke's internal alarm flipped on. "What time was that?"

"Around ten. I'm sure it was just the wind." Anne continued slicing.

"I think I'll unpack. Call me if you need me."

Anne smiled. "Honey, I always need you."

Zeke unpacked and tossed her laundry in the basket to go downstairs. Then, she removed her laptop and plugged it in. *I know I'm just paranoid, but if I'm not, no more travel. Family comes first.*

The surveillance screen opened, and Destiny's door opened. Zeke glanced over her shoulder and shut down the program and opened her email. Within minutes, Destiny appeared.

"Oh, Auntie, you're home."

"Hi. How're you doing?"

"Good. Was your trip good?"

"Yes, it was, but I'm thrilled to be home. Did I miss anything?"

"I helped Benjamin with the fence. It looks really cool."

"I saw it when I drove in, but I'd like to take a walk and look at it later."

"I'll go with you." Destiny sounded eager.

"Okay, let's go." Zeke stood.

They took off down the stairs and out through the kitchen.

"We're going to look at the fence," Destiny told Anne.

Zeke shrugged and followed Destiny out.

The afternoon had warmed up, and the front of the house and the lawn looked neat and tidy. "You did a good job with the rocks and grass."

"All the places where Benjamin put the grass seed are growing."

They continued to the gate, and Zeke asked, "How are you getting along with the horses?"

"Good. Horses are not as scary as I thought they were. Anne has taught me a lot of stuff."

"Do you want to learn to ride before you go home?"

Destiny kept walking with no answer. Zeke checked the fence attachments and waited.

"Yeah, maybe."

They walked all the way to the corner and the Bascoms' lot line. Zeke checked the ground on both sides of the barbwire, then stopped to look around toward the house.

"Auntie, are you still worried about us?"

"Worried?" Zeke turned surprised by the comment. "Why do you think I'm worried?"

"Anne told me that some bad stuff happened a long time ago and you wanted to be very careful."

They started back across the paddock. "Anne's right. Since it's related to my job, I feel responsible. And when I'm out of town, I worry more. I guess it's the price I pay for working in law enforcement."

"But aren't you just teaching now?"

"Yes, but sometimes the people we lock up hold a grudge for a very long time."

"Wow. That would be creepy."

"Yes, it is," Zeke mumbled.

❧❧❧❧

Anne was in her barn office when Zeke knocked on the doorframe. "Come in. How was the walk?"

"Good." Zeke sat on the corner of the desk. "Destiny surprised me when she asked if I was still worried about our safety."

Anne closed her laptop and leaned back in her chair. "Oh. I did explain that was the reason for reinforcing the fence. I didn't think you'd mind."

"I don't. Destiny's a lot smarter than I give her credit for, and maybe she'll be a little more cautious."

"You still look worried," Anne said softly.

"I am. I didn't look through the security tape because Destiny came out and we decided to walk. The fence looks great and sends a message."

"What else did you guys talk about?"

"Oh, I asked if she wanted to learn to ride."

Anne laughed. "So did I. What did she say?"

"She thought about it. Said she wasn't so scared of the horses and maybe she could."

"That might be a good thing for you two to try on Monday when I have my annual physical exam."

"Right. I forgot about that." Zeke leaned over and kissed her. "You get back to work. I'm going to check those tapes."

Music came from Destiny's room, and then her voice in a one-sided conversation. *Must be on her phone.* It never occurred to her that Destiny actually had friends. Huh.

She opened her surveillance program and scrolled back to the night of Susan's visit. She checked the garage cam first and saw Susan come through the trees on the path time-stamped 2110. She switched to Tree Cam #5 which showed the deck and the back of the house. She waited, then sped it up to 2200. The lights were all out, and the eastern moon cast tree shadows across the whole area that moved with the wind.

Discerning anything was hard. She continued scanning and then the floodlights went on, and there was nothing. Zeke rewound and watched again. She stopped at one point when she thought she saw a shadow that didn't move. The video continued, and she kept watching even after the deck lights went out. *There!*

Chapter Fifteen

S he rewound and enlarged the screenshot then changed her mind as it lost definition. Not wanting to holler downstairs, Zeke sent a text.

ZCabot: Would you come up here for a minute?

"What's wrong?" Anne said when she came up.

"I wanted to show you something quietly." She turned on the program and moved over.

Anne leaned on the desk and watched intently.

"Would you play that again, and can it go slower?"

Zeke watched and waited.

"One more time, please." She finished and went to sit on the window bench. "I saw a shadow, but it wasn't there when I turned the lights on. But after the lights went out I thought I saw a shadow on the other end of the deck. What was that?"

"I'm not sure. I'll need to check all the other cameras to see if someone came on the property. Was Destiny with you the whole time?"

"Yes, except for a short time when I was on the deck with Susan, but she was inside watching a movie while we were outside."

"Okay. I just wanted to see what your take was. It's the same as mine. I'll keep looking. Do you think you could keep Destiny downstairs for a while so I could finish this?"

"Sure, she can help with dinner." She walked to her door and knocked. "Destiny, would you come down and help me with dinner?"

Zeke gave her a thumbs-up and as soon as Destiny went down, she called the security company.

"Hi, Davis, it's Zeke Cabot. I have a quick question for someone. Two nights ago my partner heard a knock on the patio door around 2200. When she turned on the lights, there was no one there. I just reviewed the tape, and I'm reasonably sure I saw a vague-looking shadow on the deck before and after the lights were turned on. Would you ask someone to check everything for that evening? If there was someone out there, they had to come and go from some point."

"We'll look carefully. I'm surprised the guys missed that, but I'll let you know."

"Thanks."

⁂

Zeke paced to and from the window. "For what we pay them it sure would be nice to get a little faster response."

"Honey, you know they won't get a report until Monday. Try to get some rest." Anne reached over to turn off the light. "You're home now, and we're all okay."

Zeke grumbled something, slid into bed, and turned on her side.

Anne just smiled and closed her eyes, but she was distracted by her own physical exam. Last year, there was some concern about her kidney function. This year's tests should be definitive.

Anne knew it was too early to wake Destiny, so instead she dressed and left the house quietly to take care of the horses. It was a little foggy after a chilly night, but everything looked shiny because of the sheen of dewy moisture on the plants.

The barn was warm and the horses restless. Even though she was early, it was never early enough for hungry horses. The nickering and restless hooves increased. "I'm hurrying as fast as I can. Just hang on, you guys."

Soon they were all eating, and she decided to go to her office for a minute before letting them out. She checked online to see if her lab results from last Thursday had been reported in advance of her physical. They hadn't. A quick look at her email held nothing urgent, just a couple of inquiries about her business and how to schedule appointments. She highlighted those and began to delete the ads. A personal message from Joe caught her eye.

Hey, it feels like years since we've seen each other. I will be visiting the area next week, and we could get together? It would be fun. Joe.

She shook her head, another weirdo titillated by women and horses. She paused over the delete button and thought it through. It might be wise to have Zeke take a look at it. It could be a different kind of weirdo. She closed her browser without deleting the message.

On her way back through the barn, she caught up with Destiny. "Good morning. I was just on my way back to let the horses out. How are you today?"

"Still sleepy. I'll go back and eat after I do my chores." Her hair was wild and mussed, mascara shadowed her lower eyelids, and her clothes looked slept in.

"Thanks, I really appreciate what a good job you are doing."

They worked together and managed to get things done very quickly with little conversation.

"Let's go see if Zeke is up and planning to feed us working hands."

"I'm starved." Shayla caught up and followed them, tongue lolling.

※ ※ ※ ※

Zeke was busy in the kitchen making her Cabot family breakfast. As a child, she remembered every Sunday after church her grandmother would cook up a batch of grits, scald a thick ham slice, and scramble up a dozen eggs. Sometimes Zeke could help make the toast with homemade bread.

Everything was almost ready. The table was set, and Zeke needed to finish the eggs. She pulled a pitcher of orange juice from the refrigerator and put it on the table.

"It sure smells good in here," Destiny said.

"Come on kid, let's wash up so we can eat." Anne went to the kitchen sink while Destiny hurried to the downstairs powder room. "It really does smell wonderful. What possessed you to jump out of bed and cook?" She dried her hands and gave Zeke a warm kiss and hug.

"With a response like this, I'll jump up and cook

every morning." She pulled Anne into a hug.

Destiny returned and stopped in the doorway. "Oh. Excuse me."

Anne laughed. "You don't need to excuse yourself. You are family, and we are not hiding our relationship."

"Breakfast is ready, let's eat." Zeke carried one bowl of scrambled eggs and another of grits.

Anne put down the platter with ham and toast. "This looks so wonderful. Thank you."

There was minimum conversation as the three women dug into breakfast. Destiny asked to be excused and took her plate to the sink. As Destiny raced up the steps to her room, Anne turned to Zeke and whispered, "I got a very odd email this morning and saved it to show you."

Anne set down her phone and opened to her email. After highlighting it, she turned the phone to face Zeke. She waited for her to read it, then asked, "What do you think?"

"I'm not really sure, but let me see if I can find anything associated with that IP address." She tapped the address into her phone. "What time do you have to leave?"

"I'm going to shower and dress, and then I have to head out. Do you need anything in town?"

"No. I'll text you if I think of anything. Go ahead, I'll clean this up."

❧ ❧ ❧ ❧

Destiny changed her jeans and pulled on the western boots Zeke had given her. They weren't new; they were Zeke's old boots, but they looked really cool.

She looked in the mirror and smiled. At first, learning to ride seemed kind corny, but the more she thought about it, it could be phenomabomb.

Zeke was already in the barn when Destiny got there. "What are we going to do first?"

"I want to go over a few things first to make sure we're both safe." She brought Shadow out of his stall and tied him in the cross ties in the aisle. "This bridle is a basic snaffle bit."

Destiny was already getting confused but continued to watch the complicated routine taking off the halter and putting on the bridle that looked horribly uncomfortable.

"Doesn't that hurt the horse?" Destiny asked.

"Not really. You can't really see it very well, but horses don't have any teeth in the back, and that's where the bridle bit fits." She maneuvered the leather bridle-thing over Shadow's head and inserted that metal piece into his mouth.

"That's gross."

"Next, we're going to put on the saddle pad so the saddle will be more comfortable."

Destiny had seen this stuff hanging in the tack room but had no idea what to do with it. Zeke continued about the saddle and how it fit. Destiny watched her deal with all the straps and got confused. "Auntie, I don't get what you're doing."

"That's okay. We'll do it again with Sunny."

"Whatever."

Once Shadow was all set, Zeke took him closer to the arena and looped his reins over the railing.

"Now let's get Sunny ready." Zeke brought her out, and Destiny went to the tack room where everything was labeled, luckily.

"Good. Do you remember how we put this on?"

"Um…you put her halter on her neck first."

"Good. And then?" Zeke was holding the bridle and the bit.

"I think you slid the leather piece over her head at the same time you shoved that thing in her mouth."

Zeke laughed really hard and said, "You're right."

The saddle was still weird and heavy. But it got connected.

"Now we're going to walk them into the ring." Zeke handed the reins to her.

Sunny was really gentle and just stood there while Zeke untied Shadow and led him into the arena. Sunny just followed. It wasn't that different than when she'd bring them in from the pasture with the halter lead.

"Okay. I'm going to go around the ring once to show you what we'll do today." Zeke put her foot in the stirrup and pulled herself up and over in one move.

"Wow. It looks so easy."

Zeke took both reins in her hands. "Keep your hands here and don't hold them too tight. Squeeze your knees to hold on, then just touch your heel to his side and tell him, 'Let's go.'"

Shadow lifted his head and started walking. Zeke was still talking, but Destiny couldn't hear too well. She was getting bored and wanted to ride. She watched the birds fly in and out around the high ceiling. Looked like they were building a nest up there.

Zeke rode up beside her and surprised her. "You ready?"

"Sure." Destiny pulled on the reins, and Sunny stepped sideways toward her and crushed her foot. She screamed and dropped the reins.

Sunny bolted right into Shadow, and they both

took off. When Destiny stopped yelling, she saw Zeke half off the horse with her feet flying around. Destiny ran toward the horses. They freaked and ran in two different directions and Zeke flew into the sidewall by the door.

"Auntie!" Destiny ran up and saw Zeke bleeding from her head. "Are you okay?"

Zeke nodded and mumbled, "Towels and …"

Destiny got up and ran. Her heart pounded. "What just happened?" She raced into the kitchen and pulled open drawers looking for towels and water and bandages. With her arms full, she ran back to the barn, leaving a trail of dropped first-aid materials.

When she raced into the ring, Zeke lay in the sawdust, slumped over sideways. The horses stood very near. She dropped the stuff and ran. "Auntie, are you okay? Auntie, please talk to me." Her faced was caked with blood, and she wouldn't answer.

Destiny scrambled to find her cell phone and couldn't. "Crap!" She looked around but didn't see anything in the deep sawdust. She screamed, "Somebody help!"

That startled the horses, and they ran to the other end.

"Oh God, what am I supposed to do?"

She ran to the house and dialed 911 from the landline.

"Nine-one-one, what is your emergency?"

"My aunt is hurt badly. The horses took off when I screamed, and she fell, and I don't know what to do, she isn't talking, and—"

"Hold on, we have someone on the way. Is she breathing?"

"I don't know, I didn't check."

"Is she hurt anywhere?"

"I don't—wait. Her head is bleeding and so is her arm."

"Okay, the ambulance will be there soon. They have the code to the community gate, but I need you to go to your aunt and be on the lookout for the ambulance so you can direct the paramedics to where they need to go. Do you understand?"

Destiny threw down the phone and ran out the door just as flashing lights came around the curve on the lane. She hit the button to open the driveway gate, and the sheriff's squad car swerved in. He called out, "Where is she?"

"The barn!"

Sheriff Lafferty ran into the barn with Destiny right behind him.

"She's got a good pulse. Hand me one of those towels." He practically barked the order, and Destiny flinched.

All the supplies were in a pile and Destiny could hardly see through the tears. "Is she dead? Did I do that? Oh my God…"

"Destiny, stop it. She's not dead, but she's hurt." He snatched a towel and pushed it on the side of her head. "Go show the ambulance where to go. Hurry."

She could hear the sirens close and the horses were freaked. Still, she ran out waving her arms. "Here! She's in here. Hurry."

Three people piled out, two men and a woman. Each had a bag, and one carried a stretcher. They followed her to the arena, then the older man stopped her. "Is there a way to get out though that far door?"

"What? I don't know."

He took her by the shoulders. "You have to listen

to me. We need an easier way out than through this deep sawdust."

"Yes. There's a gate in the fence by the door."

"Great." He hurried out.

She ran over to where everyone looked busy. "Is she going to be okay? I know it's my fault, she's gonna kill me." Destiny couldn't stop sobbing. They were moving so fast—they had a big bandage on her head, had wrapped her arm tight, and they were putting a needle in her arm connected to a tube to a bag.

They pulled off her beautiful boots and tossed them aside. Destiny gasped. "Oh, no."

"We've got to get her out of here. Is Wayne here?"

"I'm here, the rig's right outside and the gurney's by the door. I think it's safer to carry the patient to the door."

"Pressure is still low. We need to go."

Sheriff Lafferty walked over to Destiny. "I know you're scared. Is anyone here with you?"

"No, I was just learning to ride. Zeke was teaching me, and Anne has gone somewhere."

"Okay, you ride with me, and we'll get your aunt safely to the hospital. Deal?" He handed her a big white handkerchief.

She looked at it.

"It's for your nose."

Just then she heard Zeke cry out when they slid the stretcher under her. "Help her!"

"Destiny come with me." He put his big arm around her shoulder and pushed her to the door. "They'll take good care of her."

Lights flashed everywhere from the sheriff's car, the ambulance, and another police car outside the fence. He opened the door for her, helped her into the back seat, and buckled the seat belt.

"Am I going to be arrested? Did I do something that bad? I didn't mean to. I love my aunt."

He knelt down beside the door. "No, you didn't do anything wrong. I'm taking you so you can be there with your aunt when she wakes up. Try not to worry."

The ambulance turned around and the sheriff led them out the gate. The last thing she saw was Shayla running along inside the fence.

Chapter Sixteen

Anne placed her order at the neighborhood Chinese restaurant. She knew Destiny loved their egg rolls as much as Anne did. The cashier asked her another question, but she couldn't hear her because of the sirens outside. She turned but just caught a glimpse of flashing lights.

"I'm sorry, yes, some almond cookies as well." The cashier took her credit card and rang up the total. Anne signed and sat down to wait. Relieved, she couldn't wait to tell Zeke that her kidney function tests had improved. It was a huge weight off her shoulders. The dietary restrictions she might have had were strict. Fifteen minutes later, she loaded two large bags in the car. As she neared the house, she saw the gate open. "Wonder what they're moving? Maybe the ATV." She pulled in the garage and Shayla ran in, panting.

"You poor thing. Did they forget to give you water? Come on in."

She stopped at the kitchen door. Every drawer was pulled out, there was stuff all over the place. "Well. This is not okay. I don't care what they're doing, do not leave my kitchen like this."

She walked around the corner and called out. "Zeke? Destiny? Somebody get down here and clean this mess up." When no one answered, she got a little bit angrier. No one upstairs, either. Shayla was still running around her.

"I'm sure you're hungry, but settle down and help me find Zeke."

When she said that, Shayla took off downstairs and Anne followed as she ran out the back door. Once in the driveway, she saw Shayla stop, then run to the barn.

Well, okay, of course Zeke and Destiny were probably engrossed in riding lessons. She walked in and saw all her towels strewn around the far end of the arena. But no people. As she got closer, she saw the blood-soaked towels on the ground. Then, a bloody streak down the wall.

She sunk to her knees. Her nurse brain tried to assess what had happened. Someone got hurt, but who and when? The towels were still wet, and there was a wheel track to the back doors. She followed them and saw the gate open. *Oh God, where are the horses?* She scanned the paddock and then the pasture. Both Shadow and Sunny were grazing near the far fence.

She pulled her cell phone and dialed Zeke's number. It repeatedly rang as she hurried back to the barn. And then she saw Zeke's phone in the middle of the arena. She picked it up and put it in her pocket, then quickly dialed Destiny's number. No reply. *The tracker.* The app opened, warmed up, and the green dot was over the house. *Shit.*

One deep breath and she dialed 911.

"Nine-one-one, what is your emergency?"

"This is Anne Reynolds. Can you tell me if you were called to this location recently?"

The wait was interminable.

"Yes, ma'am. Our paramedic team was called out about ninety minutes ago."

Anne grabbed her chest. "Do you know where

they went from here?"

"It looks like the destination was the hospital ER on Wyoming Blvd."

"Thanks." She disconnected and dialed the hospital.

"Emergency Department, how may I direct your call?"

"Yes, I need to speak with your charge nurse."

"One moment."

Endless ringing. "Pick up, dammit."

"Vasquez, how can I help you?"

Anne sighed. "Maria, it's Anne Reynolds, I'm so glad you're on."

"Hola, chica. What do you need? A job, I hope."

"No, I'm looking for my partner and my niece, both named Cabot. Zeke and Destiny?"

"Let me check. Yeah, looks like they were just admitted. I can't tell you much right now."

"It's okay. I'm on my way, should be twenty-five minutes at most. Tell them I'm coming."

She hesitated. The horses were probably okay. But not Shayla. She ran back to the house. "Come on, girl. I'll get you something to eat and drink."

Once Shayla was safe inside, Anne rushed out to her car and headed to the hospital. She tried to keep focused and not be reckless. In her mind, she screamed obscenities at slow drivers, ran traffic signals, and shoved anyone who was in the way of her getting to Zeke. Nothing else mattered. "Dear God, please let her be all right. Please, I need her."

Twenty-five minutes felt like twenty-five hours. The emergency parking lot was jammed, and she scanned every conceivable spot until a small sedan backed out and she aggressively claimed it.

Once inside, she knew the layout and skated past the desk to the nursing station. "Is Maria here?"

"Just a minute she'll be back."

Anne looked around on the off chance she could see someone.

Maria appeared and took her by the arm around the corner to her office. "Sit down, and I'll fill you in on what I know."

"Is Zeke all right?"

Maria put up her hand. "Take a breath. She's okay. She's in x-ray right now. She apparently took a bad fall, hit the wall, and hve broken her arm. Also, hit her head."

Anne gasped and covered her mouth. "Oh no, not her head."

"We're not sure of the details or if she was unconscious. The kid that came in with her was hysterical and cannot seem to give us a history."

Anne felt her throat tighten and she sucked a deep breath.

"Is Zeke talking?"

"She's been able to answer a couple of simple questions, but she lost a lot of blood, and we're rehydrating until we can get her some packed blood cells."

"Maria, radiology in the downtown location has her records, but she's had some serious head injuries in the past. The doctor may want to compare."

"That's good to know. Do you want to see the young woman who came in with her?"

"Yes, but I need to see Zeke at least for a second."

"Okay. Wait here, and I'll check what's happening over there. If the x-ray is just waiting for the radiologist, you can run over for a minute. No more. Do not get me in trouble."

Anne paced and prayed in the small office, then Maria returned.

"Okay. Down that hall, room four. Be quick."

Anne walked quickly and with authority past countless, oblivious staff. She ducked into Room 4, which was silent except for the IV monitor. Zeke lay on the gurney covered with a sheet. Her face was swollen and pale. Anne wanted to touch her to see if she was alive. An impressive compression dressing surrounded most of her head and face. Her left arm was folded across her chest, her right motionless at her side. Her chest rose and fell shallowly.

She's alive, thank God. Anne moved closer and whispered in her ear, "Honey, it's me. I'm here. You're going to be okay." She kissed her cheek lightly, and a tear fell at the same time. She carefully slipped her fingers into Zeke's right hand. She looked so weak and helpless. "Baby, we can do this. Please try, because I can't do it without you." Her throat tightened, and she fought back a sob that made her chest ache.

She heard the technician's voice.

"I'm going to get kicked out of here, but I love you, and I'll be close by."

Zeke's fingers moved around hers and squeezed. Anne kissed her again.

"Excuse me."

"I'm her partner and was sent back."

"We have to take her back to the unit."

"I understand." She gently squeezed back and left. Once she was in the hall, she hurried outside and felt her fear and grief take over for a minute. People stared, but she didn't care. Zeke was okay for now, and she would do whatever it took to bring her back. She returned inside after one circuit around the parking lot. She blew her nose and wiped her eyes, then marched back in to see Destiny.

The nurse walked her to a small exam room and explained they had to mildly sedate Destiny. "But we're glad you're here. We couldn't really keep her overnight without a diagnosis. We'd have to call Family Services." She opened the door to reveal Destiny curled up on a gurney under a blanket.

Anne just wanted to scream at her.

Instead, she walked over to the gurney. "Destiny, are you able to wake up a little?"

She mumbled something incomprehensible.

"Destiny, sit up and talk to me."

Some recognition must have filtered in because she cracked open her eyes and squinted at Anne. "Anne, you're here." She sat up. "Where's Auntie?"

"Relax. Zeke is badly hurt but will be all right. Now, I need you to tell me exactly what happened this afternoon. Start from when I left. Leave nothing out."

Destiny sat up and rubbed her face. She reached for the can of 7UP on the over-bed table. "Okay. Zeke said she'd teach me to ride. So we went out to the barn, and she showed me all about the bridle and the saddle thing and the pad. It was kind of confusing."

"That's fine, just keep going."

She yawned. "Well, she got Shadow all ready, then I had to help with Sunny."

The horses. She had to call Susan or Benjamin. "Go ahead."

"We walked them to the arena and Auntie got on and told me how to sit and what to do, then she walked Shadow around the arena and back. I don't remember exactly what…"

"Just go on."

"She was talking, and Sunny stepped on my foot, hard. And I think I screamed because Shadow took off, and so did Sunny. It was so fast, but Auntie wasn't on good and was bouncing around, and something happened and Shadow reared up, and Auntie flew into the wall." She started to cry.

"Honey, I know it's scary, but you have to keep going."

"I ran down there, but she wasn't talking, she was just bleeding so I ran in to get some towels or something. When I got back, there was blood all over her, and her eye was open. I dropped everything and went over, that's when she just whispered 'Nine-one-one' and I couldn't find my cell phone so I ran back to the house to call."

She sobbed, and Anne handed her tissues. "You're doing fine, go on." Anne felt like her head would explode.

"The nine-one-one lady said the help was coming and to go open the gate, and I did, and it was Sheriff Lafferty. He told me what I should do, and the ambulance people came. The sheriff took me in the car and I was scared he was arresting me but we all came here. But they haven't told me anything, and I'm so scared." She burst into tears.

Anne put down the side rail and sat alongside and held her. She was probably terrified. It was an accident that no one could anticipate. *What a nightmare.*

Chapter Seventeen

The sun was sliding behind the Sandia mountains as Anne pulled into the garage. She ached everywhere and was bone-tired. "Destiny, I know this has been very upsetting for you, and you must be exhausted, but I need for you to rally a little and help round up the horses and get them fed and settled."

"Anne..."

"Please help me." She opened her door and whistled for Shayla. "Let's hurry and get this done." They walked past the barn where poor Dancer was nickering. As they neared the fence, Anne spotted both horses in the paddock. "Hallelujah. At least we don't have to go find them."

She opened the gate and looked back. Destiny stood rigid and pale. *Oh, Lord. Not now.* "Honey, I know this may be really hard for you, but you will have to do it sooner or later."

"I can't." She started to cry. "I just can't."

Anne walked toward the horses, murmuring. They were probably skittish, as well. They stood watching her, and she was able to get ahold of both sets of reins.

She couldn't remember the last time she'd felt so alone without help. Susan's number went to voice mail when she called from the car, and Benjamin had requested a couple of days off weeks ago.

The horses followed her to the barn with no resistance. This was doable.

"Destiny, come in here and at least help put the tack away."

When the horses were safe in their stalls, Anne looked them over. Shadow was be first. She removed the bridle and hung it on a hook. "Destiny?" She went ahead and unbuckled the straps on the saddle and set it on top of the stall door along with the saddle pad.

"What do you need me to do?" a mousey voice asked.

"Would you flip on the overhead lights so I can check his legs? And then put his stuff in the tack room?"

The stall brightened with the light, and she ran her hands along his sides and each leg. Her voice soft and low, and Shadow relaxed under her touch. When Destiny returned, Anne came out. "He looks fine and is a little calmer. Would you give him some hay and oats along with more water?"

"Okay." She turned and immediately went for the hay.

It's probably best to keep her busy right now, and most importantly, working with the horses. She'll have a hard time with her own guilt for a while, and it will be worse when Zeke comes home.

"Sunny, are you okay, you sweet girl? You had a scare, didn't you?" Anne slipped off the bridle and then the saddle and pad. Without being asked, Destiny took the tack and disappeared.

Sunny's legs were okay as was the rest of her exam. But her eyes still had that freaky look. Anne stroked her neck and rubbed her forehead.

"Would you grab a brush when you bring the water?"

The slow, steady strokes and soft talk eventually settled her. Anne opened the stall door and slipped out. "I think she's ready to eat."

Destiny brought hay, hesitated a minute, then dropped it in her box.

"Good job." She put a hand on Destiny's shoulder. "Is Dancer okay?"

"I think so."

They walked past her stall, and the new horse hung her head out. "You poor thing, there was a whole lot of activity, and you missed it all and I, for one, am glad." She patted her neck. "Let's lock up the arena and barn, and go reheat some cold Chinese food."

When they came in the kitchen the light on the phone was flashing. "Why don't you change into your PJs and wash up? I'll fix the food."

"I'm not really hungry. Can I just go to bed?"

"Did you eat lunch?"

"No, but…"

"It's still early. Why don't you rest awhile and I'll call you when it's ready?"

"Okay. Anne…? Never mind."

The flashing light could be the hospital. Anne checked. Susan. "Just got home and saw you called. Call me back."

She went to the sink and washed her hands with hot water that felt good. What the hell was she supposed to do now?

She dried her hands and got a bottle of cold water, which she gulped down quickly. She sat at the small kitchen table, and Shayla came in and sat beside her. "You know, don't you, girl? Your mom got hurt today." She started to cry. "Oh, Zeke, please stay strong."

Her cell phone interrupted. "Hello?"

"Hi Anne, it's Maria, I wanted to update you."

"Thanks, that's sweet."

"Not sweet, I don't want you pestering my nurses all night. So, Dr. Alstadt reviewed the x-rays, the skull is okay, but there is some swelling they're going to watch. They're going to keep her sedated in the trauma unit for tonight and re-evaluate in the morning. Zeke is stable and was able to answer a few questions. Get some rest, and you can check back tomorrow."

Anne wiped her eyes. "Thanks, g'night." Maybe a little food would help, as she hadn't eaten, either. She'd be so excited to tell Zeke about her own improved labs.

The aluminum containers fit in the oven on low. On impulse, she returned Susan's call.

"Hello."

"Hi, Susan. I just got home a while ago and wondered if you'd eaten?"

"Matter of fact, no. I was just staring in the refrigerator. Jim took the boys to the Pit for a special basketball game."

"Why don't you come over and join us. I brought home a ton of takeout."

"Sounds great, give me a few minutes. Do you need anything?"

"No, just bring yourself."

She wasn't sure she'd get any cooperation from Destiny, but she went upstairs to try. "Destiny, can I come in?"

"Sure."

Anne found her in the same clothes curled up on her bed. "I'm heating up the food, and I think you might feel better if you tried to eat something."

"I just don't feel good."

Anne placed the back of her fingers against

Destiny's neck and forehead. "No fever." She sat on the foot of the bed. "I feel kind of sick, too. I'm worried about Zeke and you, but also how we'll be able to handle all this." She put her hand on Destiny's ankle. "I know you're scared and worried, too. From what you explained, it was a horrible freak accident. Horses are very skittish, and it doesn't take much to spook them. If Zeke hadn't been expecting it and had her feet out of the stirrups, she'd have had no way to stay on."

"Is she going to be all right?"

"I'm very hopeful. The doctor is going to keep her for observation because she's had head injuries before. We'll know better tomorrow, but she was able to answer some questions from the doctor."

"I didn't mean to do anything bad, it just hurt."

"Did anyone look at your foot?"

"No, I forgot about it."

"Which foot was it?"

She pointed to the right foot and sat up.

"Can you pull the boot off?"

She tried but couldn't. "It's stuck."

Or it's too swollen. "Can I try?"

Destiny nodded, and Anne carefully angled the boot and pulled slowly. Destiny grimaced. "Should I stop?"

"No, get it off. It's too tight."

"Put your other foot against my hip." As she did, Anne pulled harder until the boot was past her heel and slid off. She carefully unrolled her sock, and no surprise, her mid-foot was swollen and had a large purple bruise.

Destiny grimaced. "It hurts even more now."

Anne grabbed two extra pillows and got it as high up as possible. "I'm going to get an elastic wrap and some ice. Don't move."

She hurried downstairs and filled a plastic zip bag with ice, and went back upstairs where she dug out a new elastic bandage from her bathroom. She hoped it wasn't broken. Too bad she had to get the boot off because it had been keeping it compressed.

"This will help, and I'll get you something for pain. We won't know if it's sprained or broken without an x-ray, but let's hope the boot protected it." She taped the ice bag in place. "Do you want me to bring in the portable TV?"

Destiny still looked a little pale. "Yeah."

Anne got her set up. "Can I bring you a plate?"

She shook her head.

"Okay, text me if you need something. I'll be downstairs with Susan." She moved the phone from the desk to the nightstand. "I'll bring you something to drink in a bit, okay?"

Destiny nodded and flipped through the channels with the remote.

Anne closed the door and leaned back on it. What more? She heard the faint knock on the back door. "Susan." She hurried down and opened the door.

"Sorry, I was upstairs. Come in." Susan brought in a bag, set it on the counter, and pulled out a baggie of chocolate chip cookies and a bottle of white wine.

For the first time in her seven years of sobriety, she wanted a drink. "Do you want to eat first or sit?"

"Let's relax a bit. You sound a bit stressed." Susan helped herself to a glass and found the opener. "Want to sit outside?"

Anne smiled and nodded. She grabbed some iced tea and walked out on the deck with Susan. For the next forty minutes, Anne detailed the previous twelve hours.

Susan, although usually pretty vocal, didn't say a word until Anne finished.

"I'll be damned. You must be beside yourself. What can I do? No, scratch that. Let me stay tonight so you can get some sleep. Jim will be fine. You can't be up and down with Destiny and still rest. And I know you'll want to go back to the hospital first thing."

"Well, you're right about that. I need to talk to Zeke and see how bad she's hurt. But, unless something miraculous occurs overnight, I'll need to get Destiny's foot x-rayed. Shit. I don't have her medical power of attorney, Zeke does."

In the end, Anne could have wept with relief to have another adult in the house. Happily, the guest room was ready. Susan went home to tell Jim and came back with some things for overnight.

Anne took a small plate of food and some cookies up to Destiny. She was barely watching some scary movie and agreed to eat a little of the food while Anne checked her foot. The color was still multi-hued, but the pulses in her ankle and foot were good, and even though the swelling had spread out a but, it was no more swollen than before. Anne went for more ice while Destiny changed into a T-shirt and shorts. Then, she helped her to the bathroom.

A little more ibuprofen and Anne was convinced Destiny would sleep, but promised to leave both doors open so she'd hear if Destiny called her.

Even though Anne felt dead on her feet, she and Susan ate a little and put everything away. Anne got ready for bed in record time, because the only thing she wanted was to fall asleep sleep quickly so she could go see Zeke as soon as possible.

Anne quietly crept downstairs, hoping to get the horses and dog fed before she had to decide about Destiny's foot. She smelled the coffee before she entered the kitchen. Susan had laid out several slices of bread and was dishing scoops of egg salad on them. She looked up and said, "Good morning. There's coffee over there."

Anne could only stare.

Susan laughed. "Get your coffee, and I'll give you a report."

Anne obeyed and sat on a stool at the counter. "This is good. What all are you doing?"

"Destiny woke up a couple of times during the night—once to go to the bathroom, and the other because her foot hurt. Poor thing, that foot looks awful. Anyway, I refilled the ice bag, and she went back to sleep." She flipped another piece of bread on each sandwich and slipped them into a baggies. "Since I woke up early, I called the troops." She giggled. "The boys will feed the horses and let them out to clean the stalls. Jim will come over when you're ready and carry Destiny downstairs. She can't walk on that foot, and I figure they have wheelchairs and aides at the hospital." She stuck the sandwiches in a bag and poured coffee into a large to-go cup, then pulled a cold Coke out of the refrigerator and put in the bag.

"You are a force of nature, dear Susan. How will I ever repay you?"

Susan wiped her hands on a towel and came around the counter. "Honey, we have been neighbors for a very long time, and good friends." She wrapped

Anne in a big, warm hug.

Anne held on tight. A hug was really what she needed.

"I better go check on Destiny. Thank you for taking the helm of the storm-tossed vessel."

"Just give me a holler when I should call Jim. It might be easier to carry her out the front door."

Anne tapped on Destiny's door.

"Come in." She was dressed and watching TV with her foot elevated. Anne carefully unwrapped it. The swelling had spread up her ankle and down to her toes, along with the purple, blue, and red highlights. Pulses were still good. "How's the pain on a scale of 'fine' to 'it's killing me'?"

Destiny actually smiled. "It still hurts a lot, but it's better, and it isn't throbbing. Mrs. Godfrey came to help me. She said you were unwillingly unresponsive. Whatever that means. She said we have to get my foot x-rayed."

"I'm afraid so. We can't take a chance of walking on it if it's broken. And we may need to call your parents if Zeke isn't awake. Which I should check." She carefully re-wrapped the foot and ankle. "I'll be right back."

If she knew Zeke, that power of attorney would be filed in her file cabinet. Fortunately, it was unlocked, so she flipped through the folders. Destiny Cabot? Reggie Cabot? Powers of attorney—bingo! She had several for her family, including one for Destiny. She folded it up and slipped it in her back pocket.

She went back to Destiny. "Good news, she had the POA, no need to call your folks—yet. Are you ready?" Destiny nodded. "Okay, I'll go get the car."

"Susan, we're good to go. I'll bring the car

around."

Susan picked up her cell phone and dialed. "We're all set. Could you come and take Destiny to the car? Great. He's on the way, Anne. Do you need anything else?"

"No, I'm good. Benjamin should be here soon, maybe you could fill him in. I'll call you as soon as I know anything." She hugged her again.

Chapter Eighteen

Anne pulled up to the emergency entrance and stopped. "I'm going to run in and find a wheelchair and be right back. Are you okay?"

Susan and Jim had packed her gently in the back seat with her leg on pillows with ice. Jim even put the passenger seat belt on to keep her leg steady. They had chatted on the way into Albuquerque while eating their egg salad sandwiches. Susan had, in her own way, lifted the specter of doom hanging over the whole family. Both she and Destiny felt more rested and relaxed in spite of the circumstances.

Anne returned with a friendly, young, muscular orderly who managed to secure Destiny in the wheelchair with a little blushing on her part. Finally, some color in her cheeks. "Jeff will take good care of you while I go park. Okay? Take your Coke with you." She passed the can over.

After one futile pass around the parking lot, Anne gave up and drove up to the valet stand in front of the professional building. Ticket in hand, she jogged back to the ER. What she wanted to do was find Zeke, but first she needed to get Destiny checked out and treated. *Zeke, please be okay.*

The waiting room seemed empty, but still the staff was busy. Anne completed the necessary forms and was able to sign the release as a power of attorney since Reggie had added her name. The receptionist had her sign several other medical releases and explained the HIPPA form. Anne smiled. For so many years she was the one handing folks the forms.

As soon as they were ready for an exam room, Anne asked them what room Zeke Cabot was assigned. The receptionist scrolled through her computer. "This computer is so slow. Oh, look here, Trauma unit, bed two."

"Thanks." She rolled Destiny back away from the desk.

"Is Auntie near here?"

"Yes, the Trauma beds are behind that door." *So near.*

"Can we go in there?"

"No, we need to get you examined." She paced until a young woman came out with a clipboard. "Cabot?"

It took twenty-five minutes to have the initial evaluation. The doctor ordered the x-rays and Anne wheeled Destiny down the hall to radiology. "I'll be here when you get back. I'm just going to check if I can see Zeke."

Anne almost ran to the trauma unit. She knew visits were limited, but she had to see her. The giant door hissed with the airflow-controlled environment. The only sounds were electronic: monitors, IV pumps, pressure mattresses, and warning bells. The desk was empty. She looked into Room 2, behind the partially open curtain. She slipped in, and when her eyes adjusted to the dim light, she could see Zeke was sleeping. The head of the bed was elevated, and a faint over-bed light cast an eerie glow in the room.

There were two monitors hooked up to her and another for an automatic BP cuff. Anne came close and looked carefully. Zeke's color had improved, her hand was warm, and the monitor showed everything within reasonable limits. *Thank you, God.* She leaned down and whispered her name. "Zeke. Zeke, honey, can you open your eyes?" She watched and waited.

Very slowly the corners of Zeke's mouth moved up, and she whispered, "Of course, I can, baby." She cracked open her eyes and smiled. "I'm so glad to see you." Her hand opened, and Anne took it.

"I was so scared for you. What does your doctor say?"

Zeke swallowed and pointed to a water carafe. "He said, all things considered, I'm in reasonably good condition."

Anne handed her the cup and held her hand while she sipped.

"Thanks. I have a concussion, but the swelling is less today. I have a non-displaced fracture in my right arm right below the shoulder. And a few icky looking bruises. I'll be fine. They're trying to decide whether to stabilize the fracture or keep it in an immobilizer."

Anne stroked her face. "I was so worried. No one could tell me anything." She kissed her. It seemed Zeke's speech was slower than usual, but it could be residual swelling. She doubted they'd given her anything for pain.

Zeke's eyes fluttered open again. "How's Destiny?"

"She was pretty hysterical when I got here yesterday. I guess your friend the sheriff brought her along since no one was home." Anne sighed with relief to be talking to Zeke. "She tried to help me get the horses settled, but when we got to the house she just wanted to go to bed. When she complained that her foot hurt, I finally checked it. The boot kept the swelling down, but it certainly was bruised." Anne noticed Zeke fading a little. "She's down in x-ray, and I should get back there."

"Umm, okay…"

Anne kissed her again and whispered, "Get well. I miss you." She slipped out and hurried back to the ER and found Destiny back in the room with the doctor looking at the x-rays on the view box.

"What's it look like?" Anne stepped closer.

"Not sure. See this shadowy area here? There could be a crack in the second, third, and maybe the fourth metatarsals. It's hard to tell because of the soft tissue swelling."

He perched on the desk and tapped one of the films on his knee. "Tell you what I think we should do. Let's put you in a walking boot for a couple of weeks. Non-weight-bearing. We'll get you set up with some cool crutches and something for pain."

He walked to the door. "Keep it elevated and iced for another twenty-four hours. Judy will get you set up with PT to fit the boot and crutches. If you have any problems, Ms. Reynolds, please call." He handed her his card. "Destiny, it is important to follow the instructions carefully, or you'll end up back here. We'll re-x-ray in two weeks."

Anne felt the relief all the way to her toes. One patient evaluated and discharged.

The valet brought her car and the cute young orderly wheeled Destiny out front. Anne understood the kid was only thirteen, but she sure was flirting with this guy. She giggled. Good thing they didn't have kids.

With his help, they got Destiny into the back seat with her new walking boot. Anne rolled down the windows. She felt better knowing Zeke would soon be in a regular room where she could call. Her world was rotating back to center. Tonight, she would sleep.

❧ ❧ ❧ ❧

And sleep she did. Glorious. With a minimal argument, Susan insisted on helping out and staying overnight again. Anne made a mental note to repay the Godfreys.

She stretched her arms and yawned. Then, her arm hit the empty pillow. There was a brief phone call the night before just after Zeke transferred to the floor. Her doctor had decided on a shoulder immobilizer and would reevaluate in a month. Still, she would need to stay at least another day because of the brain swelling.

After she showered and dressed, Anne came downstairs to find Destiny helping Susan with breakfast. It was nice to see Destiny laughing again. "Looks like I'm missing all the fun."

"Oh, we are just making funny pancake faces. Come and sit down, Here's some coffee."

"You know, Susan, I could get used to this." Anne sipped her coffee. "Destiny, how are you feeling this morning?"

"I feel better. This boot is kind of weird and clunky, but the pain medicine helped a lot."

Susan set down a platter filled with very odd-looking pancakes. "I was all set to have Jim help Destiny get down the steps, but you should see this kid on crutches. She's amazing."

Destiny stuck a fork in two or three pancakes and put them on her plate. Then she giggled. "I like this one, it kind of looks like Sunny. Judy, the physical therapist showed me how to use the crutches on the stairs, and she made me practice. That was before the pain medicine, too."

Anne helped herself to a couple of pancakes. She couldn't remember the last time they made them. "These smell wonderful. I need to remember to make them more often." She took a couple of bites.

"Do you have any more information on Zeke's condition?" Susan pulled out a stool and joined them at the counter.

"Oh, yes. She called last night when she got settled in her new room. The doctor is going to treat her shoulder with an immobilizer and not surgery. She still has another night in the hospital because they're worried about the concussion swelling. But, she does sound better."

Destiny stopped eating and pushed her food around the plate.

Anne noticed and suspected the cause. "The first thing she asked me was if you were okay, Destiny. She asked me to tell you that it's not your fault and she's not mad."

"Right. Can I be excused? I want to go lay on the couch."

"Okay. I'll ask Susan if we could borrow her ATV and go for a little ride." She looked over at Susan, who nodded.

Susan and Anne cleaned up the kitchen while Destiny dozed in the family room.

"I think the old 'get back on the horse' saying is a good idea. The kid sure acts spooked about the whole accident, and she's convinced that Zeke is mad at her and going to send her home," Susan said.

"You're right. I'm going have to treat Destiny like a client. We had to work to get her used to the horses to begin with, and now she feels like she's responsible for this whole accident. We only have a couple of weeks left and I don't want her to go home feeling traumatized. The best outcome would be for her to get on a horse and ride. That'll be tricky, but not impossible." She put the dishes away and wiped the counter. "All right, we're off to the barn. Thank you again for your wonderful care, but I think your family might be missing you."

Susan laughed. "I'm almost afraid to see what they've done to my kitchen, but I'll stop by later to see how you're doing. And call if you need me. Promise?"

❧ ❧ ❧ ❧

"Good morning, Zeke," Robin Taylor said. She came around the bed in the sunny private hospital room and took Zeke's hand.

"Hi. When did you arrive? I hope it's not a referral."

"Not exactly. I had a message this morning on my voice mail from Anne. She must've left it last night. She just said that you had an accident with a head injury and thought I would want to know." She sat down in the chair next to bed.

"That probably wasn't necessary, but she was anxious. So was I, but I think it's going to be okay. The swelling has gone down, and there are no neurological deficits. The doctor thinks the shoulder injury will heal well with time and some rehab."

"She also mentioned that your niece was involved and that might be of concern. Why don't you tell me what happened?"

Zeke gave her the short version of the action. "It

was freaky and unavoidable. It turns out her foot was hurt badly, too."

"Have you been able to talk to her? I'm guessing a thirteen-year-old might be freaked out with two large horses racing around with her aunt lying unconscious. With her record, I'm amazed she didn't just take off. That might indicate some positive changes."

Zeke hadn't considered that, but the fact she stayed and got help was critical. Zeke could have been lying there for a long time until Anne came home if Destiny hadn't acted.

❧❧❧❧

Anne decided a scenic ride on the ATV—under the guise of inspecting—might give her time to talk about going back to the arena for some work. Susan brought the ATV over and parked it by the front door.

Destiny hobbled out the front door, taking long strides with her crutches. Anne shivered. "Slow down, missy. We're in no hurry."

"Well, can I drive?" She hopped in and put her crutches behind her.

"Well, no." Anne steered the ATV around the garage and down the slope. Benjamin had methodically begun thinning the trees and ground cover for fire prevention and to augment the ability of the surveillance cameras. "He's done a good job, don't you think?"

"Yeah, it looks nicer. Not so creepy."

Interesting observation. "When we finish up here, I want to go work with the horses a bit, and I'd like you to help."

Destiny started to fidget. "I don't know...I'm

pretty tired.”

"I don't want you to muck stalls, just sit and be still. I think you can do that."

"But why? That seems kind of dumb."

Anne steered close to a couple of the trees holding cameras and checked them. "Destiny, remember that I'm a registered nurse, and just because I don't work in a hospital doesn't mean I've forgotten everything."

"Yeah, I know."

"Trust me. I want you to have the best chance of returning home and having a stellar report for the judge, but we don't have much time."

She stopped by the gate next to the barn, got out, and opened it. She drove into the arena near the spot Zeke was hurt. Benjamin had cleaned up the area. "Okay, wait here, and I'll get you a soda and bring the horses in."

Destiny was sitting with her leg elevated when Anne returned with two cans and three horses clopping behind her. When the horses entered the arena, they paused, sniffed, and flicked their ears around.

Anne handed Destiny one can and sat on a nearby railing. "Let's watch them. Try not to be nervous or scared. They won't hurt you, and I'm right here." She could almost feel the energy rolling off of Destiny; she had to be nervous.

The horses walked down the far side, except for Dancer, who came directly toward Destiny. Anne smiled. That was an excellent sign for both. "Dancer doesn't know what happened, and she's aware the other two are wary, but she trusts you and senses something is wrong. Try closing your eyes and thinking about what you might say to her in secret or what you might ask her."

Destiny hesitated. Anne walked behind her. "I'm right here. Close your eyes." Anne didn't need to watch Destiny, because Dancer telegraphed a connection.

Shadow and Sunny stood on the other side watching. Dancer walked closer, paused for a minute, and then moved very near. She lowered her head briefly and stayed very still—exactly what Anne hoped would happen. Destiny was somehow sharing with Dancer, and the horse was fully engaged.

After a few minutes, Dancer huffed and shook her head. Destiny opened her eyes and smiled. Dancer took one step so Destiny could reach her. "Hi, Dancer. You came to see how I was." She rubbed her forehead and moved her face close enough to touch.

Anne's eyes teared up as she recognized the connection. Two frightened, distrusting souls had bonded. This experience would be a lifelong lesson for both. Anne didn't move and hoped the moment would last, but Dancer shook her head and took off around the arena.

Destiny sat still, smiling, as the other two horses watched intently. "That was so cool. It was like she heard what was in my head, and I could like, kind of hear her, but not words."

"That is what happened. Dancer felt your call and wanted to help you."

"Really?"

"Yup. Remember when I told you that horses were empathetic? Here's my favorite quote: 'Horses are powerful and still gentle, very perceptive but not judgmental. And horses cannot lie, cheat, or manipulate.'"

Destiny laughed. "Well, duh. They can't talk, either."

"But you said Dancer was communicating with you…"

Anne walked out through the doors to the paddock, calling the horses. When they realized where they were going, they followed her. She felt victorious. She still wanted Shadow and Sunny to forgive Destiny—for all their sakes. In spite of all the stubborn, insolent behavior, Anne had to acknowledge that deep inside Destiny held many of the beautiful qualities that Anne loved in Destiny's aunt.

On the other side of the paddock, she opened the gate to the pasture and watched them run. They enjoyed their freedom and the ability to move unencumbered. Too bad Zeke would not have that freedom for some time. That little spark of anger at Destiny's thoughtless behavior bubbled up again. Having to cancel clients to babysit when Zeke was in the hospital irritated her further.

She slammed the gate.

Chapter Nineteen

Hello."

"Hi, Annie. Is this a good time?"

"Definitely. You sound great, are you feeling better?" Anne took her phone out to the deck since Destiny was napping on the couch. When they got back to the house, Destiny could barely walk in on her crutches. Energy work could be stimulating or draining. The kid was definitely tapped out.

"We just got back from some time with the horses. Both Destiny and Dancer had a real moment of connectedness. It was amazing, and Destiny understood—finally—what I was trying to teach her."

"That's terrific. I really wanted her to understand why the equine work was so liberating."

"Hold on, buckaroo. I'm not sure we're there yet. I'll take her out there again tomorrow. I need for her to reconnect with Sunny and Shadow. They are still wary of she-who-screams."

Zeke laughed. "I wanna come home. I miss you."

"Any word on your release? I can leave to get you immediately."

"The doctor hasn't made rounds, but the physical therapist came up to show me some exercises so my arm doesn't shrivel up."

"That's a nice image."

"Well, compared to what I must have looked like when I came in…"

Anne covered her mouth. She knew very well what those kinds of head wounds looked like. And she'd seen the bloody towels strewn around. "I'm so glad you're better. It could have…never mind."

"Also, Robin Taylor stopped by to see me. She said you'd left an FYI message. I think she was delighted that I could smile and speak in complete sentences."

"And had a sense of humor. What's come over you?" Anne grinned at Zeke's silliness.

"I'm glad to be alive."

⁂

The breeze felt good on the deck. June could be iffy, but overall warmer than May had been. She closed her eyes.

"Yoo-hoo. Are you up for some company?" Susan stood at the end of the deck.

Without opening her eyes, Anne said, "No, but you are a delightful exception."

Susan sat in the chair beside her. "I just grilled a ton of chicken and burgers. I hope they'll last a little while. I put a couple in a baggy for you and Destiny."

"That sounds great. When did I stop grilling? It always tastes good."

"You grilled last year. Don't you remember the pork tenderloin? I sure do."

"You're right. This spring seems to be exceptionally long."

"How's the kid doing?"

"Actually, she had a good experience with one of the horses. I'm going to try again tomorrow because I think it's important for Shadow and Sunny to trust her again."

"Where is she now?" Susan peeked into the family room.

"She wanted to go up to her room. I managed to get some soup and a sandwich in her, but she's tired. And looks it. But so is Zeke."

"So am I," Susan agreed. "I better get back before there's a mess somewhere. Call if you need anything."

Anne waved. "Will do. Hi to the boys."

In front, she heard the sound of the lawnmower. Benjamin preferred cutting the grass later in the day so it didn't lose as much moisture. The rugged engine noise and the smell of cut grass took her back to her childhood in the Midwest. She smiled at the Norman Rockwell-esque mental picture of a suburban Saturday. Dads home for the weekend doing yard work, moms doing spring cleaning or the wash, and kids riding bikes around the block.

Sometimes, one of the neighbors would host a get-together, like a potluck or barbeque. Everyone was invited. Some of the ladies sipped gin and tonics, the men drank beer, and everybody smoked cigarettes.

She awoke to someone poking her arm. "Sorry. Do we have any ice cream?" Anne sat up and blinked. It was nearly dark. Shayla was curled up next to her and Destiny stood balanced on her crutches. "Did you look in the freezer?"

"Yeah." But it sounded like a sarcastic "whatever."

"Let me go check in the garage." She got up and looked at Destiny. "This must be really important."

Destiny clopped after her into the kitchen.

The garage freezer was on the other side of her car and locked. The meat was packed in one section, and bags of frozen vegetables on top, but underneath the were two pints of Ben & Jerry's and a quart of generic chocolate. The pints were Zeke's. She locked the freezer and brought the chocolate ice cream in for Destiny.

"Perfect. Chocolate, my fave."

Anne set it down and got two ceramic bowls and spoons. Destiny dug in with gusto. "This is pretty tasty."

"Have you called your folks?"

"Not really."

"What does that mean?"

"I sent a few text messages."

"You could try again, maybe add a picture of the ice cream so they'll know how well you're being fed." They both laughed.

Without warning, Shayla began barking loudly and fiercely. Anne had never heard her do that. "Stay here."

Anne went to the deck and turned on the floodlights. "Shayla, come!" She scanned the wooded hillside and spotted Shayla chasing a dark-clad figure running down the hill away from the house.

"Destiny, call nine-one-one." Anne ran to the hall closet for the shotgun Zeke kept there. On the way back she heard a shot and a yelp. *Shayla!* She ran out and down the steps. She followed the sound of whimpering. As she got near, she ducked behind a tree and watched for the assailant. Then she slowly crept close to their beloved pet. In the faint light, she could see blood on her right shoulder.

Anne whispered, "It's okay, baby. You'll be fine. Ssh" She stayed low and listened. I hope help is on the way. Then she heard it—noise behind her. She racked a shell and knelt behind a stump.

"Anne, it's Jim. Where are you?" The loud

whisper was indeed Jim's.

"I'm here," she said quietly.

His flashlight lit up the area, and she could see the wound to Shayla's shoulder. It wasn't too bad, but she needed to get her out of there.

"Let me look around a minute." Jim made a slow curve around her and returned. "I don't see anyone. But whoever could have made it down to the highway pretty easy."

Anne collapsed back against the stump. Her heart pounded painfully as the adrenaline drained. Through the trees at the base of the hill, she could see flashing red-and-blue lights.

"Do you think the police caught someone?"

"No way to tell. Here, let me carry Shayla up, and we'll get her to the vet." He gently picked her up. Fortunately, she wasn't large, probably only twenty pounds.

Anne led the way to the house holding Jim's flashlight. His rifle was slung across his back. As they got to the deck, Sheriff Lafferty was talking to Susan and Destiny.

Susan ran over and said, "I have some dressings. Just set her right there." She got busy checking Shayla and sweet-talking her. Shayla was a special guest at Susan's doggie bakery and well loved.

"Thank you for coming, Sheriff. Did you find someone?"

"My deputy was coming southbound and saw somebody dart out in the road wearing a black hoodie. He pulled over and apprehended him. We'll see what he has to say. Could you identify him?"

"No. Whoever it was got too far down the hill by the time I got there, and it was dark. But he had a gun and shot my dog." She began to cry.

The sheriff clenched his fists. "We'll handle it if his gun did this." He looked over at Susan bandaging Shayla. "Emergency vet in Tijeras is open late, I can call 'em for you."

Jim said, "We can take her down there. No need for you to go."

Anne wiped her eyes. "Thank you, all of you. I'd better stay here and make sure everything is all right."

The sheriff said, "Why don't I take a look around for you? Make sure everything's locked up." He stuck his notebook in his back pocket. "You two stay inside until I come back. If you could turn on some lights out there." He pointed toward the office and barn.

Anne moved Destiny back inside, as she was visibly shaking. Anne almost laughed at the absurdity of it all. This thirteen-year-old child was staying with them to teach her to make safe decisions and avoid juvie. And the person she knew best was the county sheriff. She gave her a hug. "Nice to see Sheriff Lafferty again." They both laughed. "Come on, I really need more ice cream."

"Will Shayla be okay?" Destiny finally asked.

"I'm pretty sure she will. I'll call later and see." Anne tried valiantly to keep up a brave front for Destiny, but what she really wanted was the strong support of her partner. She wanted so badly to call but didn't dare because Zeke was powerless and it would drive her crazy to not be there.

"I'm a little scared, Anne." Destiny's lip quivered. "I wish Auntie was here."

"I do, too. But I don't think I should call until tomorrow when we know for sure how Shayla is doing."

"Yeah, she would be too worried tonight."

Exactly right. "Tell you what, rather than going up and down stairs, let's have a slumber party down here. I'll get your PJs along with your pillow and blanket. And I'll get my stuff."

"Where will we sleep?"

"You take the couch, and I'll take the recliner."

From the window beside Zeke's desk, she could see all of the front of the property. The lights were still on, and the sheriff and his deputy were standing in front of her office chatting. Should be safe for a while. She gathered all the bedding and night clothes, then grabbed their toothbrushes and toothpaste.

By the time they were settled with an old movie on the television, Destiny had already nodded off. Anne went out to talk to the sheriff.

"Ms. Reynolds, everything looks pretty secure and we double checked. By the way, you got some real nice horses in there. I didn't see them last time I was here. Probably spooked by the whole ordeal."

"Thanks, Sheriff. They're much better now."

"How's Agent Cabot doing?"

"Much better as well. She will need observation for awhile, as a precaution, which is certainly warranted. If there are any other emergencies, she wouldn't be able to help. Better for her to rest up and not worry."

"Too bad she was laid up. Bet she'd had something to say to your intruder." He smiled.

"Oh, she would, indeed. I decided not to mention it until she gets home," Anne said.

He nodded. "I see your point." He pointed to the deputy. "I'm going to have John make a few passes through here tonight, so don't be alarmed."

"I appreciate it. I think Jim and Susan will be back soon, and their boys are home."

He tipped his hat. "You try to get some rest now, hear?"

She waved as they both drove out through the gate. It felt eerily quiet now, except for the calls of distant coyotes and one great horned owl high up on the mountain. The lights would stay on.

Chapter Twenty

Anne gazed out at the velvet gray dawn from her kitchen window. Even the sun seemed too tired to show up, but the coffee tasted good. Where had the past few days gone? She couldn't remember being so overwhelmed.

Her phone buzzed with a text message.

Susan said Shayla had slept well, had no new bleeding. The bullet had gone through the muscle, and they gave it to the sheriff. Susan volunteered to pick her up as soon as they released her.

She'd always enjoyed Susan's company as a friend, but when things went south, Susan stepped up every time in extraordinary fashion like they were family. One day she hoped to return the favor.

The sound of banging crutches and grumbling meant Destiny was up. At least she'd been sleeping well. Anne rubbed her face, hoping to increase the blood flow. She smiled. "Good morning."

"Morning." Destiny hopped quickly to the powder room. When she reappeared, she looked infinitely more relaxed. "I'm starving."

"Okay. French toast?"

"Yes. Any sausage?"

Anne opened the fridge and looked. "Turkey sausage?"

Destiny wrinkled her nose.

"Ham?"

"Oh yeah, much better."

Anne started cooking. "Susan said Shayla is recovering and she'll pick her up when the vet releases her."

"Yay. I even said a prayer for her. I said one for Auntie, too. But not for the creepy guy who hurt Shayla."

Anne turned to face her. "If I get a call and have to go in to pick up Zeke, I'll need you to watch Shayla. Can you do that?"

"Sure. I'll stay right with Shayla. I'll make sure she has water and cookies."

"Excellent. Susan will be next door, and Benjamin will be here, too." Anne smiled as she dipped the bread in the egg mixture. She turned the French toast mindlessly. They sat down together and tried to make small talk as they ate. The air crackled with conflicting emotions and unspoken fear.

Her phone rang. "Would you answer that?" Anne said.

"Hello? Yes, she's here, one moment."

"Who is it?"

"It's a lady at the hospital." Destiny held out the phone.

Anne rinsed her hands, dried them, and grabbed the phone. "Hello, this is Anne Reynolds. Yes, absolutely. I can be there in…an hour." She hit off and grinned. "Zeke is ready to be discharged."

Destiny started to help clean up.

"You need to get dressed for when Susan comes, and I need to jump in the shower. Do you need help getting upstairs?"

"No, I'm good. You go get ready."

❧ ❧ ❧ ❧

Anne completed the discharge rigmarole, pulled the car up, and loaded her patient. At the exit of the parking lot she stopped abruptly and pulled Zeke into a deep, passionate kiss.

"Wow. I missed you, too..."

"Listen to me. We have had to overcome some unimaginable hurdles in our relationship, no doubt about it, but times are uncertain, even for us. The past few days have pushed me out of my comfort zone, and we can talk about the details when we get home, but I can't do this alone, Zeke Cabot. And I've been scared witless. You need to marry me. The sooner, the better, and I don't need a fancy wedding. I want you to be legally bound to me for the rest of our lives because you're the most important thing in my life."

Zeke sat slack-jawed and dazed. Still coming down from her medicated state, she focused hard on Anne's beautiful eyes and tried to put all those words in context. "You want me to marry you? Is that what I heard? "

She nodded. "Was I unclear?"

"No, no, honey. You just said it all so fast."

Anne put the car in gear and turned toward the interstate. "Zeke, I'm scared. We can sort it all out when we get home, but promise me you'll think about it."

"Of course." Zeke adjusted her seat belt and opened her window. She reached over and put her hand on the back of Anne's neck and stroked her skin. "I love you, baby."

Anne took a deep breath and smiled. "I love you, too. The good news is that Destiny seems to have really stepped up. The accident woke her up and she's been helpful and cooperative. She's worried that you are angry with her. I tried to tell her, but I think you'll need to reassure her that you're not angry."

"That's great. I'm really pleased the session with Dancer worked for her. It may be the only thing that can break through."

They rode in silence for a while, and Zeke got more and more uncomfortable. Anne had something gnawing at her. "Honey, are you okay?"

Anne smiled. "Sure, I'm just…well, I have a lot on my mind. Having you home safe makes everything better."

As they rounded the curve on their road, Zeke again noticed the fence. "I'm glad we did that. It makes me feel a little safer. Oh, that reminds me, did you hear from Davis? He was supposed to call me back about the surveillance tapes."

"Nope, not a word, but Benjamin thinning the woods made a big difference."

They turned into the garage, and Zeke smiled. "I can't tell you how good this looks to me. If I never mentioned it before, I hate hospitals."

Anne leaned over and kissed her again. "Welcome home. Let's get you inside and settled."

Zeke moved slowly because of the hundred and one bruises she'd sustained being flipped off of Shadow. She chuckled. "I guess I'm going to have to get back on the horse at some point."

"Yes, you are."

The house was quiet. Zeke put down her red plastic belongings bag. "Where's Destiny?"

"I'll check, she might be napping." Anne took it and stared into another bag of bloody clothing. Zeke's previous hospital stays were a result of an attack and a shooting, and Zeke cringed at Anne's painful facial expression at being in this familiar situation yet again. Anne shuddered. "Go sit down and I'll be right back."

Zeke went into the family room and headed for the couch, surprised to see pillows and blankets folded up neatly. *Must've had a slumber party.* She sat in the recliner and tried to raise the leg portion with her left hand.

Destiny limped through the patio door and stopped. "Auntie! You're home."

"Hi. I missed you, too." Zeke grinned.

"I have to go to the bathroom." Destiny scurried through the kitchen to the powder room.

The warning lights were flashing, and Zeke felt unsettled. Something was very wrong with this picture. She looked around and didn't see anything out of the ordinary.

Anne came down, smiling. "Are you hungry? I can fix—"

"Would you sit down a minute?"

Destiny returned and Zeke pointed. "Destiny, would you sit over there with Anne and one of you tell me what I'm missing? Something is way off."

Destiny looked at Anne, distinctly uncomfortable.

Anne said, "We didn't want you to worry while you were in the hospital, but we had a little, um, incident several days ago."

Destiny covered her mouth. Then, "Little?"

Anne glared at her.

Zeke gripped the arms of the chair. "What in the hell is going on here?"

Anne sighed. "We were having some ice cream when Shayla just went crazy barking. I've never heard her like that. I turned on the deck lights and caught a glimpse of her running after someone."

"What?" Zeke spat involuntarily.

Destiny piped up. "I called nine-one-one, and Anne got a gun."

Anne put her hand up. "Okay, hear me out."

"Okay." Zeke started to shake and put both hands up.

"I ran out and heard a shot, and Shayla yelped. I ran to her and whoever was gone. Jim came over and carried Shayla up the hill. He and Susan took her to the vet, and she's okay. Sheriff Lafferty came and searched everywhere and then left a deputy to keep an eye out. They found someone on the highway, and I haven't heard if he's the one."

Zeke covered her face and put one hand up. "Stop."

Destiny offered, "Shayla will be okay."

Anne patted her knee. "Why don't you go upstairs and get your foot up for a while and let us talk?"

"I…yeah, okay." She hurried over and up the stairs.

Anne went to Zeke and knelt in front of her. "Honey, this is not the way I wanted to tell you. I know it's upsetting on so many levels." She took Zeke's hand and kissed it. "Let's take a walk out to the barn where we can have some privacy."

Zeke felt the ominous trembling inside but knew Anne was right. "Okay. Help me get out of this damn chair."

Anne held Zeke's arm, and they ambled to the barn. "I have a couple of reasons for coming out here. First, I'd like to talk privately and I want some alone time. I also thought it might be helpful to see the horses."

"I'm not so sure about the horses, but you're probably right."

"You know, Destiny is at a critical point and needs support for the short time we have left. Until we hear from the sheriff, we both need to be alert and vigilant. And I need your strength and support.

The barn felt warm and smelled of fresh hay. Zeke put her left arm around Anne's shoulder. "You are a pretty cagey woman, but I'm on to your devious means, and I love you for caring."

They embraced and kissed. Anne relaxed into her. "I missed you so much. I was scared, Zeke. Thank God for Jim and Susan."

Zeke kissed her forehead. "I'm so sorry, baby. Let's think of some nice way to thank them. You know, dinner or maybe a weekend getaway."

Anne pulled her head back. "That's a great idea." She pulled Zeke close and kissed her again. "You know, even after ten roller-coaster years together, Zeke Cabot, you still ignite a fire in my belly. I want you so badly and really wish we didn't have a house guest, worried neighbors, an injured dog, and the local sheriff poised to pounce."

Zeke laughed. "And a wedding to plan."

Anne gasped. "You mean it?"

"Absolutely. Give me some time to get more mobile, and I'm going to find the best engagement ring ever."

Anne hugged her. "Do you remember the rings we bought in Chicago that first Christmas?"

"Wow. Yes, at the small shop in Water Tower Place. Where are they?"

Anne smiled. "In my jewelry box."

"Perfect. Now, I guess I better talk to a couple of horses."

Anne just laughed and took her hand.

Chapter Twenty-one

Zeke relaxed in the recliner while Anne finished up her barn and office work. She knew how hard it had been for her to cancel clients while Destiny was with them. She'd need to make it up to her somehow, and a special marriage ceremony might be perfect.

She stretched and got out of the too-comfortable recliner. Before Destiny came back from helping Anne, she wanted to review the surveillance tapes and call Davis. Hopefully, they'd hear from the sheriff about what the lab found from the bullet the vet removed from Shayla's shoulder.

After an hour of rewinding and viewing, Zeke had no definitive answers. Thanks to Benjamin's tree and brush thinning she had a few semi-clear shots of the intruder. But even with the house yard lights, there wasn't a clear shot of his face. Medium height, average build, dark skin, wearing dark colors. He had a shiny chrome-silver automatic, which should be helpful. And was left-handed.

He ran down the hill so there was no way to tell how he entered the property. When she saw the part where Anne ran down to Shayla, her throat tightened. Anne was fearless. With the shotgun in her right hand she was cautious but focused. It was too dark to see much of Shayla until Jim came and carried her to the deck.

The fact that her doctor forbade flying for thirty days helped sealed her decision. She shut off the tape and pulled up her email. In ten minutes she'd written and proofread her resignation from teaching at Quantico. She would now be officially separated from the FBI. The next step was still unknown, but she needed to be with her family.

≈≈≈≈≈

Anne applauded as Destiny rode Sunny around the ring bareback. It had taken hours to get to that point. Fortunately, the therapist provided a lightweight molded boot for her foot, and that gave her better balance. They began her ride with grooming, then walking, then Anne leading them around, and now a victory.

Destiny was grinning ear to ear. "Call Auntie and tell her to come out here and see this."

Anne smiled and sent a text. Within five minutes, Zeke entered the barn and stood speechless. Destiny didn't see her at first, and Anne smiled as tears rolled down Zeke's face. Her face radiated pride.

"Auntie, look. I'm riding Sunny by myself."

"That's just awesome, kid." Zeke leaned against the rail and grinned proudly.

Anne decided they would have some sort of celebration before Destiny left for home. The night before they had received an email from Zeke's brother Reggie with plans to pick up his daughter the following Friday. He asked whether he should invite their dad to join him. Zeke said no. Adamantly. Anne kinda wanted to meet the tyrant.

Destiny slowed in front of Anne. "That was so

cool. Did you see how good we did? I'm so glad Auntie saw, too." Zeke joined them and, after Anne helped her off the horse, gave her niece a big hug. "I'm really proud of you, Destiny. Isn't it a great feeling?"

"Did you have to do this, too?"

"Yes, and I was blindfolded."

"No way!"

Anne interceded. "Okay folks. We need to get Sunny back in her stall."

Destiny still had one crutch but followed along with Anne to help.

"I'll meet you back at the house," Zeke waved.

Anne waved and blew a kiss.

❧ ❧ ❧ ❧

Zeke just got in the house when the house phone rang. "Hello."

"Agent Cabot, Sheriff Lafferty here. Think I could come by for a couple of minutes? I'd like to bring you up to date."

"Sure, that would be fine. I'll open the gate for you. I'm hoping you have good news." She no sooner hung up when she heard Susan calling her from outside.

"Come in." Jim was carrying Shayla, whose tail was wagging furiously. "Her bed's in the kitchen. Let's go in there."

"The vet said the gunshot missed all the vital vessels and bones. She needs to take it easy until the stitches come out in a week." Jim set her on the fluffy dog bed.

"I can't thank you enough for taking care of everyone for the past few days. It was way above and beyond."

Susan gave her a hug. "We were glad to help out, and we're happy everyone is home and safe."

"Anne and Destiny should be in from the barn soon. Do you want to sit down?"

"No, we have to get back." Jim edged toward the door.

"I'll call Anne later." Susan followed him out.

Zeke knelt down and hugged Shayla. "I'm so sorry this happened. I can't help but think it's my fault for not being here and being the source of the bad shit that keeps happening." She choked up as Shayla whimpered and licked her cheek. "You stay. I'm going to find you a treat." The refrigerator was pretty empty, but she pulled off a piece of leftover rotisserie chicken and fed it to Shayla in small bites since she knew the dog never actually chewed her treats.

The huge amount of gauze and tape wrapped around her shoulder and back would undoubtedly slow her down for a while. Once she'd eaten, her eyes got heavy, and Zeke got up and left her to nap.

Destiny came in and found Zeke at the kitchen table. She was about to lunge over to Shayla when Zeke put up her hand. "Sssh, let her sleep a bit."

"Okay," Destiny whispered. "I'll go up and shower."

Zeke nodded and waved. She headed for the front door anticipating either Anne or the sheriff. She smiled when Anne walked out of the barn as the squad car pulled up to the front of the house.

"Howdy, folks," the sheriff said as he exited the car.

"Glad you could come over. Why don't we go out on the deck since Destiny's upstairs?"

"I'll go wash my hands and get some iced tea,"

Anne said.

Zeke led the sheriff through the house to the back deck. He stood at the rail and shook his head. "It sure looks different in the daylight."

Anne joined them with a tray of tea and glasses.

"I've only got a few minutes, but I wanted to give what we got so far." He flipped open a small spiral notebook and skimmed a few pages. "The fella we got running across Highway 14 was a mister Salem Al-Fassi. He's a twenty-two-year-old carpet installer from Tempe, Arizona. Made one call and clammed up. The gun he had was unregistered. The bullet from the vet was a match." He stuck the notebook in his shirt pocket and shook his head. "We'll hold him until we hear more."

"Any chance you'd let me talk to him?" Zeke asked.

He scratched the back of his neck and cocked his head. "I'm not sure that's a good idea right now. Let's see how this pans out. I'll keep you in the loop, Agent Cabot."

"Oh, I almost forgot. The surveillance footage was dark, but the guy had dark clothes, and a chrome-silver automatic." She watched for a reaction. None. "And he was left-handed."

The sheriff pulled out his notepad and jotted it down.

Anne leaned forward. "Sheriff, is it a crime to shoot a pet?"

"Well, I suppose it depends. If a person is in fear for their life and a dog is a threat, maybe. However, if it's during the commission of a crime on someone's posted private property...I'd say probably would be." He put on his hat.

Zeke stood. "Thanks for coming over. We appreciate your attention to this."

They walked to the front door.

"I think I can say that he won't be bothering you." He drove off with a wave.

Zeke watched awhile. She glanced at Anne on the deck. "I have to run upstairs; I'll be down in a minute," she called out. Zeke wanted to get the information to Mike as soon as she could. If there were any connection to her or the case—he'd find it.

Mike was there in Beirut when the RPG hit the Hussein brothers in their car. He knew the whole story. There was absolutely no earthly reason to believe that those men posed any kind of threat, but she'd thought that in the past and was wrong. If there were any reason for concern, he'd tell her.

⁂

Anne sipped her iced tea and enjoyed the relative quiet, but imagined Zeke was not enjoying the quiet. She could practically hear the whirring brain sounds in Zeke's head at that moment either looking at the tapes or calling Davis or Mike.

Leopards just don't change their spots, not this late in the game. It saddened Anne to think that Zeke might be holding on to this for a long while and she didn't know how to help. Plus, she really wanted to share the phone call she got while she was in the barn. Nancy had called her to tell her about a former student who had a successful equestrian therapy practice in northeastern New Mexico and was retiring. She wanted to sell the practice and her home. The whole idea was sort of intriguing.

She loaded up the tray and carried it inside. This was not the time. First order was to be sure that Destiny was okay. Tomorrow she'd take both Zeke and Destiny to the doctor.

The thumping of a tail greeted her when she entered the kitchen. "Oh, Shayla. I'm so glad you're back, sweet girl. What say we take a little walk outside?" Shayla stood shakily. Anne attached her leash and slowly walked her through the garage and around the front. No need to go out back anytime soon. It was still a painfully vivid memory for her. She hadn't really had time to process everything herself. A plan surfaced.

Fairly soon, Shayla slowed and began to limp. "Okay, sweetie. Let's head back."

Shayla went straight for a drink of water and her bed. Anne gave her a couple of dog biscuits to work on. "You rest up."

She went upstairs and found Zeke—as she expected—on her computer. She leaned over and kissed her cheek. "I won't interrupt. I'm going to check on Destiny and then take Dancer for a little ride. I need some time to just be."

Zeke turned and gave her an appraising look. "I understand. Please take your phone and don't go too far."

"Yes, dear." Anne walked down the hall and tapped on Destiny's door. When there was no answer, she cracked open the door and saw Destiny sound asleep and curled around her pillow.

She changed into riding gear and headed to the barn. Dancer had been slighted by all the activity, and she needed to keep her connected. Once they were ready, she walked to the front gate. She waved in case Zeke was watching. She mounted and walked him north past the Godfreys' place. A little farther and there was a trail that wound up the mountain, the same path she took after she rescued the handsome special agent after the vicious rattlesnake attack ten years ago. She chuckled. The truth was the heroic agent actually lunged back in terror and fell off a ledge. That was the moment Anne's wounded heart took its first beat toward happiness.

❦ ❦ ❦ ❦

Dinner was a cobbled-together affair. Fortunately, Susan had provided several choices over the past few days: chicken, burgers, spaghetti, and a large pasta salad.

Destiny's ride with Sunny left her exhilarated. She even visited her before dinner. Zeke beamed gratitude. She feared that nothing would change, and Destiny would stay pissed off and end up in juvie. Happily, Anne's faith never wavered. In spite of resistance from both Zeke and Destiny, she persisted. Zeke chuckled to herself.

"Auntie, can Shayla sleep with me tonight?"

"I—" Zeke started.

Anne interrupted. "I think that might be a good idea if she wants to. And if your aunt agrees."

Since she'd never had one before, Zeke tried to be very particular about dog rules. But, Shayla was pretty traumatized, and Destiny finally exhibited some compassion to another being for a change. "It might be okay, if you agree to take her out if she needs to go."

"In that case, maybe they could camp in the family room. To avoid stairs," Anne suggested.

Zeke sat and thought about it. "Okay. We'll try

it." A good compromise. No dogs in the bedroom. No one falling down stairs.

By nine o'clock, Shayla's bed was parked next to the sofa and both kid and canine were tucked in. Zeke had already walked around the house and checked all the cameras—twice—while Anne waited in bed reading until she finally came upstairs and showered. "Could you help put this shoulder thingy back on?"

"Immobilizer." Anne got up and fitted it and tightened the Velcro straps. "Wow, this is my first chance to see the bruising." She tenderly touched Zeke's shoulder, upper arm, and right upper thigh. "How many times over the years have I cared for this same battered body?" She bit her lip and remained silent.

"What's wrong?"

"Oh, baby, it hurts me to see your beautiful body traumatized so often."

Zeke kissed her. "It's no picnic for me. But, with your TLC I always heal safely and quickly."

"Well, I wish you wouldn't do this again."

"Yes, ma'am."

They crawled into bed, and Anne snuggled close and murmured, "I'm really pleased with Destiny's progress. Believe it or not, the whole nurturing Shayla is a very positive sign of compassion. A virtue, I might add, I've not seen before."

"I hadn't thought of it that way, but yeah. Do you think she's ready to go home?"

"There's no way to know for sure. But, I'd say yes. There isn't much more I can do unless she has a relapse or new behavior." She curled around Zeke and held her close. "I've missed you so much."

"Me too. So, well, I resigned from Quantico

today."

Anne sat bolt upright. "You what?"

"We got busy, and I forgot. The doc said not to fly for a month, and I realized how relieved I was to hear that. I'm tired of the commute and being away from you. And after this last episode…well. That's it."

Anne lay back and stroked her face. "This is what you want?"

"Yes. I felt immensely relieved after I sent the email."

"I love you, Zeke Cabot."

"And I love you."

Chapter Twenty-two

W ould you please pass the syrup?" Destiny asked politely.

Zeke blinked. "Of course."

"Dad said he wanted to bring Grandpa and you wouldn't let him. How come? He'd probably like to see your house, and he could see me ride."

Anne stopped mid-bite and looked to Zeke to answer. She groaned and reached for the maple syrup.

Anne put down her fork. "You know, honey, Destiny makes a good point. I've never met your dad, and he'd probably want to see how Destiny works with the horses."

"Yeah! I'd really like to show him around and he'd love Shayla and Susan would like to meet him. Oh, and he could have my room, and I could sleep downstairs—"

"Stop." Zeke put up her hands. She hated sounding so arbitrary. "Let me think about it for a while." Her pulse pounded in her temples, and she stood to get more coffee.

Anne cleared the dishes. "Destiny, wash up and brush your teeth. We need to leave for the clinic in fifteen minutes. Zeke, I'll clean up if you want to sit outside for a few minutes." She winked and smiled.

Zeke kissed her cheek, then took her coffee to the deck, and stretched out on a lounge chair. The sun sparkled in and out of the tree branches. It gave the summer growth a polished emerald glow. The tension in her shoulders eased, and she took a deep breath. Oddly, the coffee tasted better out here. Maybe it was like camping when everything tasted and smelled better. And possibly retiring—she hated the sound of that word—would allow more mornings like this.

Anne called from the kitchen.

❦ ❦ ❦

By the time Anne had carefully deposited Zeke with the orthopedist on the second floor, she hurried to the clinic where Destiny was waiting for the physical therapist. She dropped into the chair next to Destiny. "Are you excited to see what they say?"

Destiny put down the phone and crinkled up her face. Anne could clearly see a glimpse of a very young Zeke blushing with her very first crush. Happily, the Cabot women dazzled with their dark wavy hair, cocoa and cream skin, and those penetrating amber eyes. Destiny stood nearly as tall as her aunt, only about six inches short of Zeke's almost six feet. When she wasn't slouching, she had a ramrod-erect posture. Probably inherited from the Master Sargent. The terror of both young lives. No wonder Zeke didn't want to see him.

"I hope they say 'you're all healed' and let me get rid of all this stuff."

"Cabot."

"Let's go."

❦ ❦ ❦

The ride home was more pleasant. Zeke had a smaller sling and Destiny no longer had crutches and had traded for a smaller Velcro boot.

"I had time to do some thinking about inviting granddad," Zeke started cautiously. "But a lot is riding on this visit and the outcome. You have to demonstrate that you have changed and it's permanent. If anyone doubts your sincerity, you'll be back in trouble with the court."

"But Auntie, I have changed."

"I know that, and I believe you. The reason I'm reluctant to include your granddad is that you and I are both victims of his verbal abuse—"

"Zeke." Anne touched her arm. "Is this appropriate?"

"Yes, I think it is. Destiny and I both have very similar triggers, I suspect. As excited as she is about him coming to visit, I'm afraid those triggers and the attendant anxiety might spook the horses and derail this whole plan."

Anne glanced at the rearview mirror and saw the worried look on Destiny's face. "Well, if we all agree that there's a potential problem, we can work on it now. If they only stay one night, we can do a very abbreviated demonstration as soon as he arrives. If Destiny is all ready when he gets here, I think she can do a brief demo before he has time to launch into any criticism. He might just be happy to be here."

Zeke and Destiny both laughed out loud.

Anne sighed loudly. "I am only trying to make this work for both of you. If you're not willing to help me, then we better forget the whole thing."

The remainder of the ride was silent.

When they arrived at the front gate, Benjamin was waiting with his wheelbarrow full of lawn tools.

Both Destiny and Zeke got out so Anne could put

the car away. Zeke waved. "Hi, Benjamin. Welcome back. "

"Hola, Ms. Cabot, and Ms. Destiny. I'm glad to be back, but I have much to do. We can talk later?"

"Of course. We'll see you later." Zeke and Destiny moved slowly to the front door.

"Didn't you want to tell him about our adventure?" Destiny said excitedly.

Zeke held the door open. "Some things you keep in the family. I don't want Benjamin to have to worry right now. And I don't want to tell your dad or your granddad until later."

"Why? Don't you think it's important that they know?"

"I'd rather not discuss it until we know that Sheriff Lafferty has the right suspect. I also need to know why he did it, if it is him." They both sat down at the kitchen table. Anne was fixing lunch, and Zeke thought about what she had to say. "If you tell people about an incident that happened without the details or without the result, generally everybody wants to speculate about what happened and why. None of that helps, plus it just stokes the anxiety for everyone. Does that make sense?"

"Yeah, I suppose so. I guess that's how rumors get started, huh?"

Zeke smiled broadly. "That's an excellent example. Destiny, the whole point of this visit was to teach you some coping skills so when you get home, you don't have to be so reactive. You'll be able to think through things before you react."

"You mean like when granddad is pushing my buttons about something really stupid, I can avoid blowing up at him?"

This time everyone laughed.

"Oh boy, I sure wish I had your moxie when I was thirteen."

"Why?"

Zeke glanced at Anne, who gently shrugged. "Well, it was a long time ago, and girls—especially little, um, mixed-race girls—were treated very differently. In fact, even African Americans anywhere in the south endured a lot of abuse."

Destiny looked incredulous and angry. "No way. Are you serious?"

"Of course. Why would I make up something like that?"

"So why would Granddad pick on you?"

"He wanted me to succeed and make more of myself. No matter how well I did in sports, academics, whatever, it was never good enough." Zeke laughed. "And he still pushes my buttons."

"Lunch is ready." Anne set down a large serving bowl of pasta salad and three plates. "Let's table this conversation for a while. After lunch, I think we can work on a short routine with Dancer, and once you've both got it down, we'll plan some distractions."

"This is good." Zeke took another helping. "Mike called and would like to stop by if that's okay."

"Always glad to see him." Anne nodded. "Maybe he could be one of our actors with you for Destiny's trial run? Destiny, if you're finished, would you please take Shayla for a short walk? I don't want her running loose just yet."

"Sure." She took her plate to the sink and rinsed it.

Zeke's eyebrows shot up.

Destiny grabbed the leash and gently coaxed

Shayla out the garage door.

"You know, she really has changed." Anne smiled.

"I would never have believed it from the way she started. I guess I still don't quite know how horses do it, but I know they can."

"I was skeptical, too. A lot was riding on this. Fingers crossed she won't react to their presence with old habits."

"Well, while you two are working I could try to push her buttons," Zeke suggested.

"Risky. But better to find out before we send the invitation. When does Reggie need to know?"

"By the weekend. Say, I just noticed you haven't been wearing your necklace the past few days…"

Anne grabbed her throat. "Oh my God!" She jumped up and ran upstairs.

Zeke could only hear the sound of drawers opening and closing, furniture moving, and audible cursing. It must've happened the other night. Maybe Destiny would remember.

Twenty minutes later all three were fanned out on the hillside retracing Anne's movements. Zeke couldn't remember ever seeing Anne so frantic. Benjamin joined them and suggested they wait until dark and use a high-watt search lamp because the gold would reflect better in the night.

They agreed to that, and also that Anne and Destiny could start working with Dancer. Anne excused herself and ran into the house.

Zeke put an arm around Destiny's shoulders. "That necklace holds many important memories for Anne. Just be a little respectful because she won't be herself till she finds it. Why don't you head over to the barn and get Dancer tacked up?"

"Okay, I will."

Zeke found Anne facedown on the bed, sobbing. She knew it was way more than the necklace. She curled up behind and held her very tightly. "It'll be okay, honey. I promise."

The sobbing slowed, then stopped. Anne shoved the pile of tissues out of the way and snuggled next to Zeke. "I'm sorry. I don't know what came over me."

"It's been overwhelming, and I guess this was just the last straw." Zeke kissed her forehead.

"You're right. Maybe after Destiny leaves, we could take a couple of days and get out of here. Maybe a long day trip or two?"

"That sounds divine."

They held each other for a few more minutes. Anne finally said, "I guess I'd better get out to the barn before something goes awry."

"I'll come out a little later."

"Thanks for always loving me so much."

"Always."

Chapter Twenty-three

Zeke and Mike were huddled around her computer screen up in the landing/office.

"Play it again," Mike said. "He looks like a couple of these mug shots, but the names don't match." He leaned back. "You know, we sent Hussein's cousin to prison for tax fraud. He died of cancer about three years ago. But, I agree, there are plenty of coincidences that make me suspicious."

Zeke leaned back and rubbed her eyes. "Why now? And what could they possibly want? I'm no threat."

Mike shook his head. "There are only two things I can think of. One, it's random payback from some disgruntled local, or…"

"One of the Hussein's isn't dead. Or his wife is now running things."

Mike whistled. "Well, that's a bit of a stretch, but we've sure seen weirder shit. I guess I could try to find Ben Shapiro. He'd know. I don't even know if he's still alive."

"That's a bit morbid." Zeke smiled

"You know what a crazy risk-taker he was. Listen, let me run down some of the weird shit and see what I can turn up."

"Okay. Would you play villain guy for my niece? She's doing some equine therapy to quell some of her adolescent angst. She's done really well, but when her dad and my dad show up, the expectations will rise exponentially and so will her fear factor."

"Understood. Remember, I have girls."

"Oh right. Adorable little princesses. How old are they now?"

"Tough question." He ticked off on his fingers. "Eight and ten."

"Okay. You've got a couple of years before the hormones take complete control. Come on out to the barn so you'll know what Anne does before you need her."

"Very funny."

They walked over to the barn and went around to the arena side. Anne sat comfortably on a rail while Destiny trotted Dancer around the ring. Anne coached her on when to change direction and Destiny did so without touching the reins.

Mike leaned over and whispered, "She's good, how long's she been riding?"

"Actually, just a couple of weeks. It took Destiny a while to settle down and listen."

"Is this the same as what you had to do?"

"Pretty much, yeah."

❧❧❧❧

"Hi, Mike." Anne gave him a hug. "It's been way too long since you guys were here. Ask Betsy to call, and we can set up something."

"I'll do that. This is a pretty great setup. Did you expand the arena?"

"Yes, about four years ago." She said to Destiny, still atop Dancer, "Okay, just walk her for a few minutes."

She turned back to Mike and Zeke. "Mike, the reason I asked Zeke to bring you over is that Dancer doesn't know you or your energy. But, she is watching."

He turned. "Wow, she is."

"I'd like you and Zeke to have a quiet but angry discussion. What I want you to relay is danger and menacing. I suspect she'll pick up on it and Destiny will have trouble communicating with her. We want her to learn how to do that."

"Okay."

Anne went back and whispered to Destiny, and Dancer began to canter counterclockwise. Zeke and Mike leaned together, and Anne could hear the words become more clipped and angry. The second time around, Dancer veered away from the rail. Destiny finally got her back to the rail. When they approached the arguing, Dancer balked and wouldn't go any farther.

Destiny tried to stay positive and get her to move, but finally got frustrated and yelled. Anne climbed into the ring and walked over. "What happened?"

"I don't know. Dancer got spooked and wouldn't listen to me."

Anne stroked Dancer's neck. "It's all right girl. You're fine." From that distance, they couldn't even hear the argument. "Can you hear what they're saying?"

"No, they're too far away."

"So what's Dancer upset about?"

Destiny looked across the arena then at Anne. "I'll bet she knows they're angry and she's scared."

Anne continued to stroke the horse. "So, what happened to you?"

Destiny fussed with her gloves. "I got mad cause she wouldn't do what I said."

"And that cannot happen if we invite your family to watch. Do you understand what that will mean?"

"That I haven't learned how to control myself and I'll have to go to juvie." She started to cry, and Zeke started to move toward her.

Anne put up her hand. "Excellent." She patted Destiny's knee. "Okay, we're going to go again, but this time, watch her ears. If you think she is sensing something, let her know that she's all right and that you'll take care of her, then steer her away from the danger. Stay in control."

Destiny trotted off, and Anne walked over to Mike and Zeke. "Good job, keep it up. I think she's got it now."

They all watched in amazement as the horse neared and suddenly, Destiny reversed course. Anne grinned and gave her a thumbs-up. She waved her over and smiled. "You guys can make up now."

"I don't understand what happened." Mike pointed to the horse.

"Destiny wasn't paying attention to her horse. They're prey animals, and Dancer picked up danger from your angry conversation. When Destiny didn't get the message, the horse wanted to run. This time they worked together."

"Wow. How will this help?"

"Destiny needs to pay attention to what's going on around her and her reaction to whatever. When she senses danger, she needs to avoid, not confront."

Mike scratched his head. "Is that what you had to do, Zeke?"

"Mine was more about trust." They walked out to his car. "That was cool. Listen, I'll get some details for you. Don't worry, I've got your six."

"Thanks, Mike."

❧ ❧ ❧ ❧

Zeke returned to the house while Anne and Destiny took care of the horses. The past hour had unsettled her and brought back a flood of terrifying memories; the memory of the Hussein brothers and their years of vengefulness, and all the flashbacks she endured through her own therapy.

Her hands trembled. Destiny could not see this. She pulled a package of chicken from the freezer and stuck it in the microwave to defrost. She scribbled a note that she was napping and hurried upstairs.

She leaned back on the closed French doors to their bedroom. The trembling in her legs increased with her anxiety. "Shower."

After steam filled the bathroom, Zeke stripped off her clothes along with the new sling and stepped into the large glass-enclosed shower. Multiple shower heads barraged her with nearly scalding hot water. Her back tingled from the siege.

After turning down the heat, Zeke lathered up her hair carefully and then her entire body—a ritual she developed after the episode with the homeless in Chicago. It seemed that for reasons she didn't fully understand, she felt driven to cleanse every pore to relieve her from the toxic thoughts and feelings.

All the old angst and panic threatened just like it had ten years ago when she fled Chicago for the high desert of New Mexico. Her years of undercover work for the Bureau culminated with a horrific and complicated case. The murder and decapitations of homeless victims in the name of medical research was the brainchild of Ahmed Hussein, MD.

She discovered the heinous scheme with help from a senior resident who had been murdered for her betrayal. Shayla Graham, MD.

A torrent of tears flowed for her friend and all the other lives lost.

❧ ❧ ❧ ❧

Anne pushed a wheelbarrow with hay flakes and a rake down the barn aisle. She could hear Destiny sweet-talking Dancer while brushing her.

It was always a good feeling when a client had a breakthrough, but this case was special because it was family and because it might make the difference between success and failure. Destiny initially felt that she was being sent away for punishment, but after talking to her after today's exercise, Anne genuinely thought an important corner had been turned. Time would tell. Or the judge would.

"You know, Destiny, you really went the distance today, and it was hard. I'm so pleased with your effort and the results. Can you think of something fun you'd like to do?"

Destiny stuck her smiling face out of Dancer's stall. "Yes! Do you think Susan would let me drive the ATV?"

Anne laughed. It could be worse. She might have asked to go to Disney World™. "I'll give her a call." She took her phone outside and texted Susan. Within a minute she had a reply.

SGodfrey: Of course. I'll have one of the boys bring it over. 1. Helmet 2. Low speed

AReynolds: Thanks!

When she returned, Destiny had swept the aisle and put everything away. "All done. Wha'd she say?"

"She'd send one of the boys over with it. She had two rules." Anne showed her phone to Destiny.

"Right. I knew she'd say that."

"I have a couple more: stay within the fenced property, and take your cell phone. We'll be ready to eat in about an hour. Promise?"

"Promise. Can Shayla go with me?"

"How would you keep her from falling out?"

She paused then said, "I'd put the seat belt through her storm shirt."

"Hmm, not a bad idea." Anne put an arm around her shoulder. "Let's lock up and get your stuff."

⁂

Zeke dried off, slipped on some fleece warm-ups, and crawled beneath the covers, shaking. She ran out of hot water and was more relaxed but still aware her brain circuitry was crackling and shorting out. The result, now, rendered her frozen.

The house remained quiet, so she tried to still the rising panic and sleep.

Sometime later, she heard the door open and close. She drifted until she heard, "What the... Zeke, honey, I'm sorry to wake you, but we have a problem. There's no hot water. And why are you curled up in warm-ups?"

"I'm freezing so I used up the hot water." Zeke rolled over and sat up against the headboard.

Anne sat beside her and touched her brow and neck. "Are you sick? Do you have a fever?"

Zeke took her hand. "No. I had a bit of a meltdown, and it was all I could think to do."

"Honey, what brought this on? Why didn't you call me?"

"Not sure. Talking to Mike about possible characters made all the stuff about the past and the Husseins and Shayla Graham...I freaked out. Then watching Destiny struggle just reminded me of my treatment and the other gal's suicide attempt... I thought all that stuff was gone."

Anne slid up next to her and wrapped her in a hug. "I'm so sorry I wasn't here for you. It must've been terrifying." She kissed the side of her head and felt the healing suture line. "How are you feeling right now?"

"Less freaked out, but more shaky and weak." She closed her eyes and absorbed Anne's warmth and love. The whole episode scared her more than she'd like to admit, especially since it was such a delayed reaction. "Do you think my therapy wore off?"

"No, baby, I don't. You very clearly described the triggers, and you've been vigilant since the last intrusion. Do you think Callie could help? Do you still have her number? Or maybe check in with Robin Taylor? She's seen you recently."

"Okay. I just wondered if, after Destiny leaves, I could work with one of your horses?"

"Of course. I'm not sure I'm the most qualified to work with you, but the horse is the actual healer."

Zeke pulled the covers up closer. "Would you switch on the fireplace?"

Anne nodded. "Sure."

"By the way, where's the little star?"

Anne adjusted the fan and smiled. "Her reward request was to ride the ATV—with rules. How could I refuse? I'm going to throw the chicken in the oven and make some mashed potatoes and salad. Would that sound good to you?"

"You know it does. I hate to ask, but do we still have that wretched ginger brandy?"

Anne laughed. "Yes, why on earth would you think of that?"

"The therapeutic burn it causes."

"That it does. Come down when you feel up to it. I love you." Anne left and closed the door.

Zeke rolled on her side and pulled the covers up. It helped to have talked a little and dissipated some of the anxiety. And now she had definite ideas to help.

❧❧❧❧

Anne closed the bedroom door softly and started downstairs when she suddenly stopped and sat on the steps. Now her head whirred with thoughts. Not all unpleasant, but far too many to process. She'd always felt supported by Zeke, but now it might just be that Zeke had burned out one of her functional switches. Working with one of the horses might ground her or at least provide some clarity, but it would have to wait until Destiny had been picked up.

Chapter Twenty-four

Anne heard the ATV before she saw it. She opened the door to the deck in time to see Destiny careening in large loops up toward the house. It had been about an hour, and the gas tank must surely be near empty. Fortunately, they had a container in the barn. She waved as the ATV got closer and smiled to see the happy faces on Destiny and Shayla. The dog was in the passenger seat with the lap and shoulder harness locked on. Where was her phone when she wanted a picture?

"Hey, Anne, guess what? I have a surprise for you." She stopped under the deck.

"Would you top off the gas tank before you park it? Dinner will be ready in about ten minutes."

"Okay." She steered around in a tight circle and headed up the hill to the barn.

Anne smiled. The recent changes in Destiny's attitude buoyed her spirits. It would have been heartbreaking to have sent the same delinquent back to her family and the courts. Now she'd wait to see if Zeke felt strong enough to invite her father. It had to be her decision.

Anne came back in the house just as Zeke walked downstairs. "You look a little better. Are you hungry?"

"Starving. Would you fasten this shoulder strap?"

Anne took the end and wrapped it around her snuggly, just enough to keep her arm supported and shoulder immobile.

"Did I hear the ATV?" Zeke followed her to the kitchen.

"Yes. I sure wish I had a picture of Destiny with Shayla strapped in the passenger seat." Anne laughed. "I don't think I've seen either of them this happy."

Zeke was ferreting through the lower cabinets.

Anne reached up over the refrigerator. "Here's the ginger brandy, if that's what you're looking for."

Zeke stood up with a small lockbox in her hands. "Look what I forgot about." The key was in the lock.

Anne wiped her hands and walked closer. "What is that?"

"This is a small antique revolver I got from my partner on the first Chicago assignment. It supposedly belonged to Al Capone's girlfriend. I don't think I ever fired it, but I used to clean it regularly because of the sentimental value." She opened the wood box and took out a small caliber pistol.

"Sure is pretty. Does it actually shoot bullets?" Anne asked.

"Quite accurately, in fact."

"Hey guys, we're back. And guess what?" Destiny and Shayla came in covered with dirt.

"Stop. Not another step until you shower and change clothes. We'll take care of Shayla."

"But I—"

"Upstairs. Carefully." Anne sounded much angrier than she really was.

Destiny turned and went upstairs.

Zeke chuckled. "If you could get the vacuum, I'll clean up Shayla. Good thing she had the storm shirt on."

Anne brought the vacuum to the deck with the

brush attachment. "I can hold her if you'll brush her."

"Teamwork." Zeke sat on the floor while Anne held the collar and petted her.

"What do you suppose Destiny's so excited about?" Zeke asked.

"Maybe she found some wildflowers. Have you given any more thought to whether you want to invite your dad?"

"More than a little thought. It's like watching a tennis match in my head. Back and forth constantly. I really want to invite him for Destiny's sake. It might be necessary for their relationship. But, I'm anxious that he'll go after one or more of us. If it was today, I don't think I could deal with him."

They were both silent as Shayla patiently endured her dry cleaning.

Anne finally said, "Well, you do have a new pistol."

They both started laughing, and it escalated until they were howling with goofy comments and were wiping tears from their cheeks.

Zeke dropped the brush tool. Anne reached to pick it up, and Shayla used the chance to escape. More laughter.

And with perfect timing, Destiny walked out and found them doubled over in hysteria.

"What is wrong with you guys?" She sounded horrified.

Anne took her hand. "It's okay. We just thought of something silly, and it took over and then Shayla escaped her brushing."

Destiny walked over to the railing, looked around, and whistled. Shayla came bounding back, panting and grinning.

Anne looked up and said, "She's apparently

forgotten she was shot."

They both started laughing all over.

Destiny pouted and kicked the railing. "When you two are finished, I have something important to say."

Zeke wiped her eyes. "Of course. We're not trying to ignore you. We—Excuse me, it's Mike. I have to take this." She got up and went into the house to take the call.

Destiny threw herself into a chair. "This is so unfair. Nobody ever listens to me."

Anne sat forward and cleared her throat. "Ahem. That is categorically untrue. You have been at the center of this household and our lives for nearly two months. I put my clients on hold and Zeke rearranged her schedule. You had a pretty great day topped off with an hour on an ATV, which, I might add, our neighbors graciously lent you."

Destiny sat staring at her feet. And the boots Zeke gave her.

"Furthermore, it may interest you to know that your aunt, who was recently discharged from the hospital, is not feeling well today. She pulled it together to have dinner with us but had to interrupt that to clean up the dog you took joyriding. When you came in and found us laughing, which I might consider 'stress relief,' you considered it a personal affront. Now, I am happy to listen to your good news, or we can wait for your aunt."

Destiny just sat, and Anne waited. After a long silence, she said, "I'm sorry. I was just excited because I found your necklace and I know you were worried about losing it." She stood and pulled the gold chain and Pegasus from her pocket.

Anne took it, and with tears in her eyes, pulled Destiny into a hug. "I'm sorry, too."

⁂⁂⁂⁂

After dinner, everyone pitched in to get the kitchen cleaned up, and Destiny excused herself. Zeke and Anne took their coffee out to the deck. The moon was rising over the eastern plains and casting a warm glow over the dark side of the mountain. Traffic noise at the base of the hill quieted and night birds began to sing along with the crickets.

They were snuggled together on the swing. Zeke pulled Anne closer and kissed her temple. "I'm thrilled Destiny found your necklace. She must've been looking for a while."

"Me, too. Destiny said it was behind the stump. It wouldn't have been easy to spot."

Zeke smiled. "And just when I think I've got her figured out."

"I'm more and more confident that some of her new behaviors are going to stick. I wasn't sure, but her compassion is genuine and growing."

"I agree. It's hard to remember what a complete pain in the ass she was when she arrived. So. I called Reggie."

Anne sat up. "What did you say?"

"I told him to bring Dad. But it would be for only one night. He agreed. He had a dozen questions about Destiny. I told him he'd have to wait and see for himself." Zeke chuckled." If I didn't know better, I'd say my brother actually missed her."

"When are they coming?"

"Next Friday. He'll send the details."

"Are you worried?"

Zeke paused. "Well, I have some time to get my own house in order. I think I'll be okay. Worst case: go to plan B, we invite Jim and Susan over. My father is a southern gentleman and would never be rude in front of company."

"Excellent idea. Well, I guess I'll set up some drills for both you and Destiny."

"Not together, right?"

"No. Different exercises completely."

The sky was a deep purple now with a few pink cumulus clouds on the horizon. The scores of twinkling stars were getting brighter by the minute.

"I never get tired of the western skies, night or day."

Anne bit her tongue. This might not be the right time to talk about possibly moving. "You never told me what Mike said."

"Oh, he wanted to know what else the sheriff had and whether they were holding the suspect."

Odd. "Did you know?"

"I said I'd check with the sheriff tomorrow. I'd guess at the very least they've got him for criminal trespass with a weapon, malicious negligence with a weapon, unlicensed use of a firearm, and injury to a domestic animal. That should give Mike time to do more background."

"We should turn in. I want to check on Destiny and make she hasn't run away." Anne stood and stretched. "Say, did the brandy in your coffee help?"

Zeke smiled. "You know, I think it did. No more tremors."

Once they were ready for bed, Zeke said, "I think I'll check the surveillance tapes before I turn in. I won't be long."

Anne picked up her book. "Okay, hon."

After listening at Destiny's door until she heard soft snoring, Zeke crept down the stairs. She checked all the windows and doors, then stood for several minutes watching for shadows in the back. What she'd give to see that same intruder right now.

Her service weapon was locked up, but she held tight the antique Smith & Wesson .38 Special 642, J frame. When Agent Sturgis gifted it to her at the end of a rough case involving a Chicagoland modern mobster and his white-collar crimes, she had treasured the sentiment from the rugged old cop.

As she moved back upstairs, she marveled at her own longevity, considering some of the bad actors she'd run across. She locked the pistol in the top drawer and turned on the surveillance screens, then re-ran each camera for the past twenty-four hours. The best part was the hour's worth of ATV action with Destiny. Some of it was really amusing. *That little vehicle is pretty versatile and safe. Might be worth looking into getting one.*

She re-ran the part where Destiny stopped to look for the necklace. If only she had audio to hear the conversation with Shayla. Looked very serious.

Computer shut down, Zeke slipped quietly into bed with Anne, grateful for their lives. She barely heard the low growl coming from Destiny's room. She sat up and listened for several minutes. Must've been wind.

Chapter Twenty-five

Anne put the last dish in the dishwasher. "Okay here's today's plan: Destiny, I'd like you to work on the morning chores while I take Zeke into the round pen with Sunny." Anticipating grief and whining, "Don't worry, you don't have to do everything. When we finish, I'll come help and then we can do some more work with Dancer." She closed the door and wiped off the sink. "I'd like to do this for the next three mornings so we'll be ready to give your dad and granddad a good showing."

Destiny jumped up. "They're both coming?"

Zeke nodded. "They'll be here Friday, so you will also need to clean your room for your dad. We'll put your grandfather in the guest room."

"Awesome! Anne, do you think I'm ready?"

Anne cocked her head. "Well, you have worked pretty hard, but we can't know what's in your head or heart. Do you feel different than when you arrived?"

She chewed her thumbnail. "You know, that might be why I feel happier."

Zeke nodded. "You do seem happier, most of the time. What about your impatience and anger?"

"I think that's lot's better. I'm not nearly as pissed off as I was."

Zeke and Anne both laughed.

Zeke put the bridle on Sunny and walked her out to the ring. She hadn't ridden since the accident, but Anne thought it was best to start slow with Sunny. Zeke still didn't have full use of her arm.

"How're you feeling?"

"A little nervous. Not bad."

"Why don't you loosely hold the reins and lead her around the ring and let's see how she responds to you."

Zeke started slow, and Sunny stayed alert but moved well.

"She's a little tentative but not too worried. Keep going. Concentrate on sharing with her. Try to connect and see if you can read her."

Zeke struggled to settle her mind, but some of her past training experience kicked in, and she quieted her mind by repeating a simple mantra, "Peace Within Me."

"Now drop the reins and walk to the center of the ring. Ground yourself and then call her."

Zeke followed the directions, shook her arms, and focused on Sunny.

It felt like several long minutes, but it probably wasn't when she heard the breathing behind her. She smiled and whispered a grateful prayer.

Anne waited then came closer. "Great. Do you feel like a short ride?"

Zeke took a deep breath. "Yes. Bareback?"

Anne nodded and smiled. She leaned forward and clasped her hands; Zeke bent her knee to place her foot in the cradle of Anne's hands and pulled herself up with her left arm.

"Honey, you've done this before, and it's no

different now. Trust Sunny." Anne handed her the reins.

Zeke closed her eyes and took a breath. "Okay, Sunny." She pressed her boot heels against her withers, and they moved out to the rail. After two laps, Zeke closed her eyes and became part of the rocking/swaying motion. It felt good and safe.

"Do you want to trot?"

Zeke tightened her long legs around Sunny and clicked her tongue. With the reins in her right hand, she clutched a handful of the mane and closed her eyes. It felt like flying, and she'd forgotten the experience of joy and freedom. That was it—the freedom.

After several minutes, she slowed and walked over to the rail where Anne sat grinning. "You are simply gorgeous riding with her."

"It felt delirious. I remembered my feelings and freedom. I want to do it with Shadow tomorrow."

"Good plan. Want to send Destiny out with Dancer?"

"Sure. I'll take care of Sunny before I head into the house."

Zeke returned Sunny to her stall and found Destiny sweeping the aisle. "You ready?"

"Yup. Dancer is excited, too."

"Okay. I'll take care of Sunny and see you later."

Destiny lead Dancer out and Zeke got some oats for Sunny in addition to her hay. "Thanks, girl."

❧ ❧ ❧ ❧

Destiny walked over to where Anne was standing.

"I've been trying to think about how I can create an environment for you and Dancer similar to what you'll experience with your family here. Tell me what kind of criticism you get from them that upsets you. That way you'll be ready and calm."

Destiny rattled off a dozen semi-cruel comments her granddad would use regularly. No wonder the kid was defensive. "That's perfect. Now, I'm going to follow you around the ring shouting those things. And I want you and Dancer to focus on you and staying calm. Try not to get defensive or angry. If you do, stop and we'll re-center. Okay?"

"Let's do it."

For the next ten minutes, Anne followed them calling out criticism and insults. Dancer was keenly aware, but Destiny kept control and did not get rattled. "Good. Let's take a break; I'm tired."

They sat on the bleacher seats and Dancer just watched.

Anne smiled. "Are you aware of how attached Dancer is to you?"

"No, what do you mean?"

"Whether we're working in the ring or the barn, she watches you. She doesn't do that with anyone else."

"Really? How come?"

"Do you remember when I brought you out here after you were hurt and asked you to focus on communicating with her?"

"Yeah, she came right over. It was like some version of mind-melding or something. I could hear her."

"Exactly. That happens with horses, but not all the time. A horse may pick up on bad energy and take it, but they don't always form a bond. They can have attachments, but they're not always close."

"Like with a teacher or summer friend?"

"Yes. Good example. Let's go again, and I'll try making noise. I want you to walk then trot then change direction. Keep Dancer busy even if I try to distract you both."

Destiny started, and Anne went down to a large barrel near the door. When they got close, she started hitting it with a pole. At first, Dancer shied, but Destiny kept talking to her. Anne tried throwing objects into the ring, but the kid was steady.

So, she tried shouting insults designed to make her feel like a failure. Anne knew that was how her father subdued Zeke. She watched Destiny's shoulders begin to droop. She stopped talking to Dancer and they slowed to a walk. Dancer tossed her head and nickered, trying to communicate.

Anne stopped and just watched to see if Destiny could pull herself out of whatever dark place she'd gone to inside herself. After five minutes without response, Dancer just stopped. Destiny looked up, surprised. She turned to Anne, who shrugged.

Destiny kicked lightly and urged the horse, and Anne could see confusion turning to frustration. *Please don't give in. Listen to your horse.*

Destiny dropped her hands and started murmuring. Then she bent forward and leaned her head on Dancer's neck. After less than a minute, Dancer started to walk.

Anne covered her mouth and choked back a sob.

❧❧❧❧

Zeke reread the email and attachment from Mike. She was incredulous. What he discovered was not possible. Sari Hussein, the wife of Ahmed Hussein, was the granddaughter of Emir Al-Fassi.

She looked out the window at their peaceful home, then grabbed her phone and dialed. "Hello, this is Zeke Cabot. Can I speak to Sheriff Lafferty? Yes, it's urgent."

"Agent Cabot, what can I do for you?"

"Are you still holding the trespass subject?"

She banged her fist on the desk. "When?"

Chapter Twenty-six

This is such a treat. Midweek extravagance."
Anne scooped the potato salad into a serving
bowl while Susan put out hamburger rolls.

"When Jim heard that Destiny was leaving soon,
he thought some barbeque would be a nice send-off.
You know, I'm gonna miss that little character. She's
turned into quite a delight."

"Are the boys coming?"

"No, they have practice tonight, but they sent a
memento."

"That was sweet." Anne reminded herself to run
up and get the gift certificate when she carried the iced
tea to the table.

Zeke and Destiny were setting the dining room
table.

"How come we never ate in here?" Destiny asked.

Zeke stopped. "I honestly don't know. Anne and
I always eat in the kitchen so Shayla can clean up what
we drop." She winked. "Too bad, because I always like
this room."

"Yeah, it's fancy."

"Ready? Jim's on the way," Anne said.

They all moved to the dining room, and Jim set
down a platter filled with chicken, pulled pork, and
burgers. It smelled wonderful.

Once everyone's plate was full, Zeke stood.
"My father would have a long speech, peppered with

biblical quotes. I won't. I want to thank our wonderful and generous neighbors for the kindness they have always extended to Anne and me, and by extension my niece Destiny. Her progress this visit has had much to do with your kind examples. As a small token, Anne has a thank-you for you both. Anne handed Susan the elegant envelope and gift card.

"Oh my gosh, this is too much."

Jim leaned over. "What is it?"

"A weekend at the Tamaya Resort and dinner at the Corn Maiden. I've wanted to go there for years. We've just, well, been too busy." She teared up, and Anne hugged her.

"That's real kind of you folks. Thank you." Jim coughed. "Maybe we should eat."

Everyone overindulged in the feast. When a few minutes of silence passed, Anne reminded them, "Save room for pie. I heard that Destiny's favorite was her granny's peach pie. It turns out Zeke kept the original recipe."

After the dishes had been cleared, Jim pulled out a paper bag. "The boys had practice tonight, but they wanted you to have a souvenir."

Destiny opened the bag and squealed. "Look what I got." She held up a blue and silver jersey with a Timberwolves logo. "This is so awesome. Please tell the guys I love it." She pulled it over her head and modeled it.

"Very nice. Tell the boys they scored bonus points for this," Zeke said.

Susan made their apologies and said they needed to pick up the kids. They left plenty of food, and Anne bagged it up and stored it in the fridge and freezer.

"Can I be excused? I'm totally beat."

"Sure, you worked hard today. I'm so proud of you." Anne hugged her, then Destiny went to Zeke for a hug before heading upstairs.

Zeke and Anne went out to the porch swing and collapsed.

Anne snuggled close and sighed. "This has been one exhausting day. I'm sure glad Benjamin could help with some of the heavy lifting. Remind me next year to hire a spring-cleaning crew."

Zeke laughed. "I had the very same thought about seven hours ago."

"Wow, you're a fast learner."

"Have to be with teenagers hanging around here."

"One more day. Are you ready?" Anne took her hand.

"You know, I am. Watching how Destiny has embraced her need to be ready is encouraging. If she can face the old man, so can I. Former Chief Master Sergeant Robert Cabot is no longer in charge. This is our house."

"You go, girl." Anne sighed and closed her eyes. "You know you haven't mentioned talking to Mike. Was it a dead end?"

Zeke sat up a little and cleared her throat. "Well, not exactly, just an odd detour."

"Care to expand that?"

"I'm not sure I can yet. I've put that on the back burner until the company is gone and I will have a little more time to investigate."

"That's mysterious."

"I don't want to invest any more energy into something vague." She squeezed Anne's hand. "We have a critical game-changer for Destiny. I'm hoping she can hang on to what she's learned. I'd hate to see her go down the juvie route at this stage. She's just so young."

"She is, but she's made remarkable progress in a pretty short time."

Zeke smiled. "I can't argue with that. She doesn't even resemble the wild child that showed up."

Anne yawned. "Let's turn in. We can snuggle horizontally just as easily."

"Okay. I'll lock up, you check on Destiny."

❧❧❧❧

Zeke checked with her usual care but had Sari Hussein on her mind as well as the last sighting in Beirut as her husband and brother-in-law were blown to smithereens right in front of her. Zeke vividly remembered them shouting to her, "We didn't do it!" Could she still be holding a grudge?

Zeke needed to talk to that kid who they arrested, or she'd have to find Sari herself and end this madness. She stopped at the foot of the stairs and looked up toward her sleeping family. *They don't deserve this.*

Chapter Twenty-seven

Zeke tried combing her hair away from her face. "Damn. I should've gotten a haircut." She stepped back and looked in the full-length mirror. Shirt pressed, jeans pressed, boots shined. *This is it, stay strong for Destiny.* Her throat tightened thinking about her going home tomorrow.

"Your food is getting cold. Hurry up, both of you," Anne hollered up the stairs.

Zeke tapped on Destiny's door. "Time to go." Destiny opened the door and clearly had been crying. "What's wrong? Are you okay?"

"Yeah, I'm just a little sad."

Zeke hugged her. "I am, too. I'm going to miss you, so I guess we'll have to get you back for a visit soon. Dancer and Shayla will miss you as well."

"Really? When can I come back?"

"We'll check with your dad and see. Let's go eat."

Anne set the plates out. "Sorry, I just don't want you to get tangled up in traffic." She poured more coffee. "I'm going to run to the store while you're gone. I hoped we could have a bite and then get Destiny ready to do her exercise before they get bored or critical. Besides, once the show is over, we'll all be home free. Right?"

Zeke nodded and wiped her mouth. "I agree. Destiny, do you want to use the bathroom before we go? Hurry. I'll get the car out."

Anne walked out to the garage with her. "I wish I could go with you, but it's better if I stay here."

Zeke hugged her. "I wish you could be there, too. But, we'll be all right. It's a quick trip." A light kiss. "Sure is a lovely necklace, miss. Any particular sentiment?"

Anne leaned in and whispered, "Matter of fact, my fiancée gave it to me."

Zeke choked, laughing.

"What did I miss?" Destiny asked.

"I'll tell you on the way." Zeke steered onto westbound I-40. Traffic was light, and she set the cruise control. Good thing she'd gotten the car washed after that last rain. The amount of mud she'd accumulated might have given the old drill sergeant a stroke.

Destiny fiddled with the radio. "Do you think Dad and Granddad will be glad to see me?"

"If they're not, we're keeping you."

"Riiight."

"Would you indulge your dotty old aunt for a minute? I have some last-minute thoughts."

"Sure." She turned off the radio.

"First: you've done an outstanding job at learning from Anne and applying it. And you did it in a short time.

"Second: You may face new challenges when you get home, and you need to remember that you have the tools to quiet the inside trolls and focus on what you need to do.

"Third: You have family and friends here that you can call night or day anytime. And I know from experience that Anne can talk you through a situation as if she was right beside you.

"Also, I don't plan to discuss any of the details

about your visit with your parents or granddad. That's between us."

"Thanks for treating me like a grown-up and not a little kid. It helps a lot. So…what were you guys laughing about?"

"I told Anne it was a lovely necklace, did it have any special meaning—and thank you so much for looking so hard to find it. She said that her fiancée got it for her."

There was a long pause before Destiny said, "Shut up. Are you guys really getting married?"

"Yes, we are, but I don't have any details yet."

"Can I be in the wedding?"

Zeke laughed. "I don't even know if there will be an actual wedding or just a courthouse thing."

"Well, if you do…"

"Yes, I will let you know. And this is still a secret, okay?" She slowed as they passed several terminal doors. She figured they'd probably have to go to the waiting lot. As she turned to make another pass, she got a text from her brother.

RegC: Just arrived. Headed out at Door 4.

ZCabot: Be there in 2 min. Dark brown Forester.

"Well, that worked out fine. You okay?"

"Oh yeah, I'm kind of excited to see Dad."

When she spotted an opening, she pulled to the curb and got out to open the back.

"Dad!" Destiny ran up to hug her dad, and when he leaned over, Zeke spotted an old man behind him. A frail, white-haired old man. That can't be…

"Zeke." Her brother engulfed her in a bear hug.

"Good to see you. Dad, come and say hi."

Her father stepped up and squinted through his glasses. "Zari? Is that you?"

"Yes, sir. Good to see you." She stuck out her hand, and he limply shook it.

"Welcome to Albuquerque. Why don't you have a seat in front?" She opened the door. "We'll get the bags."

Destiny chattered a mile a minute while they stowed the bags. Zeke whispered to Reggie, "What's happened to Dad?"

"Long story, but he's just gotten old."

The ride back was uneventful. Zeke answered occasional queries about where they were or the weather. Her father was amazingly quiet.

She felt wildly conflicted as she'd geared up a solid defense for the expected assault. Letting her guard down might be a mistake. She glanced sideways and felt incredulous that the imposing drill sergeant that haunted her youth sat shriveled beside her.

After opening the gate, Zeke parked in front to make it easier for everyone. She and Destiny hauled the bags in and upstairs while Reggie helped her dad into the house.

Anne opened the door. "Well?"

"You'll see," Zeke whispered.

Reggie smiled. "Anne, I'd like you to meet my dad, Robert Cabot. Dad, this is Anne Reynolds."

He held out his bony hand. "Pleased to meet you, Ms. Reynolds. I appreciate your taking care of my granddaughter. I hope she wasn't too much trouble."

Destiny stood behind him and rolled her eyes.

Zeke stepped in. "Why don't we all go in the family room." She indicated the recliner. "Dad, why don't you sit here?"

"Can I show my dad around?" Destiny said.

"Good idea. Dad, would you like to rest a little while we fix lunch?" Zeke asked gently.

"Yes, that's a good idea. Does this go back some?"

Zeke pulled the lever and handed him a throw from the couch. "We'll be right in there." She pointed to the kitchen.

Zeke and Anne talked in hushed tones so as not to disturb their guest. "And that would be the fabled Ruler from Biloxi?" Anne crooked an eyebrow.

"I know. I about fainted when I saw him at the airport."

"When was the last time you saw him?"

"Years ago, I guess the funeral. He's deteriorated so much since Mom died. Reggie insists it isn't a medical problem, he's just wearing out."

"For Destiny's sake let's hope he's run out of vitriol."

❧ ❧ ❧ ❧

Anne wiped her hands. "I want to get Destiny set up, would you finish cleaning up? I'll text when we're ready."

Zeke cleared the dishes while Reggie got their dad settled in the recliner. She overheard part of the conversation.

"Nice place they've got out here. I can see why you wanted to send Destiny to a quiet place like this."

"A quiet place? He should have been here a couple of weeks ago." Zeke mumbled into the dishwasher.

"Dad, Destiny has worked really hard to learn to work with these horses, please try to be supportive."

Then she heard it.

"And when have I not been supportive of my granddaughter?"

He's baack...

❧❧❧❧

Anne felt more nervous than Destiny appeared. So much of her future depended on how well she could perform under pressure.

They finished sweeping the barn and made sure everything was picked up. Benjamin had power-washed the place a few days earlier, and it looked spotless.

They carried the tack out to the arena. It was warm and sunny. The new sawdust left a pleasant woodsy smell, and the two other horses were out in the pasture.

"So, you understand? You'll center and get Dancer to come to you, then tack her up, and we'll do a few exercises, and that's it."

"I can do that. Don't be so worried."

Anne laughed and shook her head. "All right. You've got this." She texted Zeke. "Let's get Dancer ready. And please, if you do nothing else, remember that this moment is just between you and Dancer."

"Okay, I will."

❧❧❧❧

Zeke took them to the barn entrance and walked them through the stable. "Right now, Anne has three horses, but the client list keeps growing and we may have to expand that."

"I still don't understand what this is all about, but Destiny seems pretty excited, so I'm willing to work with y'all." Her dad grumbled. "Sure keep this barn in good shape."

Zeke smiled. He probably wanted to do a more thorough inspection. "Let's go sit on the seat over here. You'll be able to see better."

"Do they know there's a horse just wandering around loose?" Her dad pointed across the ring.

"Yes, Dad. Just keep an eye on her for a little while." She looked over and saw Anne watching from the rail. She waved and asked Destiny something.

Destiny walked around in a circle for several minutes then stooped and closed her eyes. Zeke watched Dancer, whose gaze moved between the strangers across the ring and Destiny standing in the center.

Her dad whispered to Reggie. "Is something happening? I can't tell."

"Just watch, Dad."

Very tentatively, Dancer took a step, then another, and finally walked up behind Destiny and nudged her back. Zeke watched as both Anne and Destiny smiled.

Destiny took the bridle from her shoulder and slipped it over Dancer's head and seated the bit. She walked her over to the rail and picked up the saddle pad and placed it on Dancer's back along with the saddle. Anne helped her mount and pointed to what she wanted her to do.

There were barrels placed around the ring, and Destiny navigated around with no verbal cues and minimal steering. Without a sound, they changed direction and repeated the circuit twice.

Destiny dropped the reins and put her hands up. Soon Dancer began to back up.

Zeke turned when her dad cleared his throat and started a coughing fit. Anne looked over, and Dancer shook her head. *Come on, Destiny.* Zeke watched. Anne tended to Zeke's dad. Destiny picked up the reins, patted the horse's neck, and moved on around the ring.

"No, no, I'm fine just a little cough." Anne handed him a water bottle and gave Destiny a signal. She dismounted, removed the saddle and bridle, then waited for Anne to give her a leg up.

Reggie shook his head. "Wow. What happened to my little girl?"

"What do you mean, Reg?" her father said a little too loudly.

"She's never liked animals, especially large ones. Now she's working with that giant horse like it was a puppy."

"I don't understand any of this."

Anne helped Destiny up, patted her knee, and Dancer started walking around the ring. With a gentle touch, Dancer began to trot, then a short canter before coming to a stop in front of them.

Reggie stood up, clapping, and Dancer shied a bit. Destiny took hold of her mane, looked to Anne, and then closed her eyes. Dancer stopped.

Zeke sat mouth agape. Destiny really nailed it. Complete control. Probably neither her dad or brother would understand the implications, but having done this same thing herself she realized how much power it took to focus and remain connected to her horse. She gave Destiny a fist bump.

Anne walked back to the barn with Destiny and Dancer, grinning widely.

Zeke stood. "Why don't we start back, and they will join us."

"Any more of that barbeque? I'm a little hungry." Reggie and Zeke just laughed.

"Sure."

Chapter Twenty-eight

As soon as they got back to the barn and got Dancer in her stall, Anne gave Destiny a huge hug. "You are a rock star. If we had graduation awards, you'd get most improved and fastest learner."

Destiny laughed. "Do you think my dad was surprised?"

"Judging by his reaction, I'd say yes. Let's get a treat for Dancer and go in the house."

"This may sound weird, but it felt like Dancer was kinda nervous, especially when Granddad started coughing."

"That startled me a bit. But I have to think Dancer was protecting you and she didn't understand that sound. The important thing is that you both noticed it but stayed focused on each other. You will always get sidetracked if you leave 'center,' or your space. Whatever you call it." She stopped. "Let's take an example. When you have to go to court and your caseworker or the judge asks you if you've learned anything or have a good reason why you shouldn't be sent to juvie, what will you tell them?"

"I'm not so bratty anymore."

"Well, I'd certainly agree, and it's possible that Zeke and I may be asked to write a letter. But, I think what they want to hear is, basically, that you know your behavior was bad, you were inconsiderate, and deliberately acted out to get attention—"

"Hey, wait. You make me sound like some kind of criminal."

Anne raised an eyebrow. "What are you doing right now?"

Destiny's face reddened. "Oh, wow. I just got all defensive and pissed."

Anne shrugged. "Yup. If you had stopped for fifteen seconds and thought about the question, you might have been able to stay out of the personal reactivity."

Destiny teared up. "I'm not going to make it, am I?"

Anne smiled. "You instantly went to the bad place without thinking, didn't you?"

She smacked her forehead with her palm. "Habit, I guess."

Anne put an arm around her shoulder. "It's only been a few weeks. Give it time. You know what to do. All you need to remember is to count to ten or take a slow deep breath or think about Dancer. Any of those things will bring you back to center before you open your mouth. You can practice that when anyone asks you a question. Count to five."

"Okay. Can we eat something? I'm starved."

※ ※ ※ ※

Zeke saw them come in and motioned to her brother. He immediately went over to give Destiny a hug. "Honey, I'm so proud of what you've accomplished. I had no idea you liked horses."

Destiny laughed. "I didn't."

Her granddad spoke out from the comfort of the recliner. "I'm afraid I don't understand what all that horse business was about or why you did it. Seems like you'd have been better served by a good job for the summer."

She glanced over at Anne and put up her fingers one at a time as she walked to his chair. "Well, Granddad, the whole point of learning how to work with a horse was to learn to trust."

Everyone smiled and nodded. Her granddad patted her knee and just said, "Well if you learned that, it's a pretty big deal."

Chapter Twenty-nine

Zeke pushed open the bedroom door with her toe as she carefully juggled two coffee cups. "Room service, ma'am."

Anne smiled. "Have I got a tip for you." She took one of the cups as Zeke crawled back into bed. Anne leaned over and kissed her warmly.

"Oh, but that's not all." Zeke reached into her robe pocket and pulled out a package of Pepperidge Farms® Farmhouse cookies.

"Oh my God, you really are the perfect woman." She clapped her hands wildly. "Where on earth did you find those?"

Zeke whispered, "I hid them in a lockbox in the garage the day before Destiny arrived."

"Genius." Anne scarfed down one cookie and groaned ecstatically. Then, without notice, she said, "Do you miss her?"

Zeke paused mid-bite. "You know, I do. Not all the time, because I've really missed our quiet times together."

"Me, too. I'm so happy at this moment."

Zeke pulled her into a clinch and kissed her until Anne groaned. "Madam, is something wrong?"

"Oh my, no. Your lips remain my weakness. They always have been."

"So, a wedding or civil ceremony?"

Anne collapsed with laughter. "It doesn't matter.

I just want you to be mine forever."

"I'm made a few phone calls and made some notes." She jumped out of bed and sprinted to her desk.

Anne hollered after her. "Good thing those stitches were removed."

Zeke returned with a sheaf of papers. She set them on the bed and knelt beside it. "Annie." She held up a small black velvet box with a stunning emerald-cut sapphire with two oblong diamonds along each side in a simple platinum setting. "Would you spend the rest of your life with me?"

Anne's hand trembled as tears ran down her cheeks. "Oh, Zeke, it's utterly stunning. When did you have time to do this?"

Zeke slid the ring on her finger and pulled her into an embrace. "I adore you, and I only wish I'd proposed years ago. You are the best thing that's ever happened to me, and watching the way Destiny changed under your tutelage was just remarkable." Her voice cracked. "She's going to have a bright, beautiful life now instead of a criminal record and anger issues."

"Honey, you would have done the same. Don't forget, you were my savior when my mom died."

Zeke kissed her again. "What do you say we shower and head over to The Greenside for some eggs Benedict and champagne?"

"That sounds divine. Then we can come and get back into our jammies—"

"Or, just get naked." Zeke waggled her eyebrows.

❦❦❦❦

"Hi, ladies. We haven't seen you in a while." The server handed each of them a beautiful menu.

Anne opened it. "It's good to be here, Elyse. We've had a busy spring, time to get some work done. Is this a new menu? I really like it."

"It is. We just got them today." She filled both coffee cups. "Do you know what you'd like?"

Zeke looked at Anne and winked. "I think we'd both like the eggs Benedict and a bottle of Gruet Brut."

She jotted it down. "Special occasion?"

Anne blushed scarlet. "Yes. We're getting married."

"Oh, I'm so happy for you! I'll get this order in and get your champagne. Congratulations."

Anne moved closer in the booth. "How is it that you're still able after ten years together to make me blush?"

Zeke put her hand on Anne's thigh and moved it up slowly. "For the same reason…that I still…can make you do other things."

Anne swallowed hard and took a short breath. "Honey, could we hold off until we get home. These people know us."

Zeke picked up her coffee cup and smiled. "Did you decide about what kind of wedding you wanted?"

"Well, I thought about it, and I think small, casual, intimate with champagne and hors d'oeuvres."

"That's exactly what I thought. So, where? And who you want to be there?"

"I'm not that far yet."

The owner appeared with the champagne and two stemless wine glasses. "I hear congratulations are in order."

Zeke moved over so he could sit. "Thanks, Jimmy. You know we don't like to be hasty."

"So we waited almost ten years to be sure." Anne

grinned

"Very prudent. I'm happy for both of you. The champagne is on us." He stood. "Gotta go. But, I'm really happy for you."

Zeke grabbed her napkin. "Look. Food."

Anne waited while she formed her thoughts. "Are you officially retired?"

"Not yet. There's still a ton of paperwork. The government, you know."

"Well, will you still be able to work with Mike when you leave?"

"Officially, no. I can certainly talk to him and problem-solve, but no official connections."

Anne moved her empty plate and sipped her coffee. "So how much time will you get to pursue this latest attack?" She chose her words very carefully.

Zeke wiped her mouth and folded her napkin with great attention.

Anne recognized that as one of Zeke's "tells." When she had to do or say something uncomfortable or upsetting, she stalled.

"I'm not sure. That's why I haven't raced into the office to sign off."

Anne simply nodded.

"I went back through our case notes and looked a little deeper."

"Of course, you did." Anne waited for what was to come, and her palms began to sweat. *Stay calm.*

"Turns out, before she married, Sari Hussein was an Al-Fassi."

"Why is that name familiar?"

"The kid that broke in and shot Shayla was Salem Al-Fassi."

Anne leaned back to absorb what she had just

heard. *So, Ahmed Hussein's widow has at least one cousin, and one may be Salem Al-Fassi—the same Al-Fassi that terrorized her and Destiny.* "Where is he now?"

Zeke folded her hands and said very softly, "I don't know."

❧❧❧❧

The ride home was quiet. While Zeke put the car away, Anne got out to check the horses. It could have been worse. Still could. Zeke went into the kitchen to check messages. There was one from the sheriff.

"Agent Cabot, hate to bother you on Sunday, but I wanted to let you know. Our suspect was cited for speeding just east of Gallup. And before you ask, no one was in the office when the alarm sounded indicating he'd left the zone for his ankle monitor. He was required to stay within thirty miles until his court date. So, the state patrol wasn't notified when they pulled him over. We have issued a BOLO."

She punched the Delete button and hustled up to her office, opened her computer, and shot Mike a message. They needed to wrap this up quickly. She heard the back door.

"Zeke?"

"I'll be right down." She hurried and changed into jeans and a long-sleeved shirt. Anne was in the family room with the paper.

Zeke sat next to her. "You okay?"

"Yes. You know how therapeutic those horses are."

Zeke kissed her cheek. "I'm sorry I didn't say anything sooner, but with Destiny, I just wanted to keep that between us."

"I understand. I had some news, too. But, for the same reason, I wanted to wait."

Zeke furrowed her brows and looked quizzically. "Really?"

"Yes." She poked Zeke. "Don't be so silly. I really want you to listen and think about what I have to say. Promise?"

"Yes." Zeke turned toward her and tucked one leg under her.

"Last week I got a message from Nancy, and she asked me to call. What she explained was that one of her most popular coaches was going to retire this year. The woman is interested in selling her practice along with her horses and the ranch. She is very particular and wants to find the right person." She paused. "Nancy recommended me. I'd like to go take a look and meet the woman."

"That sounds intriguing. When do you want to go?"

"I can call and see when she's available. I just wanted to see how you felt about it."

Zeke tapped her thumb on her pant leg. "I think your practice has about outgrown the room we have, which is great. I guess it would depend on how much she was asking." She leaned back. "Where is her ranch?"

Anne took a deep breath. "Well, it's up near Cimarron."

"I'm not familiar. Where's that?"

"Between Raton and Las Vegas."

The wheels clicked slowly. That sounded like the area where she had been assigned to Undersecretary Ryerson. "Wow. That's way up there. Have you thought about this?"

"A lot."

"What about our house, the horses…"

"Yes. It means moving far away from here and hopefully away from the things that keep you awake at night. Nancy did suggest that if it worked out, she could probably find someone to take over our place."

Zeke rubbed her face with both hands, jumped up, and began to pace. "That is a huge load of new information. Wow. When did you want—"

"I just want drive up and look at it and talk to her. That's all. But, I would like you there."

"Got it."

Chapter Thirty

Anne checked the map on her phone. They had just left Springer, and she saw the sign for Cimarron. "There. SR fifty-eight. There's a truck stop."

Zeke smiled. "Who knew it was so near. A jaunty one hundred and eighty miles."

"Smart aleck."

Zeke looked around at the vast open space. Nothing like their mountain hideaway. Which wasn't so hidden anymore. Anne had a good point about security. As much time and money as they spent, they were still vulnerable. And it did cause many sleepless nights. Would this be any safer? Plus, she would not have the backup she was used to having.

This is a big deal and worth checking. It could be a dream come true. Or a nightmare. But we don't have to say yes. "Since there's a truck stop I'd like to get gas and—"

"Me, too." Anne turned in her seat. "I know this is a long way from everything we know and it may take a long time to reorient. Remember many years ago we talked about moving to Colorado? I think it's doable. Besides, there's no hurry." She went to the map again. "When we get to Cimarron, look for the sign to Highway 64, the Santa Fe Trail, then turn right."

"Do you know which river we're seeing?"

"Not sure, might be the Canadian. Once we turn,

we go east until we see a sign for 'River Park Equestrian Center.'"

"Do you know anything more about this lady?"

Anne opened a small notebook. "Let's see. Rebecca Dawson, age seventy-eight, widowed last year. Husband Bartholomew, seventy-four, died following a tractor accident. He made his fortune in mining and textiles. They had two children, both of whom died in a fire as children."

"My God, that's awful."

"Nancy said that Mrs. Dawson is the original pioneer woman and a true horse whisperer. She was one of the first students and has mentored several others. She has five horses that she uses for different situations."

"How big is this operation?"

"Let's see. There's a house, barn, indoor and outdoor ring, round pen, and large pasture. They also have a small guest house with three bedrooms and a bunkhouse for the hands who work for her."

"Annie, this sounds like a big operation. You think you're ready for that?"

Anne shrugged. "Don't know. Guess I'll find out. There's the sign."

❧ ❧ ❧ ❧

Anne used the large brass knocker on the grand oak door of the incredibly beautiful ranch house, and almost immediately the door was opened by a young Hispanic girl.

"Hello, I'm here to see Mrs. Dawson."

"Please come in, she is expecting you." She ushered Anne into a spacious, comfortable living room. "I will tell her you are here."

"Thank you." She couldn't be any older than Destiny.

Anne walked around the room fascinated by the artwork. Original painting, sculpture, wood carvings, and some gorgeous beadwork. The well-made leather furniture was old and well cared for. The centerpiece was a massive fieldstone fireplace that covered part of one wall. Everywhere she looked the love and attention to detail was evident.

"Ms. Reynolds, I'm so happy you were able to come." A very energetic seventy-eight-year-old woman bounded into the living and moved directly to Anne with her hand extended. It was like seeing a favorite relative.

Anne felt herself grinning. "Mrs. Dawson, so happy to meet you."

"I understood your partner was coming."

"Oh, she did. She's wandering around awestruck."

She joined Anne on the eight-foot sofa and plopped her booted feet on the rough-hewn wood coffee table. "You know, I've known Nancy since forever. Knew her mother, too. But, I'll tell you, I have never heard her speak as highly about any one of the dozens of students as she has about you. In fact, that was part of the reason I started thinking about slowing down and passing this whole kit and caboodle to someone younger." She stopped. "Marta, would you bring us some of that lemonade?"

Marta reappeared instantly, not with beverages, but with Zeke. "Ms. Cabot."

"Thank you. Sorry to be tardy, but I just had to get a better look at this wonderful place."

Mrs. Dawson marched over and shook her hand.

"My, you're a tall one. And stunning. Mercy. Please come sit. I was just explaining how impressed Nancy has become with Anne's work."

Zeke smiled. "She has developed a keen intuition with her clients."

"Why, that's exactly what Nancy said. And what do you do, Ms. Cabot?"

"Until recently, I was a Special Agent with the Federal Bureau of Investigation. I spent the past year teaching at Quantico. But, I'm ready to retire."

"How wonderful. Thank you for your service. And so young."

Zeke smiled. "Not as young as I'd like to be."

"Ain't that the truth."

Marta came in, set the tray down, poured three glasses, and was gone.

"Alrighty. I'm not big on beating around the bush. I'd like to hear what you're thinking, and I had my lawyer put together a bunch of boring statistics, proposals, floor plans, and other schematics. I don't want to bore you or leave with a thousand questions, so I think you'll find a lot of information in there. Help yourself." She picked up a glass, drank, and set it down. Zeke and Anne each did the same.

"So. I would like to sell most of the stuff so I can build a little cottage on about five acres on that ridge behind the house. It's not on this property. I bought it a few years ago after Bart died. It has a nice road straight to town, and it's all set for water, electric, and cable." She grinned. "I still enjoy working with clients, but I've slowed down. I might teach or write, but I don't want to manage the ranch. In case you are interested, I have a very competent staff, most of whom have been here for five to ten years. It's a good job, and I think most would stay on if you wanted." She stood and walked to the piano covered with photographs. She motioned them over.

"These are a kind of historical record of the ranch. I should probably have all these photos digitized one of these days." She reached back for one photo. "This is Brutus. I raised him from a baby. I mention this because I want to sell the other four horses, but not Brutus. He's twelve, and he'll go with me."

Anne looked at every photo. "What a rich, wonderful legacy. What a life you've led."

"Thank you. It has been a joy, but I need to be practical while I still can be." She laughed.

Zeke resumed her seat. "Mrs. Dawson, you have an incredible legacy here, but I—"

"Think you don't have the experience, or money, or time to invest. I understand how overwhelming this appears. So. I want you to take the file home and read every bit of it. Talk about your expectations and what you two would like to do. Then we'll meet again and see what we can put together. There is no deadline, and I've not contacted anyone else. Does that sound fair?"

"More than fair," Anne said. "It is overwhelming and wonderful. So many possibilities. Can we look around before we go?"

"I counted on it. We'll take the ATV, and I'll give you a tour."

✦✦✦✦

Anne read aloud while Zeke drove. Zeke fought the thought demons that the name Al-Fassi was connected to the Husseins. Maybe Anne was right about leaving the area. Not that anyplace would be totally secure. "I'm sorry, what did you say?"

Anne looked concerned. "Where were you? I asked a question about five minutes ago."

"This is a huge decision, and I'm trying to cover all the bases."

"Honey, it will be much easier together."

"Sorry. What did you ask?"

Anne paused. "I don't know." They both started to laugh.

Zeke opened the windows. "It really is beautiful up here. And peaceful. I remember thinking about what spring would be like in the Rockies." She glanced over to the western sky and the mountainous silhouette of the Sangre de Cristo range. "Maybe we could take up skiing."

"Yeah. I know how you like hiking in the mountains, but this would be different."

"There's that. With the size of that spread, we'd be better with snowmobiles. Destiny would love that."

"You miss her?"

"Yes, but I also miss all the years I missed trying to avoid my father."

Anne put her hand on Zeke's neck and massaged it gently. "I didn't mean to add more worry on your plate. There's no rush, and maybe you'll need to wrap up your Hussein-related business before we make any decisions."

Zeke smiled. "Why are you so good to me?"

Anne didn't hesitate. "Because of your kissing skills."

Chapter Thirty-one

By the end of the week, Anne got back to her routine and her scheduled clients. The horses were happy with the new grass in the pasture. Benjamin decided to paint the stall doors red. She thought they looked dazzling.

Destiny called twice to let them know she was doing well, missed Dancer, and had her hearing scheduled for the following Monday. She sounded good, and Anne liked connecting via video chat online so they could see each other.

Reggie sent a long thank-you note to them extolling the virtues of his new daughter. They were thrilled with her improved attitude and helpfulness. Even her granddad grudgingly praised her new attitude.

Anne tried hard to contain her ego because that was considerable praise from her family. Yet Zeke remained distant and disconnected. It was becoming more and more frustrating. Summer was glorious, and there was a wedding to plan and guests to invite, decisions to be made. More importantly, her attitude toward the River Park Equestrian Center had soured.

Several phone calls to Nancy and Rebecca (who had insisted on the first-name address) had made the proposition much more reasonable, but Zeke held out.

"Okay, I promised you some outdoor time, and we better do it before it gets too hot." She led the horses out one at a time and watched as they ran and played in the long grass.

Benjamin was focused on repairing the paddock fences. She approached him as she still watched her charges running in the pasture. "Hi. I don't want to disturb you, but could you keep an eye on them while I run in the house to make lunch?"

"No problem."

"Thanks, there's a sandwich in it for you."

She trotted back to the house and kicked her muddy boots off by the back door. "Zeke?"

"I'm upstairs."

"Okay, just fixing lunch. You hungry?"

Silence.

"Zeke?"

"Yeah, sorry, I'll be down in a few."

Anne just shook her head and got out the sandwich fixings. What she really wanted to do was call Mike to find out what was going on, but that was not a line she cared to cross.

Zeke came down and joined her at the table, all smiles. "That looks good."

Anne took a breath. "Honey, I have an idea."

Zeke stopped mid-bite and looked up.

"You are very clearly consumed with this connection to Hussein, therefore I want you to do whatever has to be done to put this to rest. Hand it off to Mike, go to Arizona, track down Mrs. Hussein, whatever. Make this threat go away so we can live our lives. Because I have ideas, hopes, and dreams. There are things I want to do once you are legally separated from your job, but I can't do anything when you are consumed by ghosts."

Zeke put her head in her hands and took a deep breath. "I didn't know..." She got up and left the table.

Anne cleared the table and slammed her hand on the counter. "Dammit!" She hastily cleaned up, bagged Benjamin's lunch, and left for the barn, her sanctuary.

On her desk lay the schematics, financial reports, client history, and complete daily routines they brought back from River Park. Rebecca had planned for everything. In a separate folder were the statements from their financial guru who was unfazed by the offer from Rebecca Dawson. In fact, he sent her a list of questions to ask, as well as a few she needed to answer for herself about why she wanted to do this.

All of it was on hold until Zeke came back to their partnership.

❧❧❧❧

Zeke met Mike for coffee at the usual spot in the heights. She had arrived ahead of time because she wanted to avoid further discussion with Anne until she had something to say. Mike's call indicated he might have something to offer.

He arrived, waved, and joined her at a small shaded table at the edge of the patio. She'd already ordered some iced tea. "Hey, Zeke, good to see you." He set a brown envelope on the table and unbuttoned his jacket.

"Hi, Mike. Thanks for meeting me. Please tell me you have something to end all this crazy."

"I think I do." He opened the envelope. "Here's a copy of Mr. Al-Fassi's arrest record. He's been busy for a kid his age. So, we have some bargaining power. Now, the best news, I just got confirmation that Sari Hussein is back in Chicago with her kids. In fact, they moved back into the house on the North Shore. She's clean. No record. Kids are enrolled in a nice Catholic school, and many of the staff are the same."

Zeke read through the report. "Why'd you include the medical examiner's report?"

Mike smiled his boyish-prank grin. "Because I think I can fly to Chicago, get in to see Sari Hussein, and present her with a proposition. I show her proof that we had no part in the death of her husband. I think it's plausible to put it on Rafael Santiago and show that he's dead. "

Zeke was trying to follow. "Okay. Then what?"

"I don't imagine she's going to admit to any knowledge of anything, but I'll put out her cousin's rap sheet along with his future and an offer a deal. She puts an end to this vendetta against you, and we make these charges go away. Provided she makes sure all of her family are aware of this."

Zeke leaned back. "Wow. And you got all this approved?"

"Yup."

"You know I want to be there."

"I figured you would, but that can't be part of it—officially. You aren't working in the region. You're still officially part of the job at Quantico."

"But I resigned. Can't someone make a call?"

"No. Zeke, this woman tried to have you killed. It's ridiculous for you to show up at her front door."

"Mike, I have to find a way. I have to know."

"And I figured that, too. There may be a way to fly to Chicago and wait at the hotel, out of sight. I'll wear a wire so you can follow the conversation. No input."

"That's your best idea?" Her frustration was growing by the minute.

"Zeke, we shouldn't even be having this conversation, but I convinced the boss that the whole

Hussein cartel is still a threat and we no longer have tax evasion as leverage."

Zeke chewed her lip as her heart pounded in her chest. It seemed possible they could end this whole freakin' nightmare. "When are you going?"

"On Monday. I booked a room at the North Shore Hilton. One of the Chicago guys will pick me up and provide backup. The locals were also notified."

"So, if I was staying at the same hotel…visiting old friends…"

"That would be none of my business. But promise me one thing, or I end this whole thing today."

"What?"

"You will not go anywhere near that property or that family—ever."

"Mike—"

"Promise, or no deal."

"I promise."

"For your sake, you have to let this go, no matter how this meet goes."

"It's not easy to just let it go if I have to keep looking over my shoulder." Zeke really felt like grousing, and she knew Mike understood.

"Now, you do have to discuss this with Anne."

"What?"

"Come on, Cabot, you can't leave her out of the loop again."

"Fine, as soon as I get home. Listen, if anything changes, call me."

Mike looked at his watch. "Gotta go. I'll text when I leave."

Zeke sat a minute to process what he had said. Her heart rate had remained rapid, so she chose a slow walk around the parking lot before jumping in the car.

As frustrating as it would be, Mike had a good plan. Sari Hussein might not go for it, but it was there best shot.

Immediately, she had the same old flashback: a huge fireball and the ground shaking, bodies tossed in the air, Ben crumpled with a horribly deformed leg. Zeke remembered like it was yesterday, the widow standing in shock, covering her mouth. Zeke had yelled over the noise, "We didn't do this."

She got in the car and started the motor. This plan had to work. She did not want to plan her own wedding with the gut-burning fear she'd endured all these years. She had to be able to offer Annie one hundred percent of her life and her love.

This had to work.

Traffic thinned out as she passed Zuzax. Warm air blew through the open windows and Zeke inhaled deeply to get every single molecule of new air. How would she broach this trip with Anne?

She promised Mike full disclosure, and she certainly owed Anne an opportunity to talk about it. How to approach this?

While her heart rate had settled down, her brain took up the slack with multiple scenarios and what-ifs. "Stop. This is Mike's op."

The market was just ahead, and she turned in. She hustled through the store picking out some fresh flowers, two excellent New York strip steaks, a large salad, and some obscene home-baked tarts. It wouldn't fool Anne one bit, but that was not the intention. It was a real peace offering.

"Oh, a card." She ran back into the store and chose a straightforward message. "I'm sorry."

When she got home, Anne wasn't in the house.

Likely in her office. Zeke used the time to set out the flowers, the card, and the dessert. The salad went in the refrigerator, and she went out on the deck to uncover the grill.

The kitchen clock read four-twenty, so there was time to shower. By four–forty, she'd put on some clean cargo shorts and a favorite royal blue polo shirt.

Since Anne still wasn't back, she took a breath and headed out to the office.

❧❧❧❧

The figures still came out wrong. "Damn." This is why she passed on finance and chose a nursing career. No matter. By her calculation, increasing her client load would more than cover the daily expenses. Depending on what they could get for the house... "Note to self, call realtor." The land contract could be handled.

She smelled fresh, clean soap, and looked up to see Zeke standing in the doorway. Her heart skipped a few beats. Even now, Zeke Cabot remained one of the most strikingly attractive women she'd ever known. With her damp wavy brown hair, dazzling amber eyes, and that dimpled smile, Anne forgot how annoyed she'd been. She dropped her pencil on the desk and leaned back.

"Oh, my," she muttered.

"I'm back from my meeting with Mike and had a few minutes, so I stopped at the store. Are you about ready to quit for the day?"

"I'm ready. Well... Yes. Let me just check the horses, and I'll be up."

"Do you need help?"

She knew her face was red. *I certainly do need help.* "Oh. It should only take a minute."

"Okay. See you back at the house."

Anne chastised herself for her lack of control, but hormones were wicked, wicked influences. No matter how angry she got, Zeke could walk in, and without saying a word, cause her desire to bubble up like a hot spring.

The horses were fed and watered. Anne locked the door and paused. "No reason why I can't be both irritated and insatiable.

Boots in the mudroom, Anne walked into the kitchen to see the flowers and the card. Her heart threatened to explode. Zeke was on the deck fussing with the grill.

She opened the patio door. "How long will it take to get hot?"

"I dunno, maybe twenty minutes or so."

"Perfect, get it started and meet me upstairs."

Zeke dropped the tongs and looked up.

❧❧❧❧

"These steaks are extraordinary." Anne took a final bite.

Zeke cut a piece up for Shayla. "It's an old family recipe. Leave steak at room temperature for at least two hours in butcher paper, then grill by flashlight."

"It wasn't my fault the deck lights were burned out."

"That's true, but it was your fault for luring me away from a task to have your wicked ways with me. Repeatedly."

Anne coughed. "My wicked ways? I simply wanted to thank you for the flowers and thoughtful card."

"Simply? Are you going to stick with that?" Zeke started to clear the table. "Should we have coffee out here?"

Anne took several dishes. "Yes, and then you can tell me how the meeting with Mike went."

Zeke knew that Anne with a serious concern was like Shayla with her chew stick.

The dishes done, they propped their feet on the railing. The only lights were in the yard and citronella candles that dotted the railing and tables.

"Mike wanted to meet out of the office for his new idea. He had already cleared it through channels. He's leaving early Monday for Chicago and will meet with an agent from their office."

Anne focused on every word, and Zeke knew why.

"Together, they will go to the Hussein residence in Lake Forest."

"Wait, I thought they moved permanently to Lebanon?"

"I did, too. But, they kept the house and the staff. Not sure why, but Sari moved back with their kids who are back in school."

"Okay. Go on."

"He's taking the CIA report from the explosion, medical examiner's results, and her cousin's arrest record."

Anne frowned. "I'm not sure a widow would want to dredge up those things."

"Exactly. Mike plans to tell her simply that we were not responsible for the explosion, Rafael was, and he's dead. He is going to ask to drop the vendetta against me and in exchange, they will clear her cousin's criminal record."

Anne leaned back. "Sounds iffy. But, aren't you leaving out something important?"

Silence.

"I wasn't finished. You're right. I asked to be part of the visit."

Anne started to bristle and put down her coffee cup.

"Hold it. He said no, I could not be involved."

"Good thing. Tell Mike I said thank you."

"I understand that my presence might set her off, but I want to know what she has to say, so Mike agreed that I could stay at the hotel and he'd wear a wire for me to listen. I can't respond or even talk."

"Zeke, are you just nuts?" Her frustration was palpable. She stood and paced.

Better to not push it. "Well, he did say I had to run it past you first."

Anne turned around. "And you entertained the notion that I would happily send the woman I love within a thousand miles of someone who wants her dead? Seriously?"

"I guess I hadn't quite carried it to its natural conclusion."

Anne sat next to her and took her hand. "Honey, I can't prevent you from doing what you seem compelled to do, but if a part of you loves me as much as you appear to, please let your partner handle this and just call you when it's over."

Zeke had not considered that option.

"After all, it's possible Sari will say no, and who knows what will happen then?"

Zeke closed her eyes. That was not an option. This nightmare had to be over once and for all. Mike had to make it happen. She never asked what his Plan B was. "I need to turn in."

"Okay, I'll lock up."

Chapter Thirty-two

Anne hung the plat map for the Dawson Ranch on the wall behind her desk in the old barn. She had marked every building, and noted which staff worked where, plus made notes on changes she'd like to make in the guest bunkhouse. Saturday mornings were generally quiet, and so she used the time to catch up on loose ends, pamper the horses, and daydream. The last one was relatively new, but she certainly enjoyed the ideas that grew from that one visit to Rebecca's ranch.

They needed to make some decisions before taking an offer to Rebecca. She peeked up at the house and Zeke's office window. Until the planned op in Chicago was successfully completed, there would be no conversation about a happily-ever-after future for them. Zeke's complete obsession with this case precluded everything in their lives at the moment.

With a deep sigh, Anne returned her attention to the future home of Reynold's Ranch and Equine Center. In the past few days, the large plat map had been festooned with different color markers and sticky notes.

Mainly, she focused on the horse barn. Happily, the much larger barn had ten stalls so there'd be room for her horses. Evidently, Rebecca had several clients who came wanting to learn to work with their own horses.

She sat on her desk staring and daydreaming about the expansion. Maybe she could hire one of Nancy's students to be her assistant. After all, some of the women Nancy worked with were veterans. She glanced at her desk calendar and her schedule. What would happen with her clients?

She thought about Melisa Pearce's training seminar. Well, she had women come to her ranch and stay for a few days. Why not offer three-day classes? With all the room, she'd be able to house the horse and the owner.

If only.

She glanced out the window to see Zeke moping along dejectedly. Uh-oh. She must've made the call. Might be a good time for her to visit the horses.

"Hi, honey. I was just coming to see if you'd be interested in some equine PT for your shoulder."

Zeke stopped and pondered the question. "Might be a good idea. What was your thinking, that I could brush them all?"

Anne laughed. "Probably an excellent exercise, but how about some riding. Bareback?"

"That might be nice. Think Sunny might be up for that?"

"Sure. You can work in the ring for a few minutes, then I'll get Shadow and we'll take them out for a ride."

As they entered the barn, Zeke said, "I called Mike and told him I wasn't going. You know, I think he was relieved."

Anne stopped. "Thank you, honey. I know that was hard for you."

They walked the bridled horses into the ring, and Anne gave Zeke a leg up. "Just relax and let Sunny take over. She knows what to do."

At first, Zeke had her long legs snug against Sunny's sides. After the first circle, her legs and shoulders relaxed, and she closed her eyes. Sunny continued her slow, steady gait and the rocking motion was hypnotic. *Work your magic, Sunny.*

Anne observed to be sure Zeke wasn't actually asleep. After ten minutes, Anne stopped Sunny and said, "Ready to go outside?"

Zeke's eyes fluttered open, and she yawned. "Yes. Boy that was relaxing."

Anne could see the usual stress lines in her forehead and around her mouth were gone. "Good. Let's go. I'll get the gates."

By the time they reached the south side of the paddock, Anne had climbed the gate and pulled herself on Shadow's back. The abnormal snowpack had given the spring grass a head start, and it was still lush and bright emerald green. It smelled wonderful. "You know I wish I'd packed a picnic."

"It is pretty out here. Sort of forest primeval, and even with Benjamin's hard work it's still thick and beautiful."

They rode down the far side toward the road. Periodically, Zeke looked back, probably checking her surveillance cameras. Looking out from the deck made it deceptively smaller. From this vantage point, it was a pretty impressive size property. Anne should be able to get a reasonable price, if—

"We should probably get an appraisal on this place before we talk to Rebecca again," Zeke opined.

Anne stifled a whoop but did an internal fist bump instead. "I was thinking the same thing. I'll call for one tomorrow. It does look impressive from down here."

"In fact, if they want to post property pictures, they should include a couple from here."

Anne stopped. "Do you have your phone with you?"

"Sure, you want to take some?"

"Yes. I rather doubt many real estate agents are going to venture this far to take a picture and you can't see the house from the fence line."

❧❧❧❧

They brushed and fed the horses. Zeke paused. "Do you mind if I go to my office, I'm going to shoot a note to Destiny. You know, see how she's doing?"

"Of course. Are you okay?"

"Yeah, I just kinda miss her. Taking this ride made me wish we'd connected sooner."

"I understand." Anne embraced her. "I love you, Zeke Cabot. Please don't forget that."

"Never." Zeke kissed her and turned toward the house. She needed to make some calls. Tomorrow would be Sunday and no chance of making arrangements, so she left a message for Sam and Gloria to please call. They hadn't gotten together in months.

After checking her email—hoping Mike might respond—she dialed Destiny's cell number.

"Hi, Auntie! Do you miss me?"

"As a matter of fact, I do. But I wanted to see how you feel about the hearing Monday."

"It's cool. I met the court-appointed lawyer. She was nice. Gave me advice about what not to say or do. And Mom got me some new clothes to wear so I'll look grown-up and fancy, I guess. How's Shayla?"

Zeke smiled. "I think she was kinda sad for a

while. So, Anne let her sleep in your room."

"Poor puppy. I miss her, too. I asked my parents about getting a dog and Dad pitched a fit. Mom said we'll see how the next few months go."

"Destiny, do you remember some of the techniques Anne taught you to center?"

Pause. "Yeah, how come?"

"Sometimes court can get real busy and loud. I think it would help if you practiced focusing and tuning out the crazy. Know what I mean?"

"Right, you want to make sure I know what to do so I don't flip out. I get it. I really am going to try really hard. Dad said if I got off these charges, he'd find some way with you so I could come back. Would you be cool with that?"

Zeke beamed. *Hell yeah.* "I think that would be great. We'd love to have you."

"Awesome. Gotta go. I'll call you after court, okay?"

"I'd like that. I'm rooting for a great report because you deserve it."

"I love you, Auntie."

"I love you, too." Click.

Tears filled her eyes, and Zeke felt so much gratitude for the decision that she and Anne made to experiment with Destiny. After all these years, she finally had a connection to her family.

The crumpled tissue in her hand, she took a breath and looked across the yard past the large "Reynold's Ranch" sign to Anne's office. All those years ago, it had been important for Anne to build a business and a safe place for them. Time to step up and be part of the only team she needed.

Mike can do this, and I need to get to work on my

new job.

She stopped in the bathroom and splashed cold water on her tear-stained face. Her eyelids were puffy. But she wanted to report on Destiny's new attitude.

❧❧❧❧

Sunday became Operation Crunch. Zeke brought a thermos of coffee and a box of cookies to the barn and met Anne in her office. The desk was clear except for the papers from their accountant, and the details provided by Rebecca Dawson.

"All set," Anne said, drying her hands. "The horses are out in the sunshine grazing, so let Operation Crunch begin." She leaned provocatively across the desk. "If I neglected to mention it, I simply adore you for tabling your anxiety about Chicago—or at least pretending to—to embrace my dream."

"Baby, you know that sooner or later I am likely to see the wisdom in your calm, cool logic." She leaned forward to share a warm kiss. "Let's figure this out."

They each took one of the four offers Rebecca had proposed and plugged in the numbers Anne received from the accountant. When they finished one, they tackled the next.

At one point, Zeke paused to look at the large plat map. The area that was marked included twenty-seven acres of various terrains: pasture, tree-covered, hillside, flat land, and a stream. It really was perfect, the location, the property, and privacy. Another possible bonus that Rebecca mentioned as they left was the possibility of a job for Zeke with the county sheriff. That might be interesting.

Anne stood up and stretched. "I'm hungry. Let's

take these last offers back to the house and have a deck picnic."

"Sounds great. I'll put this together if you want to start with lunch."

"Deal."

Zeke watched appreciatively as Anne jogged off to the house. Riding had provided her with enviable legs and ass.

"How did I get so lucky?" She began whistling as she carefully organized the piles for each offer. After putting the contents into labeled, individual file folders, she carried them back to the house. She stopped partway back and looked around. It would be hard to leave this lovely place after ten wonderful years.

She laughed. "Well, mostly wonderful. We sure have had more than a fair share of injuries, accidents, threats, and of course, hospitalizations."

They each camped out in a comfortable chaise lounge with iced tea and a salad and a few file folders. The sun moved on over the roofline and up the mountainside. The warm temps cooled and warranted a long-sleeved shirt. Nevertheless, they carried on with their evaluation of each proposal, pro and con.

They each had priorities. Anne wanted an attractive ranch that was inviting and warm to greet clients. She had good ideas about decorating and how to promote the business to old and new clients.

Zeke was far more structural and organic. She wanted improved utilities, security, better fencing, a parking area for staff and guests. Screening and background checks for all employees. Oh yes, and more insurance. Maybe even contract a food company.

They narrowed it down to two agreements, and both contained a land contract and a contingency to sell their house. They combined their ideas and picked the one that provided the most freedom and was fair and equitable.

Anne stretched her arms overhead and groaned. "You know, if Rebecca is agreeable to most things and we can get a loan for a down payment, we could probably let our lawyer draw up a contract and have her lawyer check it over."

Zeke was rereading the last page. "I know Rebecca is willing to include all the furniture that she won't be taking with her, so are you happy with that and what would you do with your stuff?"

"I think we can use both. I'd like to redo the guest house, and the staff could use some better furnishings. Plus, we don't know about Nancy's prospective student."

"What kind of time frame do you have?"

Anne laughed. "No idea. Rebecca needs to build a place, we need to sell or rent or whatever, we'll need to decide about furniture, utilities, and moving." She sat up and dropped her feet to the deck. "Stop. This is crazy. It's too big a plan and way out of my comfort zone." She started to pace.

Zeke smiled and was about to call her out for kidding around, but stopped. Anne's face was a mask of fear. Zeke cleared off her lounge. "Come here, baby."

"I can't."

"Yes, you can. Come talk to me." Zeke waited until she walked off some of her nerves.

Anne sat at the end of the lounge. "Zeke, I just got so caught up in the dream, the fantasy of having the career Melisa does. And I'm not her. I have a dozen clients who come and go. We really haven't made any money because of the expenses, and now I want to quadruple the expenses? It's nuts."

"I don't agree. I felt the way you feel when you first mentioned it, but after reading all these offers, well, this really is a good deal. Rebecca is offering you a working ranch complete with staff and a built-in business for what amounts to about ten cents on the dollar. She is not advertising it or offering it to anyone else." She pulled Anne closer. "Honey, she's doing this because she believes in you and trusts you with her legacy." She kissed her temple. "I agree this is going to be a radically steep learning curve, but we have both been managers and Rebecca will be right next door."

Anne hugged her tightly. "You always make me feel safer and more capable. And you're maddeningly calm."

"It's not like you haven't been there for me. That's kind of what partners do. Can we turn in early? My brain is fried."

"Mine, too. We can finish up in the clear light of day and send off our response."

Chapter Thirty-three

A nne fed the horses and finished mucking the stalls, then added fresh straw. All three were happily grazing in the morning sun. In spite of being older, both Sunny and Shadow were energetic and in good condition. Dancer was only four but had good bloodlines and a sweet disposition. She watched and wondered how they would adjust to a larger area and several barn mates. Good thing Rebecca had good people working for her.

The sun moved higher through the trees creating a watercolor scene in the meadow. From her seat atop the gate she could see the house, barn, and east hillside. It was a beautiful location and a wonderful home. The previous night she and Zeke had talked until they exhausted every scenario. In the end, they both agreed to take their offer to Rebecca as soon as possible. With her holding the paper, they would avoid dealing with finance people. When they combined Zeke's savings and retirement with the profit from the sale of their house, they could do this and still have a cushion.

Anne smiled. For the first time since she got Nancy's call she felt relaxed and confident.

She hopped down and hurried in to fix breakfast. Since she'd left Zeke sleeping soundly, she wanted to surprise her with breakfast in bed.

The smell of bacon and coffee greeted her at the back door. Glorious. She kicked off her muddy boots and hugged Zeke from behind. "Good morning, you sexy kitchen goddess."

Zeke laughed. "Well, I did wonder what my next title would be after retiring."

Anne washed her hands. "What can I do to help?"

"You could set the table on the deck if you want to eat out there."

"Great idea. It's a glorious day."

Zeke brought a tray with the coffee carafe, and two plates with breakfast burritos and sliced strawberries. "I tried a new recipe. Hope it's good."

"It smells divine. What's different?"

"I added some whipped cream cheese to the eggs along with green chile. Topped it with bacon and cheddar."

Anne groaned. "Can we have this every day?"

Zeke paused mid-bite. "Hmm, we might have to ask the cook."

Anne stopped. "I hadn't thought about the staff and our loss of privacy. That might be a problem."

"How so?"

"Well, for one thing, chasing me around naked."

Zeke coughed and nearly choked. "We may need to establish some house rules."

"For staff or us?"

"Yes."

❧❧❧❧

Anne excused herself to go work on her invoices, so Zeke went to her upstairs office. Her nerves started the excitement phase before she got to her desk. In Biloxi, her niece was likely arguing with her mother about her appearance and what she could not wear for court. Her brother would be praying.

In Chicago, Mike and his team would be prepping and reviewing every contingency. She sent mental hints to Mike to keep her in the loop. Failing her resolve to stay out of it, she shot him a text.

Zcabot: Sending good thoughts to you and the team Stay safe.

Then, on impulse.

Zcabot: Destiny, big hugs from your NM fam.

She decided to strip their bed and do some time-consuming laundry. That would keep her busy. The sheets, towels, and pillows were hauled down to the laundry room where she started a load, then took the bed pillows outside for freshening. She smacked them together a few times and propped them in chairs.

The kitchen was clean, but she could empty the dishwasher. Shayla lay on her bed near the table watching every move.

"It's okay, girl, I'm just trying to keep busy. Your favorite kid is going to court today, and it's a big deal. Plus, Uncle Mike has gone to Chicago to stop a lady from trying to kill me. Also, a big deal. Very big!"

Shayla listened and then wagged her tail.

❧ ❧ ❧ ❧

Anne answered her cell phone, "Hi, Susan. What's up?"

"I hate to bother you right now, but I need your help. I tripped over the rug in the kitchen with a glass bowl that shattered—"

"I'll be right over." Anne was already running to the house. Susan never asked for any help. Ever. So she must be scared. "Zeke, Susan hurt herself and I'm taking the car just in case she needs to go to the hospital."

"I'll meet you there." Zeke took off from the deck and through the yard shortcut.

Anne backed out, stopped, ran to the cabinet, and grabbed her nurse bag. She drove out and around to the Godfreys' driveway. She hurried in the open door and found Zeke holding Susan's arm in the air while propping her up on a chair.

Blood spattered on the cabinets and floor along with broken glass. "Okay. Did you hurt anything else?"

Susan smiled weakly. "Yeah, I bumped my head on the counter. Oh, Anne, I just feel so silly."

Anne washed her hands and pulled on some gloves. "Let's take a look." She gently loosened the dish towel Zeke was pressing on her arm, and a small spurt of blood shot out from somewhere on her hand. Anne took a handful of 4x4 gauze squares and pressed them into her hand and put more on her wrist. "Zeke, would you put pressure here on her wrist so I can take a look?"

Within a minute she was able to look at Susan's hand. She had two fairly deep lacerations in her palm and thumb. She needed stitches. "Should get these cleaned and sutured. Let me call the clinic down the road. Zeke, let's prop her arm on the table and get her hand higher than her heart."

"Should I keep holding her wrist?"

"Yes, as long as you can. I'll wrap it in a minute." She made a quick call and described the injury. "Yes, we'll be down in about ten minutes. Thank you."

Susan was apologizing, and Zeke hugged her.

"After all you've done for us? Please."

Anne found a two-inch elastic wrap and wrapped a wad of gauze in the palm of Susan's hand and tightly around her wrist. "Will you be able to keep that over your head?"

"I think so." Susan smiled weakly but looked a little pale.

Zeke stood. "I'll go with you and drive. You sit with Susan."

"My purse is there on the counter". Zeke grabbed it. "Do you want us to call Jim?"

"No. It'll just scare him. Let's wait till we see what's going on."

They made it to the clinic in less than ten minutes. Anne took her in and explained the injury and the blood loss.

Anne came out to the waiting room. "Why don't you go home? No need for both of us to be here."

"Nonsense, this is where we should be. It's Susan the Indomitable. She may need support. I've got my phone." She put an arm around Anne's shoulders. "You might want to go to the washroom and clean up just so you don't scare the children," she whispered.

Anne looked down and shuddered. "Oh, my." Now she was glad she was wearing jeans and an old T-shirt. Susan was tough, but an arterial bleed of any kind was frightening. Hopefully, she wouldn't need a transfusion. Hard to tell. She did look pale.

Anne looked in the mirror. "That's the best I can do with paper towels." She joined Zeke in the waiting room. "Any word?"

"Not yet. Do you think Susan will be okay?"

Anne pondered the location of the lacerations. "Hard to say. I didn't want to waste time evaluating any functional stuff." They both turned to watch the large waiting room full of sick and injured people.

Zeke leaned over and whispered, "Do you ever miss it?"

"Nursing?"

Zeke nodded.

"Not usually, but when I'm called to play nurse, it's an adrenaline rush for a while."

Zeke glanced at her watch.

"Should you be hearing something by now?"

"Hard to say. I don't have a timeline for Mike's op or Destiny's court appearance. Could be minutes or hours."

Anne put a hand on her arm. "Waiting for answers sucks."

A woman in scrubs came out and looked around. She must've recognized the blood-stained shirt. "Are you with Mrs. Godfrey?"

"Yes."

"I'm Doctor Calhoun." She sat on the coffee table in front of them and leaned forward.

"She's stable. We were able to get the bleeding stopped, but I'm concerned about a couple of tendons and nerves. She needs a good hand surgeon, and I was finally able to convince her that she needed to go to town and get it taken care of as soon as possible. I called and talked to a hand specialist I respect, and he'll take a look as soon as we can get her there."

"We can take her."

"I know, but we've got IVs and her hand hanging from the IV pole. Her pressure is still a little low, so I think a medical transport is safer."

Anne nodded. "I understand. Can we see her for a minute? I'll need to call her husband."

Zeke and Anne waved when Susan was loaded into an ambulance. Anne wrote down the instructions, and they called Jim so he could meet her in town.

"Poor Susan. She must be scared. I don't think she's ever spent the night in a hospital." Anne stopped and looked out the window.

Zeke took her hand. "You thinking about what will happen if we move?"

"How'd you know that?"

"Because that's what I'm thinking."

Chapter Thirty-four

Zeke flung open the door and ran across the lawn to Anne's office in the barn. "Annie, great news!"

Anne took off her glasses. "What?"

"Reggie called. The judge dismissed Destiny's charges."

"That's great!"

"The judge told them he hardly recognized her. Said he'd never seen such a dramatic transformation. She still has to stay clean until she's eighteen, but then her record will be clear. Reggie was in tears."

Anne hugged her. "Oh, Zeke, that's such great news. I know how scared Reggie was. He must be relieved."

Zeke laughed. "Yeah, as a reward, he told her she could visit us any time she wanted."

"Oh, he did? That was generous of him. I don't suppose you mentioned moving."

"Well, not yet. But it might be nice to have a young person helping out."

"Sly," Anne said. "I'm done in here. Want to look at the final paperwork before I send it to the lawyer?"

"Sure, can I take it back to the house to review? I was cooking some noodle soup."

As they walked back, Zeke took Anne's hand. "I know it will be months from now, but I'm already feeling nostalgic about this wonderful place and all of the memories we made here."

"I know. I was reminiscing this morning, but we can't ignore all of the nightmares we've endured. I think about the ranch and the staff that are there, and of course, I'm sure we'll take those security cameras."

Zeke laughed. "You'd be right., Without them, I'd have to learn to watch TV. With larger areas and buildings, not to mention animals, it will be much safer. This is a big investment, and it will also be a business expense."

"Why didn't we think of that sooner?"

"Because this system is set for perimeter safety. We'll need a different setup."

Anne nodded. "And more good news. Jim called, and he's bringing Susan home. She has a huge cast, but the doctor was able to get everything reattached and functional."

"That's great."

"I'll wash up, and then I'd love some of your soup."

Zeke put out bowls and spoons just as her phone rang. The ID said "Mike." Thank God. "Hello, Mike. How'd it go?"

"Hey, hang on. I want to go outside. Okay. We got to the house at oh-eight thirty after the kids left for school. I didn't call ahead on purpose."

"Of course. Too risky."

"When the housekeeper took us back to the dining room, Mrs. Hussein looked puzzled. After I introduced myself and Tom Hendricks, her face got red, and I had to do some fast reassuring. Once she settled down, I gave her my proposition. She seemed unmoved. We waited while she ordered and prepared some coffee."

"Did she call anyone?"

"No, I got the impression that she's assumed the mantle for her family."

"Interesting."

"Eventually she asked to see her cousin's arrest record and shook her head. She told me she had not approved his visit. She agreed to the deal."

Zeke whispered, "Yes."

"I had her sign a note to that effect, gave her a copy, and apologized for the tragic accident."

"That was nice of you."

"Well, it was a horrible thing to witness. I wouldn't want my family to see that."

"Mike, you have no idea how grateful and relieved I am. I owe you one. Let's get together when you get back."

"Will do. Take care."

She hung up and began to cry.

Anne was standing in the doorway. "Honey, what's wrong? I thought it was good news."

"Baby, it is good news. I'm just so damn relieved after ten years of agony and looking over my shoulder. Let's set up a time with Rebecca and get the heck out of here." She hugged Anne tightly. "I'm looking forward to a fresh start. I'll go in and sign my separation papers as soon as I can."

Anne kissed her. "I'm so happy for you and for us. Is this when we get the happily ever after?"

"I don't see what could stop us. I love you."

Epilogue

R ebecca, your house looks beautiful," Anne said from the porch of Rebecca Dawson's new home on the ridge. "And this view is magnificent."

"I'm pleased. Still, so many details to attend to, but I wouldn't be this far along if it weren't for you two."

"We wouldn't be here to help if it wasn't for you."

"Let's sit down and wait for Zeke. My knees are back-talkin' again." Rebecca eased into the oak rocker.

"Do you want your pills?"

"Nah, I save them for real pain." She winked. "How're your horses getting along?"

Anne pointed to the pasture below them. "It's only been a few months, but as you can see, they are forming their hierarchy. I think when horses do intuitive work they develop a higher level of communication skills. I've noticed it with the clients. The horses are a little quicker with their input."

"Interesting, but makes sense. I expect horses learn from the herd, as well."

"That's logical. Previous clients of mine have commented on how the combination of different horses seems to increase the energy."

The sound of an ATV shattered the peace.

Rebecca laughed. "Must be Zeke, she sure likes that contraption. I should have suggested an electric golf cart."

"No way. Once she saw how easily she could check out any situation quickly, she was sold."

Zeke pulled up in front of the porch with an insulated bag strapped on the back. She waved and unstrapped the bag.

Rebecca leaned over and whispered, "She cuts a fine figure in that sheriff's uniform."

Anne smiled. "Yes, it fits her well." *But I think she looks good in just about any outfit or none.*

"Dinner, ladies." Zeke left the helmet on the seat and hurried up the steps. "Should I put this on the counter?"

"Smells great. Let's go on in," Rebecca said, inching out of her rocker.

Anne offered her hand. "I don't remember the last time I had Chinese takeout."

"It smells good. See, I'd never get this from Angel the Beloved Cook. Where'd you find it?"

"When I stopped at headquarters in Raton, I passed it. Called in my order and here we are."

"I didn't know you had to go to the office," Anne said. She put out three plates.

Zeke unbuttoned her shirt collar. "We had some cattle go missing. I wrote up the report."

Rebecca smiled. "Back in the day, cattle thieves got shot or hanged. Good thing we've got more law enforcement today."

"So far I haven't needed to shoot or hang anyone. It's pretty reasonable. Nothing like a day in the Bureau."

Rebecca took a few bites, then paused. "Are you bored out here in the sticks?"

"Heck no. I'm enjoying the job. It's only three days a week, and Anne is a much tougher boss."

"Hey!"

"Just kidding." Zeke regaled them with a couple of her adventures while they cleaned up the dishes. "If you're ready, I'd like to go and drop off the boys' paychecks."

"It's real nice of you to hand-deliver them. I'm sure they appreciate the effort."

"In reality, I do it so I can learn everyone's name and face. Anne has the advantage of seeing the staff every day."

"Well, thanks for stopping by. I enjoy your company." Rebecca waved as they rode off.

Anne leaned close. "Rebecca likes the way you look in that uniform. So do I."

"Hush, woman. People will start talking."

"I don't know what's to talk about. After all, you made a huge announcement on the first day. We are affectionately known as 'the ladies.'"

Zeke parked in front of the bunkhouse and took a canvas bag with the pay envelopes inside. "*Buenas noches.* I have your pay." She pulled out and read each envelope and tried to match it to a face. It always made them laugh.

"Manuel?" She walked to the end of the table and a silver-haired man. "Robert?" She looked and picked the youngest.

"Si, Gracias."

"Carlos?" The heavyset man in front.

"Where's Juan?"

"In the barn con los horses."

She smiled, hoping she got them right. "*Gracias, muchachos.*"

As they left, Anne said, "You know if you get one wrong they just wait until you leave."

"Seriously?"

Zeke was up early and went downstairs to make coffee. They had arranged for the cook, also known as Angel, to come in at eight o'clock so that they could have some time together before the day got started. She was very accommodating and prepared the staff food the night before so they could heat it.

So far, it was working fine; each one of Rebecca's employees made an effort to be incredibly gracious and helpful. Zeke and Anne made it clear that the house staff, including the cook and housekeeper, were to help Mrs. Dawson one day a week, and it would be included as part of their salary.

Of course, Rebecca pitched a fit but negotiated some of her time to help Anne with clients. It was a win-win.

Zeke sipped her coffee as she stood on the back porch and watched the many moving parts of a working ranch. Manuel seemed to be the senior staff and refused to be the foreman, but everyone listened to his soft-spoken instructions.

She was still surprised how quickly they had adapted to the broader, more complex lifestyle. Anne got used to a different facility for her clients, with Rebecca's guidance. The regular clients continued to come for training or individual work. Nancy had come out twice to observe and suggest. Happily, they had found the perfect couple to buy their East Mountain house. The woman had owned horses all her life and just retired from the Air Force. Her husband managed a small bank in Albuquerque. They had two young boys and meshed well with the Godfreys.

Anne still missed Susan terribly, more so since there were no close neighbors, except for Rebecca who became a surrogate mom for them both. They were pleased, and lucky. The only thing on the to-do list was still the wedding. She'd tried a couple of ideas, but once the wheels started to turn for the ranch and the move, well, things moved the wedding off the list.

She went back for another cup and ran into her fiancée. "Good morning, beautiful." Zeke kissed her warmly.

"Well, aren't you romantic?" Anne filled both of their cups. "Hungry?"

"Not yet."

"What's on your list today?" Anne asked and sat at the table.

"I just added something to the top at number one."

"Do tell."

"Our wedding."

Anne sighed. "How did that get lost, especially after I browbeat you into wedlock?"

"When I get to Raton tomorrow, I'm going to do some research."

"Wouldn't it be easier to plan something in the East Mountains or Albuquerque?"

"I suppose. Do you have any requests or ideas?"

"I'd like it small and simple with a few friends, some nice food, and a delicious cake. We already have the rings, and I don't intend to wear a fancy white dress. Been there, done that."

"The only thing is, I think I'd like to show off this place. No one's seen it yet."

"Good point." She glanced toward the window. "You know, there's room for six in the guest house, and we have two extra bedrooms here. We could do a weekend thing so nobody has to drive back."

"Wow, that would be kinda cool. If it was during the semester break, Destiny could come."

"Jim and Susan for sure. I think you'd want to include Mike."

"Yeah, I do owe him a lot."

"Oh my gosh, what about Sam and Gloria?"

"They'd kill us if they found out through the grapevine."

"Well, I did call before we moved and told them we'd have them over." Anne went to the counter and grabbed a pad of paper. She started writing furiously. "Pick a date, invitations, find a baker." She paused. "Do we cater or ask Angel?"

"Why don't we see what Rebecca would suggest. I'm sure this is exactly the kind of thing she'd love to be in on."

"Rebecca! We have to invite her."

"You know she might know a local magistrate or Justice of the Peace. Just don't let her take it over."

Anne jotted it down. "Anything else?"

"Flowers. I'd like some nice flowers."

"Why Ms. Cabot, I had no idea."

"Names. What are we going to do about names?" Zeke chimed in.

"Well, keep our own, pick one, or hyphenate."

"Hmm, I vote for hyphenate."

"Reynolds-Cabot? Or Cabot-Reynolds?"

In unison, they said, "Cabot-Reynolds."

Anne underlined it. "Okay, I have to get ready for my first client." She kissed Zeke. "I'll see you later."

Zeke watched her run upstairs. A wedding. It was something that had never been on her to-do list ever. Of course, that was after years undercover with the

Bureau and a series of short, unexciting relationships. That was before Anne Reynolds captivated her from the very instant she spotted her in a drugstore on North 14. She fell hard, and that was even with the traumatic brain injury. She laughed. If not for her incapacity, that newly divorced and stunning blond-haired, blue-eyed goddess would have been in deep trouble.

As it was, she had to fall off the side of the mountain and be rescued on horseback by said beauty.

Their budding relationship teetered on so many occasions it scared her. Zeke cringed, thinking about the harrowing situations her job had created.

She stood and grabbed the list. She'd make this the best damn wedding anyone had ever attended. She hurried out while dialing Rebecca's phone number.

"Good morning, Zeke."

"Hi, do you have a few minutes to chat?"

"Why sure, I'll pour you a cup." She laughed.

When Zeke came to a halt at the new house on the hill, she spotted the grinning Rebecca Dawson in her royal rocker.

"Thanks. I could use your help."

"Well, then I guess you better sit down and start from the beginning."

For the next half hour, Zeke poured out the story of her and Anne's lives—which was never her intention.

"I'm sorry. I never meant to do a true confession, but you see why I want to make this wedding ceremony the most wonderful, loving remembrance of our lives."

"Zeke, I'm honored you trusted me to share this wonderful event, and I do remember how deep and wondrous true love can be." She squeezed Zeke's hand. "Now, let's get to work and not a word to Anne. You just tell her you've got it taken care of."

Zeke sighed. She could have wept. For the next hour, Rebecca gave her a list of tasks and who to contact. Whatever date they chose, these were the thing that should all be in place. Zeke jumped up and hugged her. "Rebecca, I don't know any other person I could have called…well, thank you."

"You're welcome. Now get busy, and keep me apprised."

Zeke revved the ATV and took off for home. She had a lot to do, and since Anne taught until at least noon, she had time to make some calls. The first email went to her brother. She wanted to tell him the good news but doubted the whole family could make the trip because of his teaching schedule and Maura's work schedule. But she really wanted Destiny to see the new place and be there for their wedding. She was part of their ranch family.

Rebecca gave her a couple of phone numbers, so she called the cake decorator first. Reportedly, she booked in advance for months.

"Hello, my name is Zeke Cabot, and Rebecca Dawson gave me your number. We're planning a small wedding, and I need an estimate for a cake and how soon you need to know."

"Rebecca's a darling. And your name was Zeke?"

"That's correct."

"How many people, layer or sheet cake, type of cake and frosting, a location of the event, estimated date?"

"I'd say twelve to fifteen, layer, I'll have to let you know about the flavor and frosting, here at the ranch, thirty to sixty days from now."

"Excellent. Give me your email, and I'll send an

estimate. Say, how fancy do you want this?"

"Not fancy, just delicious and pretty."

"Okay. Got it, I'll get back to you. Oh, my name is Joan."

Zeke ticked off the box for cake. Next up, Justice of the Peace. It might help narrow their choices of dates to have his schedule.

"Ralph Hendley's office, how may I help you?"

"Hello, I'm looking for dates to plan a small wedding and thought I'd better start at the top."

"Excellent idea. When are you thinking?"

"In the next thirty to sixty days."

"That's quick. Let me see…"

She read off available dates, and Zeke copied them down. "Thanks, I'll get back to you as soon as I can."

"Check."

She looked at her watch, and there was still time, at least two hours. Anne's jewelry box sat on the dresser, and the two matching gold rings they bought in Chicago were inside. She smiled. As soon as Anne picked a date, she'd take them to be polished and inscribed. Meanwhile, it was probably safest to leave them in the box. The jewelry made her think about the Pegasus necklace. What would be a meaningful wedding present? She sat on the side of the bed and looked around.

Their new bedroom was much more significant with its fieldstone fireplace. There were French windows and doors, one of which opened onto a covered balcony on the north side of the house with nothing but a view of the mountains and the long driveway. Every day they made discoveries around the ranch. When Rebecca and Bartholomew built the home nearly forty years ago, everything had to be shipped from Colorado or Santa Fe. The architect deliberately selected wood and stone from the hills and valleys and riverbeds nearby.

Zeke admired the craftsmanship. She'd never been especially handy or creative, unlike Anne who could make anything. The small writing desk by the window held an ornate leather-bound notebook. Anne used it to jot a note about her day every evening before bed. Lately, however, they both dropped into bed as soon as possible. The days were busier than she imagined, but it was good, satisfying work. *Work!* She needed to add another cake for the staff. Adding each person by location, Zeke counted eight. *Note to self.*

⁂

Anne walked Dancer back to her stall as her last client drove out with her trailer in tow. Juan immediately stepped up.

"I will take her, *Señora*."

"*Gracias*, Juan." She watched him take Dancer out to hose her down and brush her. The horses loved the attention, and as a bonus he was gentle and caring with them. He said it was because he didn't want the barn to smell bad. To that end, he cleaned the stalls frequently. He was right. The barn did not smell bad.

The walk up to the house was farther than she had been used to compared to their old home, but it was an excellent opportunity to stretch her legs. She left her boots by the back door and Angel greeted her.

"Hola."

"Smells good, what's for supper?"

"Chicken enchiladas and rice. Pie for dessert."

"You are an Angel, gracias!"

Anne hurried upstairs hoping to catch a quick shower. She found Zeke asleep on the bed pen in hand, notepad beside her. She looked adorable.

Fresh and clean, she woke Zeke with a kiss. "Time for supper, honey."

"My gosh, what time is it?"

"Nearly five thirty. You must be tired, but no worries. Are you ready to go down and eat, and you can fill me in on your notes?"

They sat on the long couch in the living room while Angel set the table.

"I gather you've been busy."

Zeke smiled. "I'm proud to say, we're in good shape. I found an e-vite site online—don't judge yet—it's attractive and fast. No waiting for the turn-around of snail mail. I saved a couple for your approval. Got all the email addresses, so all we need to do tonight is pick a date, send out the e-vites, and decide on the cake type and frosting. And I figured we should get a small sheet cake for the staff."

"Oh, I'm glad you thought of that. You've been busy." Anne grinned at Zeke's enthusiasm.

"Also, once we decide on the date I can let the Justice of the Peace's office know." She pulled out a note. "These are the dates he's available in the next two months."

"Wow. This wedding is getting real. Fast."

"If I have time tomorrow, I'll check on chairs and tables, flowers, and the food. Rebecca said that Angel loves to make fancy dinners and seldom gets the chance."

"That would be great, then. How many are you counting?"

"You, me, Rebecca, Destiny, Jim and Susan, Mike and Becky, Sam and Gloria. Ten?"

"Great. We can easily fit in the dining room."

"Where shall we have the ceremony?"

"If it's okay, Rebecca asked if she could plan that and make it a surprise."

Anne started to stay something and stopped. "Why not? I love surprises, and I completely trust Rebecca."

"That's what I thought."

"Did you think about where to put people?"

"I did, but decided to see who responds and wants to stay."

"Zeke, we're going to have to plan breakfast on Sunday and probably a light lunch Saturday. Plus, snacks, beverages—"

"Rebecca is working on that."

"That woman is amazing."

"And I suspect, a little bored."

"Good point."

"Dinner ready for you," Angel announced.

❧ ❧ ❧ ❧

The September morning dawned bright and clear. The light rain the night before left everything shiny and new. Rebecca had provided written instructions for the staff regarding the landscaping, fall cleaning inside and out, and that everything must be complete by Friday afternoon. She designated two of the guys to help the cook with serving food and two serving drinks.

Zeke grinned at how magical everything looked. Rebecca managed to find some blue and white bunting, which matched the other decorations and the sign at the front gate, the one Anne had not seen yet.

They had agreed on white slacks and white Mexican wedding shirts with hand-stitching in royal blue. Zeke sat on the porch watching Destiny and Shayla ride the ATV around, exploring. She'd arrived two days earlier, and they had listened to stories of her success at school, a part-time job at a stable, and the promise of a car when she turned sixteen.

Anne was the first to comment on how she'd lost that adolescent waif-like look and looked more like a young Zeke. She was right, and Zeke liked the comparison that Destiny was beautiful and far more mature.

Soon the messages from guests began pouring in. Susan and Jim were on their way; Sam and Gloria stayed the night in Santa Fe and would be here soon as well. Mike and Betsy decided to take the scenic route up to Highway 64 from Angel Fire. They had just called for local directions.

Rebecca forbade the happy couple from going near the barn since yesterday afternoon. Anne worked on final touches in the guest house, which also got a coat of paint.

Zeke felt tremors vibrating through her legs. Excitement and terror battled for supremacy. Anne waved as she rounded the corner of the house. "I need to shower. Are you about ready?"

"Yup, my clothes are laid out ready to go."

"Come keep me company, I'm getting nervous." Anne tugged her hand.

Zeke followed, happy to have Anne nearby to soothe her nerves.

"Rebecca has done an amazing job getting the house…the whole ranch sparkling. I would never have had the nerve to ask so much in such a short time." Anne turned on the water and squealed.

Zeke laughed. "You have to wait a little longer for hot water." And under her breath, "If there's any left." She hung up her clothes and dressed in her wedding duds, happy she'd showered much earlier.

She opened Anne's jewelry box and removed the rings. She took two jeweler's boxes from her top drawer. After exhaustive brain-wracking work on the ring designs, Zeke decided to add two small diamonds close together on each ring. The jeweler did a beautiful job. She placed one ring in each box, one white and one blue. Anne's was white.

As soon as they arrived, she'd give the rings to Mike. They had forgotten about witnesses until the secretary for the Justice of the Peace asked for the names. Anne quickly called Susan and Zeke called Mike. She debated about Destiny, and then they decided she'd be the lone flower girl.

Anne came in wrapped in a towel and stopped. "Mrs. Cabot-Reynolds, you still take my breath away. Now, come here and kiss me, then get downstairs and find Destiny."

Zeke hugged her and kissed her gently, and again after whispering, "*Je t'adore*".

She had just hustled Destiny inside when the Godfreys arrived. "Susan, Jim, welcome. Follow me over to the guest house. Anne's got you all set in the Azure Room." She started the ATV and they followed her the short distance. One of the grooms came out and took their luggage. "I'll be back with the next group," she said as she spotted Mike's car turn in.

She hurried over and asked Mike to follow.

"I hope we're not late. That took longer than

expected."

"No, the Godfreys just arrived, and we still have Sam and Gloria."

"Hey, love that new sign," Mike said

"Thanks. Anne hasn't seen it yet." She turned the ATV around and led them back to the guest house where the groom stood waiting to take their bags. "I'll see you soon." She watched as another one of the staff came down from the house with a champagne bucket and several glasses.

That should take care of things for a while. It was nearly one pm, and the ceremony was planned for three. She drove back to the house and met Anne coming out.

"Mike and Betsy, Jim and Susan are settling in, the only others are Sam and Gloria." She climbed off the ATV and started up the porch steps as Anne stood gaping.

"What's wrong?"

"Zeke your white pants, they're covered with dust!"

"Shoot I didn't think about that. I'll try to—"

"Let Tina put them in the dryer on air only."

Sure enough, ten minutes and they were fine. Ah, the wonders of synthetics.

She re-dressed, walked out, and met Destiny coming out of her room. "Wow." The kid looked radiant. Rebecca had set her up with a light silver velvet shirt. A long navy-blue broom skirt and a silver and turquoise Concho belt with a matching necklace completed the look. She had polished her old boots and looked beautiful.

"Destiny, you look amazing. What a great outfit."

"Rebecca gave it to me because she said she'd

never wear it again. What do you suppose she meant?"

"I don't know, but that was nice. She's been so helpful getting this whole wedding together. Let's go find Anne."

They walked out on the porch as a bright red Mercedes convertible pulled in.

Destiny gawked. "Who is that?"

Zeke laughed. "Those would be our dear friends, Sam and Gloria." She could see Gloria driving with her classic scarf and huge sunglasses. They honked, and Juan appeared on the ATV.

Zeke waved. "Just follow Juan."

"They look fun. Where'd you meet them?"

"Anne used to work in surgery at the hospital with Sam, who is a surgeon. Then, quite by surprise, we ran into them at the Georgia O'Keefe museum."

"I've heard of her," Destiny added. "She dressed funny, was real old, and a great painter."

"In a nutshell, yes." Zeke laughed.

Tina came out and asked, "Cook has questions for Miss Zeke."

"Okay. Destiny, keep an eye out for Anne." She followed Tina down the hall to the dining room. The beautiful hand-hewn oak table had been set for ten with a gorgeous royal blue runner down the center of the sparkling white damask tablecloth, four silver candelabras, and a small glass vase at each seat with wildflowers and evergreens. Crystal wine goblets and cobalt blue china completed the gorgeous table.

Angel rushed into the room. "*Señora*, we need for you to put out the place cards and Miss Rebecca asks if Mr. Hendley will stay for dinner?"

Zeke took the cards from her but thought it best to let Anne do the honors. "I will find out for you. This looks so beautiful. Thank you."

The living room contained additional seating, and a bar was set up with ice, glasses, whisky, vodka, wine, fruit juice, along with a cheese and cracker tray.

"Zeke." Anne hurried down the stairs. "Is everyone here yet?"

She looked breathtaking. Anne seldom wore makeup, but when she did she pulled her blond hair up into a loose French twist. Zeke could only stare and allow happy tears to leak from the corners of her eyes. This woman had asked her to marry and today was the day.

"Are you okay? Honey, talk to me."

Zeke took her hands. "I don't think I have ever been happier than I am at this moment. I'm so proud that you want to spend your life with me." She hugged her tightly.

"I love you, and I'm so excited and nervous, and God, you look hot."

"Thanks. So. Are we all set?"

"Everyone is here and settling in at the guest house. By the way, Destiny looks incredible, thanks to Rebecca, and Cook wants the place cards set out and wants to know if the Justice of the Peace is staying for dinner."

She took the cards. "We'll check with Rebecca. Tell her to have a place setting ready just in case. We can squeeze him in next to Rebecca."

The sound of a different vehicle filled the air. It didn't have the loud rumble of their ATV but still was noticeable. Right in front of the house sat a bright red ATV with a truck bed and a bench seat with a silver-haired woman in all red, including a western hat.

"Howdy folks. How do you like my new ride?"

"That's cool," Destiny said, running down the steps. "Can we go for a ride?"

"Later, honey. We got more work to get ready." She shut it off and climbed out. "This one's easier to get in and out of."

Zeke just smiled.

Anne went down to hug her. "You look fabulous. Do you want some tea?"

"Sounds good. I'd like to see what the girls fixed up for you."

Anne and Zeke led her into the house and showed off everything. "Oh, Cook wanted to know if Mr. Hendley would be staying for dinner."

Rebecca paused. "I kinda doubt it. He'll probably accept a cocktail then be off." She checked the table in the living room and moved to the dining room. She clapped her hands and smiled. "This looks perfect. I hope you approve."

"Absolutely. They did a wonderful job. Any thoughts on place cards?"

Rebecca looked at each one and pointed to a seat. Once they were all placed, she said, "All right, your guests will want to say hi before the ceremony. Best hightail it on over to the guest house. I'll give the kid a ride." She winked.

Zeke and Anne went out the front door after her and found a long swath of indoor-outdoor green carpet running to the guest house and barn.

"Guess we follow the green brick road."

❦ ❦ ❦ ❦ ❦

All six of their guests were pleasantly buzzed and getting on famously telling personal stories about the brides, who barely had time to talk before being ushered to the barn. Zeke quickly handed off the rings to Mike.

The grooms led the guests out first.

Anne whispered, "I hope Mr. Hendley arrived."

"I'm sure he's been here before. He sounded very familiar with the Dawsons."

Juan came for them. "Miss Rebecca asked that I take you over to the arena." He followed the path to the rear door and peeked inside. "Okay." He held open the door.

There in the center of the arena was an elevated round platform, and everyone stood around it in a circle. Mr. Hendley was on one side between Mike and Susan. There was a small table set in the center under a suspended spotlight and a tall white candle, with two smaller ones, and a leather folder.

Everyone held a candle. Destiny waited for them and preceded them with a basket of flower petals which she scattered on the carpet running to the platform. She then joined the circle.

Zeke took Anne's hand tightly and walked forward. They climbed two steps and took their place in the circle.

"Welcome." Mr. Hendley opened a book and read the formal state-required questions of each of them, professional and impersonal. When they had answered his questions, he closed the book. "Zeke Cabot and Anne Reynolds you are here today to be joined in holy matrimony. It is my pleasure to provide the service that will forever bind you to one another. And now, I'd like you each to light a candle and then light each candle in the circle. Then together you will light the wedding candle, exchange rings, and pronounce your vows."

Zeke winked at Anne, and they picked up a small candle. They went around the circle and whispered to each guest. When they got to the table in the center, they stopped briefly to share a smile, and with trembling hands, they ignited the flame on "their" candle.

"Zeke, would you start?" Mr. Hendley whispered.

"Annie, I think I've waited my whole life for this moment, and now I can't find strong enough words to express my love for you." She teared up and stopped.

Anne smiled and took her hand. "My life with you has never been dull." Everyone laughed. "But with every single obstacle thrown in our path, my resolve strengthened. Whenever some stranger tried to take you from me, I became even more determined to love you harder and make you stronger, because today, we are together. Forever."

Mike handed the ring boxes to Mr. Hendley, and he gave Zeke a ring in the white box. "Please repeat, with this ring I thee wed."

Zeke slipped the ring on Anne's finger and whispered the words. Anne did a double take.

He handed Anne Zeke's ring, and she repeated the words as she held Zeke's hand.

"By the power vested in me by the state of New Mexico, I pronounce you each, Mrs. Cabot-Reynolds. You may—"

Too late. They needed no permission. And while their friends clapped and congratulated, Zeke and Anne kissed.

The grooms were quick to gather the candles as the happy couple signed the papers. Zeke turned to Rebecca, "Could we borrow your ATV for just a minute? Anne hasn't seen the sign."

While everyone followed Destiny and Rebecca, Zeke took Anne past the house and down the long driveway very slowly.

"Honey, we can't run away yet, we have company waiting for us."

"I know. I just wanted a few minutes alone." She drove out the gate and down the road a short distance. She stopped and pulled Anne into an embrace. "I hope you know how much you mean to me."

"I think I do. Our ceremony was perfect. And the rings! My God, when did you have time to do that?"

"Check the engraving."

She slipped off the ring, and read the inscription, then said, "I love this and you. I'm so disappointed that your gift didn't arrive."

"That's okay."

"I wanted it for Monday. It's a special-order Stetson, chocolate brown with the Colfax county insignia. I hate that cheap one they make you wear."

"That's a wonderful idea. I'm just not sure the chief—"

"It's okay, I called him and asked permission. He thought it'd go great with the tan uniforms. Might ask all the guys to get them."

"Then I can't wait to get it and be the first!"

Zeke turned the ATV around, and in the afternoon light, the large white sign over the entrance glowed with the dark blue printing and a horse-head silhouette. "Cabot-Reynolds Equestrian Center."

Anne got out and walked closer. "Oh, Zeke, it's utterly perfect."

"Let's go and thank our friends."

About the Author

Barrett Magill is a Golden Crown Literary Society Award Finalist who published five novels starting in 2011 including: Damaged in Service, Defying Gravity; Dispatched with Cause; Deliver Us From Evil; Balefire; and two novellas Windy City Mistletoe, and Flights of Fancy before joining Sapphire Books.

Her YA novel entitled The Dreamcatcher was released January 15, 2017. Balefire was re-released in June of 2017 and her next novel, Highland Dew was released in April 2018.The Audible version of Highland Dew was released in June of 2018.

With the New addition—Destiny's Child, Book Five—due for release in July 2019, Sapphire Books will be re-releasing the original four Damaged series eBooks one book per month March through June at deeply discounted prices.

Barrett is a member of the Western Women Writers of New Mexico, the Land of Enchantment Romance Authors, Romance Writers of America, Golden Crown Literary Society, Sisters in Crime, the Petroglyph Guild, and the F.O.W.H. #251.

After retiring from a busy nursing career, she moved west. Now, Barrett enjoys the inspiring mountain views from two acres of prairie in New Mexico's high desert. Her devoted pack includes a hyper border collie mix, and a sweet young blue eyed husky mix. Her current other hobby is transforming prairie driftwood into whimsical art pieces.

barrett-writes,

https://twitter.com/BarrettWrites,

http://www.sapphirebooks.com/barrett,

http://highlanddew.com/,

https://www.facebook.com/pg/Barrett-Writes/

Check out Barrett's other books

The Damaged Series

Damaged in Service - Book I - 978-1-948232-61-6

Zeke Cabot is smart, tough, and one of the top Special Agents in the FBI's Chicago Field Office. She's also recovering from a traumatic head injury and months of being undercover on the mean streets of the Windy City. She agrees to an extended vacation in New Mexico to help her recover from her physical and emotional duress.

She meets Anne Reynolds, a home health nurse, who is recovering from a failed sham marriage. Surrounded by the breathtaking New Mexico landscape, they are pulled into the horror of a serial murder case that Zeke thought was closed.

JZeke's PTSD runs dark and deep and threatens to overwhelm their fledgling relationship. But every once in a while, two opposing energies can merge to create a stronger alloy-but the laws of physics, like love, can be fickle.

Defying Gravity - Book II - *978-1-948232-62-3*

Special Agent Zeke Cabot and Anne Reynolds are both excited and a little wary as they take steps to commit to their budding relationship. But like the unpredictable weather in the mountains of New Mexico, their path to happiness is anything but smooth. Zeke continues to struggle against debilitating bouts of PTSD and flashbacks.

Anne still copes with the lingering pain from her divorce and wonders if she's ready to take another chance on love, especially with a woman.

A danger from a past case Zeke thought was closed threatens both their safety and the strength of their trust. But Zeke and Anne are determined to overcome their personal obstacles and learn to defy gravity enough to keep them grounded in love.

Dispatched with Cause - Book III - 978-1-948232-63-0

Special Agent Zeke Cabot begins her new assignment in New Mexico and soon has a confrontation with her dangerous nemeses, which triggers her barely concealed PTSD symptoms.

Anne Reynolds reluctantly accepts a less stressful home healthcare office position as she settles into a life with Zeke, but it's not easy living with someone whose job is filled with dangers that threaten to destroy their relationship. Their serendipitous meeting and immediate attraction had been too good to be real, and now secrets and dangers make reality almost too much for them to bear. Zeke and Anne have to face their personal demons and make tough choices for their love to prevail.

The Dreamcatcher - ISBN - 978-1-943353-67-5

High school is rarely easy, especially for a tall, somewhat gangly Native American girl. Add a sprinkle of shyness, a dash of athletic prowess, an above-average IQ, and some bizarre history that places her in the guardianship of her aunt. Then normal high school life is only an illusion.

Kai Tiva faces an uphill struggle until she runs into Riley Beth James, the extroverted class cutie, at the principal's office. Riley shows up for a newspaper interview, while Kai is summoned for punching out a classmate.

Riley is the attractive girl-next-door-type whom everyone likes. Though a fairly good student, an emerging choral star, and wildly popular, she knows she'll never live up to her older sister. She makes up for it with bravery, kindness, and a brash can-do attitude.

Their odd matchup is strengthened by curiosity, compassion, humor, and all the drama of typical teenage life. But their experiences go beyond the normal teen angst; theirs is compounded by a curious attraction to each other, and an emerging, insidious danger related to the mysterious death of Kai's father.

Their emerging friendship is tested as they navigate this risky challenge. But the powerful bond forged between them has existed through past lives. The outcome this time will affect the next generation of Kai's people.
Balefire – ISBN – 978-1-943353-91-0

Silke Dyson is a free-spirited artist and teacher struggling with a vision impairment as a result of a physical altercation. Kirin Foster is a pragmatic Type A writer for a travel magazine with great opportunities for travel, and a growing restlessness.

Their lives intersect at thirty-thousand feet during a tropical storm. With plans lost in the ensuing confusion, they form an unlikely friendship. The relationship strengthens in the warm tropical sunshine of the Belizean Cayes.

To their surprise, they discover a real connection with backgrounds in Milwaukee. Back home they continue an easy rapport with common interests and mutual friends.

Sometimes a random spark of kindness or caring can kindle a small flame. With patience and serendipity, a small flame can grow into a balefire—a beacon of hope to guide a pair of lost soul's home.

Highland Dew – ISBN – 978-1-948232-11-1

Bryce Andrews, west coast sales director for Global Distillers and Distribution, is tired of the corporate hamster wheel. She needs a change.

A craft whisky trade show offers her inspiration and a chance to revisit Scotland and the majestic scenery of the Speyside region—best known for the "Whisky Trail." Bryce and her coworker, Reggie Ballard, need to find a wholly original whisky for their international distribution division by visiting a number of small distillers.

A blind curve, a dangling sign, and weed-choked driveway draw Bryce directly into a truly unique opportunity. She discovers a struggling family, a shuttered distillery, and a spitfire of a daughter called home to care for her confused father.

Fiona McDougall—the only child and heir to the MacDougall & Son legacy, had her career teaching in Edinburgh curtailed by fate...or serendipity.

When the stars finally align, the two women work together to resurrect a dream for themselves and the family business—if they can weather the storms of unscrupulous business practices in the competitive whisky market.

Other books by Sapphire Authors

McCall - ISBN - 978-1-948232-32-6

Sara Brighton is a quickly rising culinary star in Savannah after Food & Wine magazine named her restaurant Best New Restaurant of the South, until it burns to the ground in an accident and she impulsively packs her truck and heads for McCall, Idaho, the last place she remembers being truly happy.

Sam Draper, head of the Lake Patrol division of the McCall PD, knows the last thing she needs is another entitled tourist making her life difficult on the water. However, after Sara surprises her by helping her avoid a near professional disaster, Sam teaches her to drive a boat. The chemistry between them is hot and instant, and as the summer heats up, Sam finds herself fall-ing in love until Sara buys her late father's iconic diner and turns it into the newest hotspot for pretentious culinary tourists.

Can the love Sam and Sara found on the water survive the lingering ghosts waiting for them back on dry land?

Silver Love – ISBN – 978-1-948232-51-7

Jill, Dory, Robby, and Charlene are a fantastic foursome that embodies the varying experiences that come with being Lesbians of a Certain Age. They are vibrant and vulnerable, wise and foolish, introspective and outgoing. The close-knit friends fight aging at every turn—or just ignore it altogether. These four will never go quietly into the night, redefining life after fifty. They are the new mature woman.

But along with twenty-first-century attitudes come twenty-first-century problems. Public office candidate and retired judge Charlene is confronted by a wannabe blackmailer, Jill's passions threaten to swamp her common sense, Dory's best-selling book could turn out to be a national disaster, and Robby must confront the hard reality of learning that her wife may not be the woman she thought she was. Steadfast in their faith in themselves and each other, and bolstered by the rich history of their friendship, the four women struggle with twists and turns as they try to navigate a landscape generated by the actions of others as well as their own choices, proving that experience does not always pave a smooth road.

In a world where everything increasingly seems relative, these women remind us that some things don't change—like the bedrock of relationships. Silver Love is all about love; love among friends, love between lovers, and the unexpected role of love with acquaintances who may not always be what they seem.

If you can keep up, join the ride and follow these ageless heroines as they pursue their adventures in the modern world.

www.ingramcontent.com/pod-product-compliance
Lightning Source LLC
Chambersburg PA
CBHW051630180726
48284CB00006B/1669